BOOK 5

THE TANGLED TREASURE TRAIL

A 1920s MYSTERY

BENEDICT BROWN

COPYRIGHT

For my father, Kevin,
I hope you would have liked this book an awful lot.

NOTE TO READERS

This is my twelfth mystery novel in a little over two years. I try to be truly original in my books and, for that reason, I wouldn't be happy if I wrote the same story each time. In an attempt to keep things interesting, The Tangled Treasure Trail is not just a simple whodunit but a whydunit – with even more twists and turns than in previous outings.

The next Lord Edgington novel will be about an eccentric family in a grand country house, but this one is a bit different. Set across London and featuring the notorious Bright Young Things of the 1920s, Edgington finds himself out of his element. So far, my readers have loved the change of pace and extra dose of intrigue, and I really hope you do too.

This is another spoiler-free story and doesn't give away any of the mysteries from previous entries in the series. At the back of the book is a glossary of unusual terms, a character list and notes on my research and inspiration.

Vol. XXXI   **The London Chronicle.**   [393]   Issue No. 1224

FEBRUARY 13th, 1926

Bright Young People at it Again: Late-Night Treasure Trail Terrorises Sleeping City

Though it may not be high season for the Mayfair set, it seems that some young devils have returned to the capital early this year in search of hijinks. Perhaps the pleasures of the countryside wore thin for these frolicking free-thinkers as they convened once more for a high-speed chase across London. Starting at midnight in Sloane Square, this decidedly modern steeplechase stretched into the early hours of this morning.

The Metropolitan Police were forced to caution two members of the nocturnal society after complaints of unruly behaviour in the neighbourhood of Saint John's Wood. Drunkenness, cavorting and the singing of bawdy shanties led to the despatch of a small team of constables to deal with the matter.

Earlier in the proceedings, luminaries of the London scene – such as enfant terrible Fabian Warwick, artist Augustus Harred and his charming fiancée Lady Pandora Elles – were on hand to add a touch of glamour to the event. There were even reports of an appearance by The Prince of Wales. The question on the lips of this reporter, and every last person in the capital, is what new diversion will these Bright Young People engage in next?

Police at the scene of the accident in Richmond.

Industrialist Dies of Heart Attack After Engaging in Youthful Pursuit

Baron Terence Pritt, owner of the Eastern Steel Ingot & Aggregate Company, died unexpectedly this morning while participating in a high-speed treasure hunt which streaked across the capital in the early hours of the morning. Pritt came to the public's attention when his metal and aggregate company spearheaded the road-building boom of the last decade. Although he was a hugely successful businessman, accusations of industrial espionage and worker exploitation dogged his career. He leaves behind no children and is said to have been estranged from his wife, Baroness Ermentrude Pritt.

The incident took place on a quiet road at the edge of Richmond Park. The baron is believed to have lost control of his Bentley Blue Label tourer which narrowly missed another motorist. Police at the scene confirmed that little damage was done to the vehicle. By the time Stone's body was found by another competitor in the treasure hunt, he had been dead for some time.

The industrialist was a divisive figure but had become recognized as one of the bright, though not so young, people on the London scene over the last year. He was a regular fixture at the popular Gargoyle Club on Dean Street and spent the season in a flat in St James's Square. Questions will surely now arise about the identity of the beneficiaries of his substantial estate.

Trouble in the Pits

Price of coal soars as supply outstrips demand due to extraction issues in northern mines.

Full story **page 9.**

10th Anniversary of Traitor's Execution

Lord Septimus Marchant served his sentence a decade ago today. The notorious infiltrator's accomplices were never brought to justice.

Full story **page 4.**

Huddersfield Town's Winning streak Continues.

Is an unprecedented third consecutive league title really within their grasp?

Full story **page 19.**

CHAPTER ONE

My father always tells me that only boring people find themselves bored. I suppose that must mean I'm mind-numbingly, brain-fizzingly dull.

Oh, how I missed the excitement of the Christmas holidays. January had been a cold, wet month with little to thrill a young gentleman on the cusp of adulthood. There hadn't even been any snow since we'd returned to the milder climes of southern England. I longed for the chance to build a snowman again, or at least encounter a nice, puzzling murder to solve.

Which isn't to say that I wanted anyone to die, but it had been six whole weeks since the great detective Lord Edgington and I had stumbled upon any wicked crimes, and it was becoming tiresome. Where were the despicable characters creeping out from behind the wainscoting to settle old scores? Where were the money-hungry black widows and silver-tongued charlatans? Why had all our adventuring dried up for the season? I was desperate for a break from the ordinary, but instead…

"Hmmm… There's an interesting article in the financial pages of today's paper," Grandfather mumbled one night after dinner, as I sat opposite him in the library of our family's grand estate at Cranley Hall. It was the first thing he'd said in over an hour. "There's talk of unrest in British coalmines."

"Interesting," I replied, though I very much doubted this was the case.

I, too, was reading. I'd scoured the old man's selection of books on detective work, crime solving and police protocol for something that didn't look too dull. With 'A Beginner's Guide to Ratiocination' in my hands, I hoped that it would level the playing field between my distinguished forebear's famous mental skills and my own, well… not very advanced reasoning. Failing that, I thought he might at least notice what I was reading and think me rather bright.

Lamentably, I would have no such luck, and another thirty minutes passed before he spoke again.

The truth is that such weekends with my grandfather were still far more entertaining than my days at school. All our teachers wanted to talk about was the high cliff that we would jump from at the end of our final year – the safety net that would be pulled out from under us – leaving us at the mercy of the big, bad world. There were exams for which to prepare and universities to visit. Personally, I thought it jolly unfair that unworldly seventeen-year-old boys should have to make such life-changing decisions. I struggled to decide what I wanted for breakfast most days; how on earth was I expected to choose the path that the rest of my life would take?

"Hmmm," the esteemed chap finally uttered once more. "Now, this *is* interesting. Tell me, Christopher, have you heard of Baron Terence Pritt?"

"What? Where? I can't see anyone." I bolted up in my chair and peered through the window, as though this were entirely normal behaviour. It's possible that I had nodded off. Our footman, Halfpenny, was pouring tea and I hadn't even heard him enter.

"In the paper, boy. Here in the newspaper!" My grandfather gave the immense broadsheet a resounding thwack with the back of his hand. "There's an article about Terence Pritt. I met the chap back when I lived in London."

"How fascinating," I replied, with my eyes growing heavy once more.

"I'd say! He was the talk of the town in those days. A man of industry and a bit of a rogue with the ladies, by all accounts. We tended to run in the same circles, you see. I had just been promoted to superintendent, and he always wanted to be associated with the right people."

"That's nice. So how is he these days? (And why is it so important that you decided to wake me?)" I considered asking this last question but didn't have the nerve.

"He's dead!" Lord Edgington pronounced these words with some satisfaction. "The Chronicle claims he had a heart attack at only fifty years of age."

He tossed the newspaper through the air so that it landed face up in my lap. I read the headline aloud. *"Bright Young People at it Again: Late-night Treasure Trail Terrorises Sleepy City.* Well, that does sound like fun. Perhaps we could-"

"That's the wrong article, Christopher. Look at the one on next to it."

To avoid piquing the old bear any further, I read the suggested column in my head.

__Industrialist Dies of Heart Attack After Engaging in Youthful Pursuit... Baron Terence Pritt, owner of the Eastern Steel Ingot & Aggregate Company, died unexpectedly this morning while participating in a high-speed treasure hunt which streaked across the capital in the early hours of the morning. Pritt came to the public's attention when his metal and aggregate company spearheaded the road-building boom of the last decade. Although he was a hugely successful businessman, accusations of industrial espionage and worker exploitation dogged his career. He leaves behind no children and is said to have been estranged from his wife, Baroness Ermentrude Pritt.__

"Hmmm..." I replied once I'd finished the whole thing. I genuinely didn't know what else to say on the matter.

"Hmmm, indeed," my grandfather concurred, and all this hmmming was becoming ridiculous. He kept his eyes on me, clearly hoping for a bigger reaction.

I plumped for, "I'm very sorry to hear such bad news about the poor baron. Fifty is terribly young to die these days. If he was in his seventies, it wouldn't be quite such a shock, but–"

I should have kept my mouth shut. His stare had become a glare, and he took exception to my response. "I'll have you know, Christopher, that it would be just as a great a tragedy if the man were in his seventies. In our modern world of hospitals and advanced medicine, people can live past a hundred. In fact, the king sends out telegrams for every centenarian's birthday, and I fully intend to receive one."

That put me in my place. "Yes, Grandfather," I responded somewhat sheepishly. "I'm terribly sorry for you and your friend."

He seemed placated by this and took a sip of freshly poured tea in order to spit it back out again. "Friend? The man wasn't my friend. Where would you get such an idea? He was a preening, pompous blowhard, whose only topic of conversation was himself. I wouldn't go so far as to say that I'm glad he's dead, but England is certainly a quieter place without his self-important prattling."

There were days when it seemed that every word I uttered would offend my grandfather. This was clearly one of them. At such times, the only options were to seek out a room in that immense house where he would never find me – I considered the coal cellar a particularly good choice – or accept that I would have to endure his wrath.

I chose the latter. "Why show me the article if you don't even like the man?" I was a little more awake by now and tossed the paper back to him. Well, that was my intention. Sadly, I've never been much cop at throwing. I hit the tea tray and upturned the silver teapot so that a steady stream of amber liquid poured across the carpet.

Our aged footman had already left the room and, though I rang the kitchen bell, no one would respond for several minutes. Grandfather looked unimpressed as I jumped into action. I righted the teapot and, with nothing else to hand, used the misaimed projectile to soak up the stain on the carpet.

"Most enterprising, my boy," my companion said with just a hint of sarcasm before answering my question. "I showed you the article because it strikes me as strange. A heart attack at his age? The man was as fit as I am!"

This really was saying something, as the sprightly septuagenarian was as healthy as a horse.

"You think he was murdered?" I practically yelped with joy.

He took a moment to stroke his long white beard before answering. "I'd like to know one way or the other."

"But why would anyone kill him?"

"Didn't you read the article? It should have provided you with at least two motives, even if that was all you knew about the man."

"Oh…" I replied as, evidently, I had failed to extract such information.

"Come along, Christopher. Haven't I taught you anything?"

As my mentor, the former luminary of Scotland Yard had instructed me on any number of matters over the last year. In addition to tips on police work, I'd learnt that it was never a good idea to combine a spotted cravat with a stripy pocket handkerchief. He'd also gone into great detail on the correct way in which to tie a four-in-hand knot, though I doubted that either of these pointers would help when it came to determining the reason for a man's death.

"You can read the article again if you wish." He crossed his arms and looked up at the oaken panels on the ceiling. "I will wait."

I tried to do as he'd suggested, but the newspaper was now sodden. The article in question had melded together with another page. "I don't suppose it has anything to do with Huddersfield Town's seemingly unstoppable run towards a third consecutive football league title?" The messy black ink was all over my fingers and this was the most I could extract from it.

"No, Christopher. It does not." He stood up and began to pace about in front of the window, as was his wont. "Allow me to remind you of what you read a mere two minutes ago." He cleared his throat and began to recite the article as if it were a great work of poetry. "*Although he was a hugely successful businessman, accusations of industrial espionage and worker exploitation dogged Pritt's career. He leaves behind no children and is said to have been estranged from his wife, Baroness Ermentrude Pritt.*"

"So…" I decided to get to my feet in the hope that it would jolt my dozy brain into action. "Well, his wife and he were estranged for a start. That could explain things."

He furrowed his brow, as though he thought my nervous pacing was intended to mimic his own. "Correct. I remember Baroness Pritt from decades ago, and she was quite the character. What else did you notice?"

"Industrial espionage!" I rather liked this word and so I said it once more. "Espionage could mean he had enemies and rivals. It could mean he was spying for Great Britain's foes."

"That's the wrong kind of espionage, I'm afraid. But I appreciate your enthusiasm. Did you notice anything else?"

I'd become overexcited at the mention of something so thrilling as *espionage* and forgotten what the rest of the article had discussed. "I believe it mentioned metal and something about Richmond Park and–"

"No, no. What you should have noticed is that Pritt left no children. If he really was murdered, and his wife wasn't behind it, who's to say there's not some distant cousin waiting in the wings to sweep in and claim a fortune?"

There was no time to answer as our part-time butler, full-time chauffeur and all-round impressive chap, Todd, walked in just then to respond to the bell.

"M'Lord?" he enquired with his usual efficient brevity.

"We'll be needing a car, Todd. Bring the Alfa Romeo RL to the front of the house."

"That's a two-seater, M'Lord," he reminded us with a bow of the head.

"Yes, that's all we require. Christopher and I are heading out this evening. We're going into the city."

"Very good, M'Lord." The smart young employee looked a little sombre, and I got the definite impression he would have liked to join us on the adventure Grandfather had planned.

I somehow managed to contain my joy for the seven or eight seconds it took for Todd to retreat from the room. "Oh, this is just marvellous! I thought we might not come across another crime until I was old and bald."

Grandfather shook his head disapprovingly but was soon just as enthused as I was. "The question is, if we're hoping to investigate the possibility of foul play, what should our first step be? In our investigations thus far, we've always been on the scene when the victims died. It's not as though we can drive up to the grieving widow's door and say, 'It's awfully nice to see you again after all this time. Would you have any objection to our rummaging through your house on the off chance your husband was murdered?'"

"You may have a point," I conceded. "But what about your contacts on the force? Couldn't one of your old colleagues from the Metropolitan Police give you access to the case?"

He perched on the windowsill, which was covered in piles of ancient books. "What case? If it has already been reported in the newspaper that the man died of a heart attack, you can be sure that the police won't want anyone to complicate matters. I might be able to ask some old friends to show me their notes, but I'm not going to do anything official for the moment. This may come as a surprise to you, but I made a number of enemies on my days as a police officer and I'm uncertain what sort of reception I'd get in Scotland Yard today."

This came as absolutely no surprise to me, especially after recent events, but I wasn't about to tell him that. "Gosh, really?"

Luckily, he was distracted by the conundrum we were facing and didn't notice my abysmal acting. "We need a way into Terence Pritt's world."

He had that look on his face which said, *Well? What should we do?* I could tell that he wasn't going to give me the answer before I'd had another stab at it myself.

I had a good long think and, once I'd drawn a blank, opened my mouth to see what might come out. "You said that Pritt was a man about town. He was on a treasure hunt with the society of Bright Young People when he died and so…"

"Yes?" This was the most animated I'd seen him in a month.

"And so, perhaps…"

"Yes, Christopher?"

"Perhaps we could… No, I'm sorry. I haven't a clue."

He let out a groan and explained, "In order to infiltrate the smart set of London society, we need a Bright Young Person of our own."

"You mean–" I was about to reel off a list of my more fashionable cousins when he surprised me.

"I mean, I'm calling your brother Albert."

I couldn't think what to say to this. With a slightly bewildered expression on my face, I finally managed a "Hmmm?"

CHAPTER TWO

The newspapers' obsession with Bright Young People had begun a year or two earlier. It's hard to say precisely why a group of folk letting their hair down in curious new ways caught the attention of the national press, but countless articles soon appeared, replete with lurid details of this hedonistic new generation's wickedness. *The Bright Young People Tear Across London in Convoy! The Bright Young People Have Their Day in Court! The Bright Young Things Abroad!*

After four years of war, and the resultant hangover the unparalleled conflict had brought with it, you would think that the nation could do with a jovial pick-me-up. Sadly, though, the denizens of the Fleet Street presses viewed the revellers' pursuits as a sure sign of the downfall of western civilisation. Everyone from bankers and bakers to housewives and hair-dressers were taught to loathe and fear these despicable young creatures, lest their own children should follow suit.

I, on the other hand, thought that the Bright Young People were the flea's eyebrows! With their all-night games and themed parties, their luminous clothes and daring manner, they were everything I dreamed (and doubted myself capable) of becoming. They were thoroughly wonderful.

By the time Grandfather had learnt what he needed to know from my brother, and I'd bundled up warm in every woollen scarf and overcoat that I possessed, Todd had the car purring on the driveway.

"All I'm saying is that Albert wasn't the obvious person to call," I insisted, for the third time, as we stepped out of the grand front entrance of Cranley's oldest wing. The cold stung me like an electric shock, and I would have turned on my heel and gone back inside if I'd thought for a moment that Grandfather would let me get away with such cowardice.

"Your brother is comparatively *young*, isn't he?" He marched down the stone staircase, as though he hadn't noticed the frosty air jabbing at his skin like a fistful of syringes.

"Not at all. His soppiness aside, my brother was born with the spirit of an elderly accountant. And as for bright! I've met smarter seals in the zoo than Albert. Why didn't you ring your first-born grandson?

Now there's a man who has his finger on the pulse of the city." My oldest cousin had earned his reputation as a hellraiser and was forever out on the town.

"The fact you'd even ask proves that you don't know very much about the Bright Young People." Taking the keys from our chauffeur, Grandfather eyed his red Italian sports car like a wolf gazing at a house made of straw.

"Are you sure you won't need a lift home tonight, M'Lord?" the truly bright young chap asked in an aggrieved tone; he hated missing out on our escapades. "I could always follow in the Aston Martin and collect you when the night is over."

"That's very kind of you, Todd, but I'm sure we'll be fine. And besides, we will not be home until very late." The illustrious lord had a twinkle in his eye as he said this, and I was terrified of whatever plan he had devised.

I climbed into the cockpit (which is the perfect word for it, as the car was little more than a plane with the wings and tail cut off) and we rumbled away down the drive with the gravel flying out behind us.

"Don't look so glum, Christopher. I have no wish to insult your intelligence," the old man insisted. "All I'm saying is that you haven't considered the facts. The fashionable clique we hope to meet tonight is largely composed of former Oxford University students, where your brother is still in attendance. By calling a friend of his at the Gargoyle Club in Soho, Albert delivered the time and location we need. There's another treasure hunt tonight, and we're going to be right in the thick of things."

He'd managed to cheer me up. In fact, I was warming to the idea of our excursion – despite the plunging temperature – when we pulled off the Cranley estate and the force of the engine glued me back against my seat. With his foot to the floor and the wind attacking us, Lord Edgington couldn't make a sound but turned to look at me with an expression of pure glee shaping his face.

"The road, Grandfather!" I managed to squeak. "Keep your eyes on the road!"

Somewhat miraculously, we avoided any major disaster and, upon leaving behind the leafy lanes of Surrey, he reduced his speed to a mere forty miles per hour. Evidently Todd had noticed the pulpy mess

I'd created in the library as he'd placed an extra copy of The Chronicle in the glove compartment for me to peruse. I soon found the page that Grandfather had shared with me and took my time to read the other article on the "treasure trail" as they quaintly chose to describe it.

Though it may not be high season for the Mayfair set, it seems that some young devils have returned to the capital early this year in search of hijinks. Perhaps the pleasures of the countryside wore thin for these frolicking free-thinkers as they convened once more for a high-speed chase across London. Starting at midnight in Sloane Square, this decidedly modern steeplechase stretched into the early hours of this morning.

The Metropolitan Police were forced to caution two members of the nocturnal society after complaints of unruly behaviour in the neighbourhood of Saint John's Wood. Drunkenness, cavorting and the singing of bawdy shanties led to the despatch of a small team of constables to deal with the matter.

Earlier in the proceedings, luminaries of the London scene – such as enfant terrible Fabian Warwick, artist Augustus Harred and his charming fiancée Lady Pandora Elles – were on hand to add a touch of glamour to the event. There were even reports of an appearance by The Prince of Wales. The question on the lips of this reporter, and every last person in the capital, is what new diversion will these Bright Young People engage in next?

I read the story three times to make sure I hadn't missed any significant details – and then read it once more, as I was certain that I had. It seemed that, at the time the article was written, the writer had been unaware of Baron Pritt's demise. There was no by-line to tell me the name of the journalist, but I found the judgemental tone in both pieces typical of the London press.

Thanks to Grandfather's dangerous driving, we were in the centre of London in the time it takes to say *Peter Piper picked a peck of pickled peppers*. I was most surprised when he pulled the car to a stop in front of Buckingham Palace. Though, perhaps even more remarkable, was the selection of expensive cars that had already assembled in the late-night gloom. There were countless Rolls Royces (of course!) along with a number of Bentleys and Crossleys on show. And in the centre of this unexpected congregation was a sort of ringleader, firing off instructions to his audience.

"Settle down, gang! You know the game, but tonight is going to be rather special."

My eyes were drawn to him even before Grandfather had turned off our engine. I doubt that I'd ever met anyone so instantly magnetic, not only for the curious outfit he wore, but the verve and energy that emanated from him. He was dressed – entirely inappropriately, it must be observed – in a pale green suit with a metallic sheen to it. As he gestured about with wild abandon, the thin material caught the palace lights and shimmered like liquid mercury. Equally alarming was the fact that he wore no shirt or thermal vest but had a thin silk scarf tied around his otherwise bare neck. The man was clearly insane.

"I have handed over the running of events to Mr Cyril Fischer. His capable assistant, Marjorie, will be handing out the information you need. There are three clues to solve tonight and only one pack of information per car. No matter how you might try to inveigle me, I can give you no hints."

I descended from our chariot to get a closer look at the chap. Or, to be more specific, I walked over like a somnambulist caught in a dream. I can't say exactly what I found so enchanting about him, but he was like no one I'd ever met before and instantly eclipsed all my prior acquaintances. His arms flew out in every direction as he spoke and, standing on the bonnet of his Alvis 12/50, it was as though he were a singer upon a stage.

"Oh, go on, Fabian!" a young lady in the crowd shouted, causing our leader to bellow out a laugh. "I'll give you a bottle of champagne when we finish if you whisper me the answers?"

"Tut, tut! It will do you no good. Even I don't know what tonight has in store for us. We'll have five minutes to study the clues and then my associate, Cyril, will lead the countdown."

There was a murmur of discussion and several young fellows dashed back to their cars to give themselves a few extra moments' advantage.

I noticed that the young lady had called that enigmatic character "Fabian" and I had to wonder if this was the *enfant terrible Fabian Warwick* whom the paper had mentioned. I wanted to go over to the man to find out all about him, (and perhaps ask him what he thought I should study at university) but I was interrupted on two fronts.

"This is more like it." My Grandfather had joined me from the car and now placed a firm hand on my shoulder. "Let the games begin."

"Oh, hello," a fair-haired creature in her twenties said when she caught sight of us. "Were you invited?"

Grandfather looked a little embarrassed that he would have to explain who he was. He cleared his throat and said, "No, I'm afraid we don't have a formal invitation, but my name is–"

"Lord Edgington!" The glamourous woman who had heckled Fabian Warwick cut through the crowd to address us. "My goodness, what are you doing here?"

Blushing at the attention of yet another young lovely, Grandfather bowed in greeting and admitted his breach of protocol. "I was rather hoping to join tonight's hunt. Though, I must confess, I did not realise an invitation was required."

The woman stared at my grandfather for a good ten seconds without saying anything, and I wondered if she felt quite the same about the old lord as I did about Fabian Warwick. I suppose that enigmatic people will always hold such power over us lesser mortals, but she finally managed to respond.

"I'm Pandora Elles. My parents were friends of your wife. We used to visit you when I was a child and I thought you were quite the most–"

"Do come along, Pandy," a gaunt chap with extremely blonde hair, a knotty beard and a faint scar down his cheek came to yell. He looked a good ten years her senior but had a rather gentle manner about him. "There'll be no sense in following the hunt if we don't get started now. Fabian's already quite drunk and will slow us down. I need your help if we're to stand a chance."

He was pulling on her arm, and she could only resist for so long. As she disappeared into the crowd, she shouted back to us. "Marjorie, they're my guests! Give them what they need."

"As you wish, Lady Pandora." The round-faced assistant, who was far more sensibly dressed in a thick coat and scarf, smiled obligingly and handed us one of the envelopes she was tasked with distributing.

"I'll have one too, please," a newcomer said, with her hand extended over my shoulder.

Marjorie turned surprisingly hostile on the matter. "Clear off. I know who you are, and you're not welcome."

Grandfather examined the envelope as I turned to study the rejected party. I don't think I'd ever seen so many pretty girls in one place in my whole life. She was dressed in a tweed suit and had lustrous brown ringlets and a hefty camera around her neck.

She looked thoroughly disappointed, and I felt I had to say something to make her feel better. "Why don't they want you here?"

She pointed to the camera and grumbled, "Nobody likes a journalist."

I was awfully tempted to invite her along with us, then remembered that we only had a tiny sports car with barely room in it for two. Before I could say anything else, a pole-thin, sweaty man in the monstrous car alongside ours let out a grunting enquiry.

"You're one of mine, aren't you?" He looked the journalist up and down like a prize turkey hanging in a butcher's window.

"Yes, Mr Twelvetrees. I work for The Chronicle. I'm Peggy Craddock."

The brusque character was ensconced in a Mercedes Double Phaeton with its roof firmly closed. My grandfather could chatter on endlessly about his favourite automobiles, and so I'd picked up a thing or two in our time together. The 37/95 was known in its day as the most powerful car in the world and was beloved by European royals like Kaiser Wilhelm of Germany.

As far as I was concerned, the intimidatingly black vehicle looked like some chariot of death and, sitting within it, was the grim reaper himself. The ashen, sickly fellow mopped his brow with a handkerchief and stuffed it angrily into his pocket. I'd never seen a man sweat in freezing temperatures before, and I was rather impressed.

"Then what are you waiting for?" He barked out every word. "Take some photographs of the madness unfolding around you, then run back to the office to write the story."

"Yes, sir. Only, I was thinking I might–"

Wrapped up warm in his Mercedes, that swine didn't give his employee a moment to talk but shouted straight back at her. "I'm not interested in what you think. Get on with it!"

The poor girl bowed her head and, looking thoroughly defeated, turned to leave. If there's one thing I can't stand, it's seeing people treated like they're less than human. I opened my mouth to let the awful character know exactly what I thought of him, and a stream of invective cut through the air.

"How dare you speak to another person in such a way? You may not give them any credit, but it's employees like that fine young lady who have made you as rich as you are. Your attitude appals me!"

Admittedly, I wasn't the one to utter this bold statement but, had I not been standing there gawping, this is almost exactly what I would have wanted to say. Instead, it was my grandfather who could claim credit for the well-worked dressing down, and the victim of his verbal assault could do little but splutter in response.

"I... Well... Well, the same to you!"

Grandfather stood up straighter, and a smile crept across his lips. "I'm sorry, but that doesn't make any sense. My employees don't make me rich. If you were looking for a strong retort, you might have said something along the lines of, *You're one to talk, Lord Edgington. You inherited your money on the back of centuries of oppression of the working classes.*"

"Oh, right... Ummm... So there you go then." Twelvetrees looked most perturbed and couldn't muster another word in response. Instead, he turned the ignition and Grandfather waved him off.

"Oh, that was wonderful!" I had to say when the monster in the gigantic automobile had rolled away. "You certainly showed him what's what!"

"No time for that, Chrissy," my dear grandfather said, as he navigated through the throng of cars to our own agile vehicle. "We've a race to win."

I bolted after him and he threw me the envelope. It looked as though I was to be the navigator.

CHAPTER THREE

Several cars had started circling the monument to Queen Victoria, but there was a small problem to resolve before we could begin. Evidently, someone within the palace had got wind of the scene outside and panicked. A battalion of tall-hatted soldiers marched out of the gates towards us with their rifles at the ready.

"Don't fire. We come in peace!" Fabian Warwick explained, once more standing atop his polished aluminium car. He raised his hands in the air, but the guards were not appeased by the gesture, and they continued their advance.

The company came to a halt and the captain, or what have you, walked a few steps closer on his own. "State your business."

Pandora Elles was parked nearby and leaned out of the passenger side of her white Lancia Lambda to smooth things over. "There's nothing to worry about. I'm an old friend of the Prince of Wales. Tell Eddie that Pandy and her pals are off on one of our jaunts from outside the palace. We certainly aren't looking to start a war." The glamorous nymph, with her blonde curls bobbing, let out a tittering laugh, but the soldier remained suspicious.

"Tell me what you're doing here this moment, or drastic action will be taken."

Fabian jumped from the bonnet to the boot of his car. "I'll tell you what we're doing here." He pulled the purple scarf from around his neck and held it high above him in the winter air. "We're leaving!" Engines around the circular concourse began to rev, and he commenced the countdown. "Three, two, one, and off we go!"

There was a deafening screech as several of the sportier cars spun their wheels. Horns were honked in exaltation, and those beautiful automobiles shot off in every direction. In their neat red and black uniforms, the poor King's Guards looked terrified. They pointed their guns after the escaping merrymakers, apparently uncertain whether to shoot or retreat.

Fabian had jumped from his car and proceeded to dive through Pandora Elles's rear window. His legs were still protruding as the fellow I took to be the young lady's fiancé drove them away. I could see now that the slug of a man, Twelvetrees, had positioned his car in the direction of travel and positively shot off at the head of the pack. We, on the other hand, were caught up in the mess of vehicles on the far side of the monument and could do nothing but wait for the traffic to clear.

"Read the clue, Christopher!" Grandfather commanded, as our Alfa Romeo jerked into life.

I pulled the first page from the envelope, which was more difficult than you might think with two pairs of gloves on and my fingers still frozen.

"*Where do the wallaboo, mingos and polars roam?*" I read aloud and, as soon as Grandfather spotted a gap, he nipped between two Austins to speed us onwards.

"And the answer is?" The wily chap was testing me again.

For once, I had an answer for him. "That's an easy one. Drive to the zoo. Christopher Robin gets the names of the animals all muddled in A.A. Milne's poem 'At the Zoo'. He talks of potamuses and nosseruses and gives buns to the elephants. I must have read it a hundred times."

"Excellent!"

He apparently knew the answer, as he'd already taken Constitution Hill and we rocketed along it in the direction of the Wellington Arch. The horse chestnuts of Green Park flashed by on one side of us, with the palace on the other, as Grandfather weaved in and out of the other motorists.

"If you open the glove compartment, you'll find the map I gave you for Christmas."

I did as he told me and extracted the folded map of the capital. The gift had puzzled me when I'd received it, but it suddenly made sense. "You planned this all along, didn't you?"

For once, he kept his eyes on the road. "I don't know what you mean."

"You knew you were going to take me on a treasure hunt. That's why you bought me the map."

"Ridiculous!" He winked on the left-hand side of his face, but his voice remained serious. "Now chart our route, boy. We don't want to be left behind."

I folded out the impressively detailed plan of London and, for a moment, I felt like a bird swooping over the city. London Zoo was to the north, and so we would need to take the Edgware Road before turning off towards Regent's Park. It was a simple route, in fact, but–

"No, no, boy," my driver said before I'd got the words out. "The Edgware Road veers northwest. The zoo is further east. When we get to Marble Arch, we'll take Great Cumberland Place and then zig-zag our way up to the park. It's really not so complicated and will save us time."

"If you knew which way to go, why did you ask me?" I probably sounded a little disgruntled, but… well, can you blame me?

"Because you've learnt something new. If I'd told you myself, it would have meant nothing. But now, you'll always remember."

I had to laugh at his reasoning. "Ah, I see. So the more you get on my nerves, the more I learn. Is that how it is?"

His smile disappeared. "There's no need to be facetious, Christopher."

"Very well. I bow to your wisdom. We'll take Great Cumberland place, as you said."

We did just that and, inevitably, had to wait for traffic to pass at every road junction we crossed. I could see how irritated it made him to be wrong, and when we finally reached Regent's Park and drove towards the zoo, several other cars had beaten us there.

"There's no need to be alarmed, my boy," Grandfather told me, perhaps mistakenly believing that *I* was the one who'd been bashing the steering wheel in anger. "Though we may have fallen a little behind, we now know the state of the game. Very few of the players have managed to decipher the first clue. We're in a select group, you can be sure."

As he said this, the rude, skinny man we'd spotted at the palace zoomed past us in the opposite direction. "Perhaps 'select' isn't the word for it," I felt I had to point out.

Grandfather gave a short laugh. "That would depend on your criteria. Do you know who the man in the black Mercedes is?"

In truth, I hadn't a clue, but I was in a belligerent mood and wasn't about to tell him that. "Of course I do. That's the press magnate – Twelvetrees. He owns The Chronicle." I'd discovered this much from the conversation I'd overheard with the young reporter.

"That's right – Leopold Twelvetrees." Grandfather took a quick peek at me without moving his head. Perhaps he was checking that I really was his grandson, and that I hadn't been replaced by someone with more than a quarter of a brain. "And he doesn't just own The Chronicle. He's one of the wealthiest men in Britain. He controls half of the local newspapers in this country."

"Well, I don't like him." I sounded very much like a sulky eleven-year-old when I said this, but he didn't seem to mind.

"Neither do I."

"Good, so put your foot down, and we might yet beat him."

He looked a little startled. "Christopher, I believe this is the very first time you've asked me to drive faster."

I couldn't help smiling. "You had better make the most of it. It may well be the last."

He did not disappoint and, with the svelte Italian machine pushed to ever greater speeds along the quiet roads through the park, we soon reached our first destination.

I've always loved the zoological gardens. When I was very young, it was one of the few places that we would all visit together as a family. No matter how busy my father was at work, he'd take the time to join us at lunch and we'd spend an hour or three strolling between the cages to see the monkeys and bears.

Of course, the zoo was closed at night, and we would not be stopping. Grandfather needed only to slow the car down in front of the high iron gates before we spotted what we required. A large sign had been hung from a lamppost with the words *Butcher's Hook* painted upon it in messy red letters.

"Come along, Christopher. You should have the clues ready to read. What's the next one?"

I extracted another piece of paper from the envelope. "It says, 'More apples and pears than ___ ___' and then there's a space. What do you think it could mean?"

He was already turning the car around to head east. "We have the two pieces of information we need. Now we must put the phrases together. *More apples and pears than butcher's hook.*"

"Oh, how silly of me." I should probably utter these words more often than I do. "*Apples and pears* and *butcher's hook* are Cockney rhyming slang. Our next port of call must be in the East End." I had a think for a moment, though, based on my grandfather's driving,

I was fairly certain he knew where we were going. "*Apples and pears* means stairs. And to have a *butcher's hook* means to have a look at something. So what famous stairs are there in the East End?"

He gave me no hint as to whether I was on the right track. "Continue."

"I've got it!" I felt like clapping my hands together or doing a little dance, but he shifted gear just then and, so I clung on for dear life instead. "Head towards St Mary-le-Bow church in Cheapside!"

"What on earth for?" This was not the response I had anticipated.

"They say that a true Cockney is born within hearing distance of Bow Bells. Surely *apples and pears* must refer to the stairs which lead up the bell tower, and if we have *a butcher's hook* there, we'll find the final clue."

In the end, it was my grandfather who gave a round of applause. Luckily, the path we were on was relatively straight and the car stayed on the road. "That is exceptional reasoning."

My smile had returned. "Do you mean it? Did I get it right?"

He put his hands back on the wheel and shook his head. "Sadly not. But I'm proud of you for trying."

"Oh, I give up." I genuinely considered throwing the papers out of the window then.

"Now, now, there's no need for pessimism. Just think for a moment. The temptation with a clue such as this one is to look for the hidden meaning, but in this case, that's far too obvious."

I listened patiently, trying not to be offended by every last word he said. "Very well, go on."

"Everyone knows the meaning of *apples and pears* and *butcher's hook*. They're quite the most stereotypical Cockney phrases you could imagine."

"Well?"

"Well why would the organisers have included such an easy task in a treasure hunt?" He had a point. "Think more literally. Where in London might you associate with actual *apples and pears* but not a real *butcher's hook*?"

He'd made me think, I'll give him that. My mind was suddenly awhirl with possibilities. I grabbed hold of my map and searched out potential destinations in the light of the passing streetlamps.

"Spitalfields is the main fruit and veg market in London," I finally declared. "Smithfield is the meat market, so it won't be there. Follow the outer circle of the park and then turn left on Euston Road. It can't be more than five miles away. We could be there in ten minutes if there's no traffic."

"That sounds like a challenge to me!"

CHAPTER FOUR

It would be inaccurate to say that I was getting used to my grandfather's reckless driving. The fact remained, however, that the lurching sensation in my stomach and the occasional prayers that I'd been saying, ever since the day I'd first sat beside him in a motorcar, were becoming less frequent. In fact, it was almost pleasant to zip through the park at his side, though I rather wished he had slowed down when we re-entered the city. At least I had the map to hide behind. Such moments are far less harrowing when I keep my eyes screwed shut.

"This is the stuff, my boy! You can't say you'd rather have stayed at home tonight."

I let out a feeble whimper and pretended to be focussing on the next clue. I think we probably arrived at the market in a little under eight minutes, which – though now past midnight, with many streets free from other vehicles – must surely have been some kind of record.

When the car pulled to a halt in front of the unassuming row of Victorian shopfronts which concealed one of the largest fresh produce markets in London, I had to stay in my seat for a good minute to recover.

"Chop chop, Chrissy. This is no time for dawdling."

I raised one hand to silence him as my tongue had apparently retreated to the base of my throat.

He either didn't notice or didn't care, as he continued chattering. "There's no sign of the others yet, so we may be in luck. Perhaps they fell for the same trick that you did."

I pulled myself up to take an experimental step out of the vehicle. It appeared as though my legs were still working, so I took a second and a third and so on.

"The market is a vast place," he continued, as we passed through a gigantic archway into the building on Commercial Street. "Perhaps we should split up to cover more ground."

I gave a resounding shake of the head and was frankly surprised when he didn't try to convince me otherwise.

If anything, the air seemed cooler inside than out, and I pulled one of my scarves higher and my woollen hat lower so that all anyone could see of me was a slit around the eyes. I still wasn't warm enough even then.

There were traders packing up after a long day's graft and others preparing for the next one in the endless slog of the working world. A group of children ran about the place, some of whom couldn't have been much older than toddlers, and I imagined what my life would have been like if I'd grown up deprived of the luxuries with which I'd been blessed. The very idea of being out of my bed at such an hour on a Saturday was faintly horrifying to me but, for these young lads, it was a part of their day-to-day existence. It certainly made our task for the evening seem frivolous.

"I don't suppose you've seen a sign painted in red, have you?" Grandfather asked the nearest scruff, who was using a large turnip as a football and had stacked up some empty boxes to make a goal.

"What's in it for me?" Though he couldn't have been more than ten, he had an intimidatingly deep voice.

"The knowledge you have helped an old man get one over on a bunch of toffs?" My chameleonic grandfather roughened his voice and hunched his shoulders a little to give the impression he was at home in this insalubrious part of the capital.

The smart young urchin didn't fall for his subterfuge. "How about five bob?"

"Make it two and we have a deal." My grandfather seemed rather proud of this negotiation and fished in his pocket for a florin.

"Done!" The young chap beamed with joy as he seized the two-bob bit, and it reflected back to us in his wide, blue eyes. I think it was clear to everyone involved that he would have lowered his price substantially if Grandfather had so demanded.

"Well?" Lord Edgington of Cranley Hall only had so much patience and urged the boy to answer. "Have you seen a sign painted in red lettering?"

"Yeah, course I have."

"Very well. Where is it?"

Still not taking his eyes from the reward, he pointed to the hoarding behind us and wandered away, whistling.

"*Bolton and Sons Greengrocers. Established 1894,*" I read with much delight.

"That is not what I had in mind," Grandfather called, but the boy had disappeared from sight, perhaps afraid that the old man he'd just gulled would demand his money back.

"That was cheating anyway," I said, feeling more alive again. "It's not much of a treasure hunt if we ask someone for the answer now, is it? Let's keep looking."

He nodded his assent and, without another word passing between us, we began to explore the long aisles of stalls and tables, the majority of which would remain deserted for some hours.

"Anything?" he asked when we reached the far end of the two parallel rows we'd explored.

"I saw some cracking prices on parsnips if Cook is running short."

"Very helpful, Christopher. You'll make a fine detective yet." He said this in an exaggerated manner, as though he were doing an impression of himself. It was rather accurate, in fact.

As he finished speaking, several of our fellow-treasure hunters appeared from the various entrances around the central hall. Fabian Warwick and his friends ran to the centre of the market but had no more knowledge than us of where the next clue might be and peered about wildly.

Twelvetrees wasn't far behind and popped up beside the closed-off wing where workers were building a new extension. He didn't bother looking about for himself but wandered along to where the largest concentration of his competitors could be found.

"Lord Edgington, isn't it?" Fabian came to enquire. "I heard you had joined in with our shenanigans." He turned to look at me with a perplexed expression on his face. "And you appear to have brought some kind of... polar explorer with you?"

"This is my grandson, Christopher. He is prone to wander about in such a getup. I can only conclude that he believes himself allergic to the cold."

Lady Pandora Elles floated over with her fiancé. "Leave the poor boy alone, Fabian." She wore a green velvet gown with a swooping decolletage but was apparently not so impervious to low temperatures as her friend. "Just because you have ice in your veins, that doesn't mean we should all go about scarfless. I rather wish women could get away with such practical clothing."

"I rather wish men could," Augustus Harred added. "Now, are we going to find this treasure, or should we give up and head to the Gargoyle?"

"Well, I am feeling a little parched. But don't worry, I brought supplies." Fabian reached into the inside pocket of his glistening suit jacket and extracted a slim metal flask. "Young Shackleton, would you like a swig to ward off the cold?"

He held it out to me and, even if I'd wanted to drink, my mouth was covered over by all three scarves. "That's terribly kind of you, but I think I'll go without."

Grandfather had been observing the scene with quiet interest but was eager to get us back on track. "So, none of you have the faintest idea where the next clue might be?"

"Sadly not." Augustus scratched the jagged scar on his cheek before explaining. "Fabian put another chap in charge this evening so that we could enjoy the thrill of the chase."

"There!" I pointed to the high black post in the centre of the market, to which several electric lights were attached. There was something hanging from one of them.

"What about it?" Fabian replied with a laugh. "A piece of blank paper isn't going to get us far."

Grandfather rushed away with his usual brisk intensity, and the rest of us followed in his wake. "It's not just one piece of paper, there's a number of them. But why would anyone have tied them up there?"

This was exactly what I'd been thinking, and I felt exceptionally clever to have replicated my shrewd grandfather's thought processes before he'd even experienced them. Maybe the book I'd been reading back at Cranley had improved my mental abilities after all.

"You're right." Augustus accelerated past us to be the first to the pole. "It makes no sense that someone would have gone to the trouble of shimmying up there just to tie a few scraps of paper to a lamp. Fabian, give me a hand, would you?"

Though dressed far more formally than his friend, in a black dinner jacket and white shirt and gloves, Augustus set about working his way up to the sheaf of papers which were tied to the lamp with a piece of stationer's twine. Even though he was a relatively athletic type, it took him a good minute to make it all the way up, and I spent that time worrying that it would be my turn next.

The hubbub this caused meant that our rivals were soon alerted to our find. The odious Twelvetrees slunk around the periphery like a wartime spy, and several of the more boisterous Bright Young Things shouted up half-hearted requests for Augustus to do them a favour and pass more of the sheets down. He ignored them and returned to solid ground.

I looked at my seventy-five-year-old grandfather and he looked at his podgy seventeen-year-old grandson. I imagine we were about to have an argument about what to do next when Augustus presented us with a blank piece of paper of our own.

"It only seems fair," he explained. "You did point us in the right direction."

Fabian let out an excited laugh. "You're fraternising with the enemy, Auggie. You know we'll never stand a chance against the legendary brain of Lord Edgington. Our youth and athleticism were our only advantages and you've just thrown them away!"

"It was so lovely to see you again," Pandora told us, placing a hand on Grandfather's arm as she ran past on the way back outside. "It's a shame we have to beat you, but I'm terribly competitive." She had a most musical voice, as though every word she spoke was a line from a song.

"Now all we have to do is work out what this clue means, and we are sure to win," her fiancé said, while the electric Fabian Warwick danced along the aisle of fruit and vegetable stalls as though he'd just entered a West End club.

"Christopher, with me," my *sidekick* (ha!) declared, and I scampered along behind him like a good boy. Once we were out of earshot of the other treasure seekers, he pulled me into an alcove near the exit and examined the paper by the light of a dim bulb that was fixed to the wall.

"What do you think it could mean?" I felt compelled to enquire.

He turned it over and upside down, searching for some suggestion of what we were meant to do now. "Did you bring the next clue with you?"

"No."

He rolled his eyes. "Really, Christopher, I did warn you to be prepared."

"Which is why I have it memorised. It said, *This symbol of fire is topped with a golden* something."

"A golden something?"

"No, a golden *something.* There was another blank line that we have to complete."

He peered away from the sheet of paper back towards the main concourse of the market. "How peculiar... unless..."

He thought for a moment and, as I rarely learn my lesson, I decided to fill the silence with a dose of my usual rambling. "Perhaps there's some hint in the words that will help us work out what we have to do next. A symbol of fire could be a painting or a sculpture representing... ummm... fire, for example."

Grandfather was in a sort of trance and ignored me entirely.

A thought miraculously appeared in my brain. "No, wait. I've got it! There must be a secret message hidden on the paper and, if we expose it to heat, the words will appear."

He finally snapped back to his surroundings and sniffed the paper in his hands. "Christopher, I've got it. There must be a secret message. We'll need a heat source to reveal the final part of our clue."

My jaw fell open, and I failed to contain my frustration. "I just said those very words!"

"Did you?" He didn't sound as though he believed me. "Well, bravo. Great minds think alike and all that. I don't suppose you have a book of matches upon your person?"

Not being a smoker, or a pyromaniac, I could not be of assistance. "No, but I know a man who might." I'd spotted a guard, as we'd entered the market, who was huddled in his cubby hole with only a candle for light. That would surely do the trick. I sped over towards the stable doors and, sure enough, the large, red-nosed character was still there.

"Hello, my good man," Grandfather began, laying on the charm as thick as it would go. "I don't suppose we could borrow your candle for a moment. We'll return it forthwith."

"Five bob!" he immediately snapped, but Grandfather had learnt from our earlier encounter with a member of the Spitalfields mob.

"I'll give you a shilling."

"Five!"

"Oh, bother." Grandfather produced a crown piece and reluctantly handed it over.

The grubby chap pocketed the coin without even glancing at it and shuffled aside to give us access to the prized flame.

"The message was probably written in lemon or orange juice. That's what spies used during the first years of the war," Grandfather explained, as he held up the paper to the light and faint lines began to emerge. "You could do the same trick with oil or vinegar perhaps, but this *is* a fruit market after all."

He had to be careful not to get the clue too close to the candle or our hope of discovering the final destination would go up in flames. The heat slowly penetrated the paper, and a single word appeared in large brown letters.

"*Pineapple*," I read. "Fitting for a fruit market, once again. But where is there a golden pineapple in Spitalfields?"

"Not here, boy. Not here!" He was already pushing past me to speed towards the car. "We'll discuss it on the way."

CHAPTER FIVE

The problem with his plan was that, until we'd worked out the clue, we didn't know in which direction we should be driving. Fortunately, I am a genius and, back in the car, I amazed him once more with my intelligence.

"*This symbol of fire is topped with a golden pineapple,*" I repeated.

"What about a fire station?" He pulled his driving gloves on as he spoke. "We should head to Lambeth, where the London Fire Brigade has its offices. Perhaps the pineapple is on the crest of one of their uniforms. Maybe–"

"That's a good attempt, Grandfather." I pulled my scarves all the way off my face so that he could see just how pleased I was. "But the clue says, *This symbol of fire is topped with a golden pineapple.*" I repeated the information one last time in case it would jog his thinking. "There's no greater symbol of fire than the monument to the Great Fire of London. And from looking at the map, I'd say it's only a mile away."

"You brilliant boy! You're right." He wasted no time and turned the ignition to kick the Alfa Romeo into life again. A moment later, I heard a second engine starting and looked behind us to see the sweaty figure of Leopold Twelvetrees, sitting in his own car, waiting to follow.

"That sneak," Grandfather proclaimed. "I really do detest men who cheat at sports. Don't worry, we'll soon lose him."

I don't think that grandfather checked his mirror before driving away, but neither did Twelvetrees, who nearly crashed into a ragpicker's cart.

"You see," Grandfather bellowed with great glee. "The good shall vanquish the wicked every time."

His point was undermined by the fact we then had to stop to allow a double-decker bus to pass. We were forced to roll along behind the big bumbling thing at little more than ten miles an hour. As a result, Twelvetrees soon caught up.

"It's the Monument, isn't it?" he shouted through his open window as he pulled closer. "I knew it from the first part of the clue. If I'd gone on ahead, I'd already be the winner. But the hunt isn't over yet."

I couldn't imagine what he meant by this, but then he pulled out from behind us, and his glossy black Mercedes went hurtling past at great speed on the opposite side of the road. Another car was approaching and so he darted back in behind the bus. It was only a moment before he could shoot off again. I'm fairly sure I heard his smug laugh carry back to us, as the black cloud of burnt gasoline that puffed out behind him made me choke.

I'd assumed that Grandfather would accelerate once more, as he rarely stuck to the twenty mile per hour speed limit. Driving the wrong way down Bishopsgate on a Saturday night, with plenty of pedestrians milling about the place, was a line he would not cross, though. I braced myself for the cursing and complaints that would mark his frustrated endeavour, but instead, he just laughed. It was a great, full-throated noise, which deafened me, even over the engine of the B-Type bus.

"I really don't think we have much to worry about, Christopher," he informed me as we calmly pootled along. "When he gets to the Monument, he will have to ascend its three hundred and eleven steps to a height of two hundred and two feet. I very much doubt that a man of Leopold Twelvetrees's physique will be capable of *rising* to the challenge." His laughter ignited once more. "If you'll excuse the pun."

The bus finally made a stop opposite the church of St. Botolph-without-Bishopsgate, and we were free to sail onwards, down towards the Thames to where the Monument to the Great Fire of London stood taller than the buildings which surrounded it.

His words had stirred a question that I felt I had to ask. "Grandfather, how do you know how many steps there are in the Monument? Or exactly how tall it is for that matter?"

He waved a nonchalant hand through the air. "Everyone knows that it was built exactly two hundred and two feet from the source of the fire that nearly destroyed the city back in 1666. As for the number of steps, I used to run up them twice a day to stay trim when I was a young policeman. I can't tell you how many times I counted them, but I am sure there are three hundred and eleven in total." He peered up at the sky for a moment to ruminate on days long past.

While he was in a good mood, I thought I'd put another query to him. "And what about the man's death that we're supposed to be investigating? How exactly will winning this race get us any closer to discovering the truth?"

His expression changed, and he pulled himself up to his full height, as though I'd offended his pride. "Well, for one thing, by completing this challenge, we will announce our arrival on the scene to a group of young people who should know more about what happened to Baron Pritt last night than anyone else."

"And?"

"Full sentences, Christopher!" He rolled his eyes but did not force me to rephrase the question. "And for another, I'm simply having too much fun to stop!"

This was his cue to force the sporty red car faster down the lively thoroughfare. I could barely make out Twelvetrees's Mercedes in the distance, but Grandfather was perfectly serene. When we parked our car alongside our rival's, the wise old chap strolled towards the staircase that led up through the interior of the immense Doric column.

As we began our ascent, he gave a brief summary of the Monument's past. "London's most beloved architect Christopher Wren designed this towering memorial with pioneering geologist, cartographer, palaeontologist and architect, Robert Hooke. The Monument was completed in 1677 at a cost of over £13,000, and was to be a symbol of London's rebirth after the terrible fire, which, as everyone knows, originated in…?"

"A bakery?" I was approximately sixteen per cent certain.

"Correct." He spoke as though he were a guide in a museum or, even worse, a history teacher. "The object which resembles a *golden pineapple* on the top of the column is, of course, not a piece of fruit, but a brass urn, spewing out fire to remind us of this area's claim to infamy. Are there any other questions?"

I wasn't aware that I'd asked him for such an explanation, but there was one thing I had been wondering. "Yes. Why don't you leave me here and go on ahead?" I looked up at the stairs, which spiralled above us into the darkness. "I'll only slow you down."

"Not a chance, my boy. Not a chance. I want you with me to celebrate our success."

He was full of energy and took the steps two at a time, barely pausing to get his breath back as we approached the wheezing figure who still led the hunt. I really wasn't a great deal healthier than old Twelvetrees and, by the time we were halfway up, I'd had to remove several of my coats and every last scarf.

Grandfather showed no mercy and sauntered past the weary figure. "See you at the top, dear chap." He clearly didn't like our fellow competitor. "I'd see a doctor about that heavy breathing if I were you. A fellow I knew died of a heart attack at fifty."

Twelvetrees had come to an absolute stop and was clinging to the banister for support. "If you're talking about Terence Pritt, he didn't die of any heart attack. The man was a whippet."

This clearly shocked my grandfather and his previously breezy demeanour turned to ice. "Pritt was a friend of yours?"

"Of course not. I barely knew him, and I can't imagine that he had many friends in the first place. Which is all the more reason for me to think that someone did away with him."

There was little light in that drafty stairwell, but the feeble glow of a bare bulb, a turn of the spiral above us, picked out my grandfather's features on one side of his face. It made him appear quite haunted and caused me to think of Dr Jekyll and Mr Hyde, combined in one person.

"What do you know of his death?" The former superintendent employed his official tone, and the words echoed about us.

In the shadows, Twelvetrees looked barely more human. He had a devilish cast, only emphasised by his receding chin and sharp eyes. "I know that he'd made a lot of enemies over the years through his business."

"I discovered that much myself in the paper this morning."

"Yes, but I saw him last night before he died and, if you let me win the treasure hunt, I'll tell you what I know."

Grandfather scoffed at this, but I could tell he was torn between a rock and two hard places... Wait a moment. That doesn't sound quite right.

"Preposterous! It wouldn't be winning if we let you go ahead of us. Why is it so important to you? What are you doing here with this pack of young cubs?"

Even in the darkness, I could make out Twelvetrees's sneer. "I could ask you the same question, but I have a feeling I know the answer. You're here because you think that Pritt was murdered and, if you're going to solve such a mystery, I could be very helpful."

Grandfather's whole being seemed to pause, as though the world had momentarily stopped turning. When he came back to life, he had formed a resolution. "Very well, my grandson and I will help you to the finish line on the condition that you tell me everything you know about Pritt."

"It's a deal." Twelvetrees moved to continue his ascent.

"You didn't let me finish. You must tell me all you know about Pritt, but also your reason for participating this evening."

He was hobbling up the stairs again and let out a joyless laugh. "That's obvious, isn't it? My papers are viewed as stuffy and old-fashioned. I obtained an invitation this evening from someone who owed me a favour, and I made sure there was one of my reporters on hand to cover the story. If I win the treasure hunt, it will be the cherry on the top and a real coup. I can see the headline now, "Leopold Twelvetrees; The Brightest of Bright Young People.""

The sallow chap was still sweating out rivers, though I suppose it made a tad more sense now that he was actually doing some exercise.

My grandfather descended the stairs to help him. "What vanity. You're not young and, from the state of you this evening, you don't look particularly bright."

"It's not vanity," he insisted as I took his other arm. "It's for the sake of my newspapers. Such stories will attract a new generation. Sales have been flagging since the war, and we need new readers to help us grow."

Grandfather seemed disappointed that our first mystery had been solved in such a mundane fashion, and we continued up to the summit of the Monument like a team of three in a four-legged race. "What about Pritt then?"

"He was scared, I can tell you that. They started the hunt last night in Sloane Square, and I spoke to him briefly because I've rarely seen a man look so frightened. He could barely get his words out and was constantly glancing over his shoulder. I think his past had come back to bite him like a rabid mutt."

"Why do you say that?" I asked. I'd been watching him as he spoke, and there was something curious about the way his expression continuously seemed to shift, as though he didn't know how much he should tell us on the matter or was, himself, frightened of the consequences.

"Because… Because, in my line of work, I hear rumours. Nothing I could print in the paper, mind you, but reliable rumours that the formula for the road treatment that Pritt patented was stolen from a chemist who went off to war and never returned."

I might have let out a small gasp at this. Well, in fact, I definitely did. You see, until this moment, I'd believed that our investigation was as much a game as the treasure trail we'd followed. I was willing to enter into the spirit of things but, in the back of my mind, I believed my grandfather had constructed this mystery to give us a reason to leave Cranley Hall in the middle of a long, harsh winter.

I could see from Twelvetrees's hesitant manner that he genuinely believed Terence Pritt had been murdered, and it changed everything. My grandfather must have been chewing over a similar thought. He made no response in the time it took us to reach the top of the stairs and then, with his hand on the door to the viewing platform, he asked another question.

"I don't suppose you know the name of the chemist whose work Pritt hijacked?"

Twelvetrees's expression turned graver still. "I haven't a clue. But then I'm not the person you need to talk to about such matters. It's the Baroness who will know all his dark secrets. She hated her husband more than anyone else I've met."

His face as expressive as a slab of marble, Grandfather nodded and opened the door for Twelvetrees to step through. Lord Edgington was as good as his word and made no attempt to steal victory from the jaws of… ummm, victory? Instead, he stepped back and watched the press magnate's sickly face transform with the knowledge he was about to be crowned champion.

I was rather sore that we had come so close and lost, but my ever gallant companion put his hand on my shoulder to comfort me.

"Don't worry Christopher. We may have lost the race, but we can still win the war."

I wasn't sure I approved of his muddled metaphor but, once our rival had disappeared around the bend of the central column, we stepped out into that icy night.

"You knew, didn't you?" Twelvetrees fumed as we arrived.

Standing a little way beyond him were Fabian Warwick, Lady Pandora Elles and Augustus Harred. They'd brought a bottle of champagne with them and were taking turns to swig from it.

Grandfather finally smiled. "How could I have realised that you were not the first to arrive? I certainly didn't spot their car parked on Pudding Lane."

"Oh, cheer up, Twelvetrees," Fabian said, with the bottle of Moët et Chandon extended in his direction. "Second place is almost as good as first. And it's not as though you need the money." He was fanning himself with a small bundle of ten-pound notes, and there was an empty envelope nailed to the wall behind him.

The owner of The Chronicle looked as pallid as fresh paper stock at that moment, though that was nothing new. He threw his hands in the air and rushed towards the exit, leaving my grandfather free to take a gulp of champagne.

I was instantly frozen to the bone and busied myself by re-donning the pile of clothes I was carrying. It could have been worse. I could have looked down over the sheer drop in front of me and realised that we were hundreds of feet off the ground. Which is exactly what happened next. I sat down on the stone-cold floor – just to be on the safe side.

Despite my fears of imminent hypothermia and falling to my death, it was a truly beautiful night. The Thames looked like a chunk of sky that had fallen to earth in the middle of the city for Tower Bridge to trap in place. I looked out across the capital at all those rooftops, chimneys and spires. With only the moon and stars for illumination, I felt quite privileged to be up there – petrified of falling to my death, but privileged, nonetheless.

"You did rather well for a man of your age," Fabian told the legendary detective.

Grandfather just laughed. "And you did rather well for a man of your age."

With the hunt complete and the temperature dropping by the minute, I was terribly glad when Lady Pandora suggested we move on somewhere that was both warmer and lower.

"Let's get a drink, shall we?"

Her fiancé peered at the bottle he'd just been handed and looked bemused. "What's this if not a drink?"

"Champagne makes me sleepy, darling. You know that."

"Of course, my love." There was something rather sad about Harred's manner: a world-weariness to everything he did. Even in this joyous moment of their victory, he seemed lost and lonely. "We'll head to the Gargoyle. The others will have given up and headed there by now anyway."

"Sounds like a plan," that bright spark Fabian intoned before performing a quick lap of the platform and reappearing on the other side to pull me up to standing. "You're with me, Shackleton. We'll get there first and nab the best table."

He sprinted off down the stairs and, though I was just about as tired as I believe it's possible to feel, his energy and exuberance were such that I managed to race after him.

"We'll take your car, Lord Edgington!" he screamed up the stairwell. "See you there."

CHAPTER SIX

I'm still not entirely convinced that the whole evening wasn't some indescribable dream.

As though our twisting path through the capital on the way to the Monument wasn't exciting enough, I was about to visit a new dimension – a special form of reality reserved for those pioneers and rule breakers who might reasonably be described as *Bright Young People!*

The sparkling enigma that was Fabian Warwick was, by all accounts, even wilder behind the wheel than my grandfather. So it was a good thing he didn't have the keys to either of the cars. Instead, we jumped into the Lancia with the others and Grandfather followed in his Alfa Romeo.

I'm not sure I've ever really felt a part of *something* before. I suppose I was a member of a family, though only in a very formal sense. And I went to a school where the teachers constantly informed us what it meant to be a good Oakton boy, but I never felt like I belonged there. In the car, as we navigated our way along Victoria Embankment, beside the black mirror of the river Thames, I felt... included.

Everything that Pandora did was beautiful and full of light. She smiled at me in the back seat whenever I spoke and seemed quite charmed by my presence there. Augustus offered a more sombre, mature view of the world, but his conversation was filled with tantalising ideas and highbrow concepts, and I thought I would like to listen to him for ever more.

But it was Fabian in whose orbit we had become entwined. He was truly the dazzling star of his day and each word he spoke was an explosion of hope, passion and joy. He was a guru, a philosopher, a magnet whose pull I simply could not resist. And though I hadn't consumed a drop of alcohol, I felt the buzz of the moment. I felt bright and young, just like them.

It was almost a disappointment when we arrived at the club and that inspirational excursion came to an end. Not that the Gargoyle could ever have disappointed, of course. I was about to breach the inner sanctum of that luminous new generation and what a wonder it was. We all four of us piled into the metal art nouveau lift and bashed the door across, leaving peals of laughter in our wake. I think I was possibly more terrified being pulled up against gravity in that rickety box than I had been looking out across London from the Monument. But we made it to the upper floors in one piece and spilled out in the direction of the muffled music that emanated from the nearest apartment.

"You're going to love it here," Pandora promised, as I suppose I must have betrayed some hesitation at entering the sort of place my father would have described as *a den of iniquity*. "It's paradise."

Fabian rapped his knuckles on the door, and it swung wide to grant us access to a large entrance hall, complete with Moorish ceilings and brightly coloured modern portraits hanging wherever I looked.

"Matisse helped design the interiors, you know?" Augustus informed me when he saw me peering into one of the frames. "Henri Matisse. He's a friend of mine." He managed to say this in a very blasé manner so that he didn't sound like he was showing off, but merely stating an everyday fact. One of the greatest artists of our generation was a friend of his; it was really nothing to make a fuss about.

As soon as we entered, Fabian was swallowed by a sudden wave of friends and well-wishers. He raised his hands in the air, presumably in celebration but, to me, he looked like a man being dragged out to sea. I wondered if I would ever catch sight of him again.

As I stood gawping at the glamourous space in front of me, my grandfather appeared and received much the same treatment as my new friend had. The celebrated Lord Edgington disappeared into the rowdy restaurant, and I reflected that I could never imagine myself being so adored. My faithful guide Pandora took me by the arm to deposit my many outer garments with Marjorie in the cloakroom, while Augustus signed his guests in with the tough-looking doorman.

"I hope the bill wasn't too steep," Augustus joked and, in reply, his paramour tutted fondly and led us across the hall.

"Everyone who is anyone has been to the Gargoyle. There are authors and politicians, impoverished artists…"

"Like me!" Augustus put in.

"…and even the odd American star." She'd led me over to the immense dining hall and paused to scan the clientele. "There you go. I won't point, but over in the corner is Adele Astaire and I'm sure Tallulah Bankhead will be around here somewhere. She was wonderful on the stage in 'They Knew What They Wanted'. Truly revelatory."

In his usual unpretentious voice, Augustus had his own claim to fame. "I had an interesting conversation with Virginia Woolf here last summer and, the very next evening, Noel Coward kicked the band off the stage and entertained us for hours. I've never had so much fun."

The names came thick, fast and, in some cases, were quite foreign to me, but it didn't matter. I was impressed by the stories even if I didn't fully understand them. I'm not sure I spoke a word for some minutes, overwhelmed by the fact that this nocturnal playground could exist behind the respectable exterior of a Soho townhouse. I was fairly certain I had no right to be anywhere near such a place, but my companions were only too happy to show me around.

"Oh, we must dance, Auggie," the young aristocrat declared, and it didn't surprise me in the least that her introspective fiancé had other ideas.

"I'll get some drinks, but I'm sure that Chrissy will accompany you."

"Oh, yes. Please do!" Pulling me up the extravagant, metallic staircase towards the ballroom, she didn't give me the chance to refuse. To a seventeen-year-old schoolboy who had seen very little of the world, this was a fantasy made real. Every other person there stared at me, jealous of the extraordinary being I'd had the good fortune with which to collide. I had to wonder once again whether any of it was real.

The space reserved for dancing was nothing like the ballrooms I'd seen in the houses of my family and friends. The ceiling was painted gold, and the walls on all four sides were tiled with squares of mirrored glass. Even more than the décor, though, it was the people inside who brought the place to life. Every soul there appeared to be dancing in a different manner. Three tall gentlemen of African extraction, who I soon learnt to be real-life Americans, had a space to themselves beside the elaborate fountain in the middle of the room. Everyone was dancing around them, with arms and legs flicking here and there to the music of a small jazz band on the stage.

When each song finished, someone would shout out a request and the musicians would strike up their instruments before the same fervent movement broke out once more. I would normally have been mortally afraid of participating in such an event in public, but it was clear that there were no rules to the electric display and, when Pandora pulled me into the throng, I listened to the music and moved my body in whichever unusual way entered my head.

"That's the spirt, little man," Fabian appeared from another room and began to dance around the pair of us in something approaching a high-speed solo tango.

He was hypnotic, and a space had soon cleared for other less-adventurous revellers to observe his wild performance. Augustus joined us a while later with four bright green cocktails trapped together in his large, capable hands. There were flecks of paint under his nails and even on the sleeves of his dinner jacket, and I remembered that the newspaper had described him as an artist.

"I got us all Grasshoppers," he explained, and I was unsure whether drinking an alcoholic cocktail was a wise step for me. I had bad memories of the time I'd consumed half a Pimm's Cup and a man had ended up dead. The two events were unconnected, but my father did always warn me that drinking was a fool's pastime.

The decision was taken off my hands after a well-timed interruption from my grandfather.

"I'll have that. Thank you." He swiped the tall glass and offered me a tumbler in its place. "I bought you an orange juice, Chrissy. I thought it would be more to your taste."

This was as much as I saw of him for the next hour and, when my glittering friends had tired of dancing, we went up to the top floor of the building to get some air.

"You're such a killjoy, Augustus," Fabian said as we reached the roof terrace, a vast open space with another dance floor and even a large garden planted in neat beds. The walls on either side of us were covered with a vibrant mural depicting the main floor of the club.

"It's fantastic," I had to declare, running over to the closest one. "Did Matisse paint it too?"

"Oh dear me, Augustus," Fabian replied with a laugh. "Paying a poor, innocent boy to praise your work is really below the bar."

"This is yours?" I was genuinely impressed but, looking humbler than he had all night, Augustus was unmoved by the comment.

"I was never very happy with it, as it goes." He cast his gaze across the rooftops of Soho.

"My beloved husband-to-be is too modest for his own good."

48

Pandora put her hand out and I took it. For a moment, I thought she might jump from the building to take me flying up into the air like Peter Pan and Wendy (which, I suppose, would make me Wendy). Instead, we followed the wall upon which the mural had been painted to an unassuming black door hidden behind a small potted tree. "This is Auggie's studio. He's a wizard with a brush. Those in the know say that he could be the next Picasso."

The artist in question caught up with us but was unconvinced by the claim. "You are the only person who has ever said such a thing, darling."

She winked at him, and I enjoyed the playful nature of their relationship once more. "Exactly, my love. And who, pray tell, is more in the know than *moi*?"

He wisely refrained from replying, and I began my tour of the messy studio. There were piles of canvases all around, some half-finished, others ready to be hung in the National Portrait Gallery – and they certainly were good enough. I suppose he'd chosen regular figures from the club as his subjects, as there was a commonality to them, a glamour and grace that I did not associate with most portraiture. Though I thought I might recognise some of the figures I'd seen in the restaurant, they were in a wispy, implicit style which left the viewer to decide who or even what we were seeing. I didn't know much about art, but I knew that they were extraordinary.

"I love them," I got out in a whisper. "Every last one."

"The founder of the club likes to do his bit to support struggling artists and kindly donated this space for me to work on my paintings."

I had stopped paying much attention, as I'd just found my favourite portrait. A girl in a long red dress was peering out at me through sapphire eyes.

"It's you," I said, looking back at Pandora.

For the first time that night, she seemed a little shy. "I'm going to find Fabian. We haven't danced nearly enough." She spun on her pretty heels, and I turned back to her watercolour substitute.

If I hadn't already come to adore Pandora, it was a foregone conclusion after I saw that composition. I'd never seen a painting capture someone's essence so cleverly. If the pair of them hadn't been engaged, I might just have asked the artist whether he'd sell it to me. Though where I'd have found to hang such an artwork at Oakton

Academy for Boys is beyond me.

"Really, Augustus, I mean this most sincerely, you have an unparalleled talent."

He came to stand next to me and scratched the long scar on his cheek as he examined his own creation. "I've seen better." He let out a low laugh, as though he didn't want to offend the girl looking back at us, and then gently coerced me towards the party.

Pandora was true to her word and found a group of her friends with whom to dance, while Augustus and I sat talking. I can honestly say that the conversation was so scintillating that I no longer noticed the cold. Fabian joined us and we talked about art, love, history, music, literature, travel and everything in between. Though I couldn't imagine I had the slightest thing of interest to say about any of the wonderful subjects these intellectual giants might raise, they responded to my rambling as if I made a lot of sense. They were either very generous or exceptionally good actors.

As the terrace emptied and people began to disappear off into the night, I wished that I could stay there talking for ever. With sleepy eyes and tired limbs, we eventually retreated downstairs to look for my grandfather, who we soon discovered fast asleep in a deserted lounge. He was snoring loudly, and I had to conclude he was quite drunk.

CHAPTER SEVEN

There was no way he could drive back home to Surrey in such a state, so we had to spend the night in a suite at Claridge's. I've never taken my family's wealth for granted, but I must say I was terribly grateful that we could afford such simple luxuries as a nice warm bed (and butler service) when away from home. I'd half imagined myself sleeping on the steps of Victoria Station, waiting for the first trains to run, though nothing in that brief nightmare had any basis in reality.

The hotel was known for its high-class clientele and, with our two bedrooms and private dining room, complete with grand piano and roaring fire, it would suit me just fine.

"How do you know I was intoxicated?" Grandfather asked me over breakfast (well, more like brunch, in fact). "Who's to say that I wasn't putting on an act in order to extract vital information on the death of Terence Pritt?"

I considered his point... for approximately three seconds. "Unless you were putting on the same act for me, I very much doubt it. You were still singing 'The Boy I Love is Up in the Gallery' when we got back here."

Far from grumpily denying my claim, as I had expected, he had a little laugh at this and burst into song once more. He was clearly still inebriated.

> **"The boy I love is up in the gallery,**
> **The boy I love is looking now at me,**
> **There he is, can't you see, waving his handkerchief,**
> **As merry as a robin that sings on a tree."**

As he recited this verse, he held his hand out to an imaginary beau, who was floating about somewhere in space.

It was terribly vexing when I had to be the sensible one, but he would have gone on like that all morning if I hadn't interrupted.

"A virtuoso performance, Grandfather. But perhaps we should focus on the case of the murdered industrialist."

He looked like he was planning to ignore me, and so I adopted a sterner expression and rang for coffee. Clearing his throat a little guiltily, he finally conceded, "You may have a point."

"So?"

"Full... sentences... Christopher." I thought it was a bit much of him to pick on my grammar when he was the one who was as drunk as a pig in an orchard at eleven on a Sunday morning.

"So... what did you find out in the Gargoyle last night?"

He munched on a piece of toast which our private butler had just prepared. The man was dressed rather flamboyantly for my liking. In all his frills and frippery it appeared as though he'd been magically transported out of Regency England, though he certainly knew how to toast bread!

I thought, perhaps, that my grandfather had forgotten the question, but then he came back to himself with a start. "Last night? Oh, yes, of course, last night! Well, I struggled to find anyone who liked Baron Pritt – just as Twelvetrees had informed us. What I found most interesting, however, was that it was the younger people there who knew him best. Your friend Fabian Warwick appears to have some connection to the dead chap, the nature of which I failed to establish."

"You're slipping, old man. I expected you to have the case sewn up by now."

"Very droll." He did forget what we were talking about this time and started whistling the same ditty as before.

"Grandfather!"

He looked over his shoulder in a panic, as though I had just warned him of some imminent threat. "What's wrong? Why did you... ah, yes. Terence Pritt. Well..." He raised one finger as if to make an incredibly serious point, but then crumpled into his seat. "I'm afraid I'm not in a tip-top state to investigate a murder this morning. I may need a nap."

"May I suggest a posset of raw eggs, nutmeg and treacle, M'Lord?" the exceedingly plummy butler asked, and it made me miss our staff at Cranley Hall. "It does wonders when one has over-exerted oneself."

"You may," Grandfather replied with a bow of the head, "but I certainly won't drink it."

The snooty chap straightened up at this and realised that the moment had arrived to occupy himself elsewhere.

Lord Edgington took his cup of coffee and rose from his chair to walk around the dining table. He reminded me of a man winding a clock as, after several turns of the room, he appeared to be in working order once more. "One thing I did discover is that Baroness Pritt and I have a close friend in common. That should be enough to warrant us an audience at her Mayfair *pied à terre*. We'll have lunch at The Criterion and then call in to see her." His voice suddenly became more urgent, and he stopped in his tracks. "But before all that, there's something I simply must do."

This burst of assertiveness had re-energised me, and I shot to my feet. "Whatever it is, Grandfather, you can count on me to be at your side."

He frowned and pulled his neck in. "No, boy. I told you. I need a nap."

Evidently, this was not something with which he required my assistance, and so I stayed behind to enjoy the impressive spread that the hotel had provided. As my favourite detective investigated the case of the very sore head, I set to work examining croissants, egg tarts, and fried bacon. It was certainly a step up from the breakfasts I was used to at school and, at Cranley Hall, our cook's experimental tendencies meant you could never be sure what you would end up eating.

Once my stomach was full, and Grandfather was back to his best, it was time for lunch. I won't bore you with the details of the beautiful, gleaming restaurant in which we ate. Suffice it to say that, by the time we left, I was a stuffed pepper.

"You'll have to let me take charge of the conversation with the Baroness," Grandfather insisted as he marched through the Burlington Estate on our way back to Mayfair.

All I could manage in way of response was an "Urrrrrr" sort of noise, as I clutched my tummy and tried to move my legs.

"Keep up, my boy. Keep up." Apparently recovered from his own ordeal, he had absolutely no sympathy whatsoever for just how tight my trousers had become or the war of attrition that was taking place within me. "There's nothing like a walk in London on a sunny winter's day."

He looked around the leafy street we were on and breathed in deeply as though he were enjoying fresh country air.

I was some yards behind him, tottering along as best I could. "I thought that you'd fallen out of love with London. The last time we visited, you regarded the city as a deadly trap that was eager to snare us."

"'Love' is just the word for it, my boy. London is my old flame, and we have had good times and bad, but my heart will always belong to her." He nodded to himself, clearly pleased with the phrasing, then frowned and changed his mind. "Or perhaps I am her jilted lover. It hurts to see her again, yet I am intrigued to discover her latest excesses and failures. Or maybe–"

"I think I understand, Grandfather. You have mixed feelings on the topic."

"Well, yes. That's just it. London felt like my own private kingdom for forty years. I didn't just live here; I patrolled the streets, employed by the Metropolitan Police – by the city herself, you might say. She is a beautiful behemoth, an elegant beast and she can neither be trusted nor ignored."

He was becoming overly poetic, and I drifted away with my thoughts. At least this took my mind off the indigestion I was experiencing. When I clicked back into what he was saying, we were standing in the south-east corner of Grosvenor Square.

"…And that is why I will never drink green tea again for as long as I live."

I rather wished I'd heard the rest of his story, though I was too polite to reveal that I hadn't been listening.

He looked up at the Victorian red-brick building we were standing before. "Remember, Christopher, I will talk, and you will stand quietly beside me like the obedient grandson that you are. The Baroness will like that. We'll need to win her over if we've any hope of finding her husband's killer."

We entered the building and were met by a porter who demurely enquired of our business, then escorted us up to the second floor. He even knocked on the door of the widow Pritt's apartment before bowing and returning to his post downstairs.

Grandfather and I waited to be admitted and, in those few seconds, I realised something dreadful.

"Remember, I'll take the lead," he whispered as the door swung open.

The words burst out of me before I could stop myself. "Please may I use your bathroom?"

The middle-aged lady in a pink feathery gown looked taken aback but shrugged and let me pass.

She pointed to a door at the end of a short hallway, and I yelled my thanks to her whilst attempting to walk like a normal human being.

"Lord Edgington?" I heard her utter in a deep, husky voice. "Were you unable to find a public facility so felt compelled to call in at my abode?"

I did not catch my grandfather's response, as I was a little busy at that moment. My father had always told me that I should learn my limitations.

Once I was relieved of that particular discomfort, I followed the sound of voices along a crooked corridor and discovered the Baroness in an opulent lounge. "It was just terrible what happened at Chandos Grove. I couldn't believe it when I heard the news."

Grandfather was sitting on a plump sofa opposite her. "Ah, Christopher," he said on catching sight of me. "Baroness Pritt is an old friend of the Professor's. I've been telling her all about you."

I might have blushed at this. "That must have been a short conversation."

The old detective glared at me then, as if to say, *remember the plan!* But after the business with the toilet, I'd assumed that we'd moved on to other things.

I sat down beside him, and the cushion sank beneath me as though it had a puncture. The room we were in had been decorated with little restraint. It was all pink, gold and cream, with great bundles of pampas grass poking out of expensive vases in every corner. A pink marble fireplace held a modest fire, which was the only thing in there that didn't scream, *Look at me! Am I not wonderful?*

There was an uncomfortable silence which lingered for a few moments before the Baroness decided to get down to business. "It's a pleasure to have you here, of course, but would you mind telling me the purpose of your visit?"

She certainly didn't look like a woman mourning her husband's death. She had eschewed traditional widow's garb and wore a full face of makeup, though merely lounging at home. What's more, there wasn't a chrysanthemum or lily in sight.

This was one occasion when I was happy for Grandfather to speak on my behalf. "I'm going to come straight to the point," he began. "I have reason to believe that your husband was murdered."

She froze for a few moments and then, to my surprise, burst out laughing. "Oh… Oh, that's just too marvellous. Do you really think so?"

Grandfather was clearly perplexed by her attitude, and he hesitated over his reply. "We cannot be certain, though we have information which makes it a strong possibility."

"Fantastic!" she clapped her hands together. "Do you know if he suffered?"

It was rare to see my eminent mentor so confounded. "I'm afraid I cannot tell you that. I'm here in a purely *amateur* capacity." He struggled to get these last two words out, and I'm certain he never considered himself anything of the sort. "I am no longer affiliated with the police."

"Well, I blinking well hope he did. The intolerable swine. I was married to that man for thirty years, and what did I gain?" I thought about mentioning the luxurious apartment in which we sat, or the fact that she counted two dukes and a prince among her neighbours, then decided it was a rhetorical question and held my tongue. "Terence was a cheat, a liar and I hope someone put him through the mill. My only regret is that I wasn't the one to do it."

My normally headstrong companion seemed lost for words at this brassy woman's speech. I, meanwhile, thought she was quite the character and decided it was time to forget Grandfather's plan altogether.

"As it happens, that's the biggest piece of evidence we've found so far. The very fact that your husband was so unpopular, added to his apparent good health, suggests that foul play could be to blame for his demise."

She was perched provocatively on her chaise longue but swung her legs to the floor as she became more involved in the discussion. "Yes, Terence amassed enemies the way some men collect stamps. I could list a hundred people who would have wanted to hurt him."

I waited for a moment in case my grandfather should wish to contribute, but he was still gazing uncomprehendingly across the room.

"And is there one person in particular whose name comes to mind?"

She didn't think for long. "The First Earl of Scunthorpe, of course. That's Terence's brother Bertie."

"Gosh, really?" I failed to contain my response. "My brother once took my binoculars without asking me. I was quite furious about it, but I very much doubt we'd ever try to kill one another."

She looked vaguely amused by my babbling and provided an explanation of the brothers' bad blood. "They quite detested one another ever since their father disinherited Terence. I think it explains my husband's ruthlessness. He liked to say that he was a self-made man, though, in my mind, he stole everything he ever owned – from the discoveries that made his company such a success to the money he *borrowed* from old friends to get started. He was a rogue. For a period when I first met him, I thought that was charming, but the appeal didn't last long."

I took a deep breath, as this was a difficult question to put to someone. "Do you really believe that Baron Pritt's brother was involved in his death?"

She rolled her eyes as though I was being dim. To be fair, I probably was. "No, of course not. Bertie spends the winter shooting in Scotland. Unless he paid someone to do the job, which really isn't his style, I can't imagine he even knows that Terence is dead yet."

I'd rather run out of questions now, so it was lucky that Grandfather had something to say at last. "Madam, if you don't mind my asking, we heard the story of a young chemist whose work your husband… appropriated. Do you know anything more about him?"

She produced a fan, seemingly from thin air, (though presumably from her sleeve) whipped it open and began to cool herself. Her jowls jiggled with each movement, and I thought for a moment that she looked like a pampered turkey. "Of course I do. Terence never stopped boasting about his good fortune. He was a young lad – quite the genius by all accounts. Well, he'd created some new formula for a hard-wearing road surface and wanted Terence to invest in the idea. He might well have done, but the war broke out and the poor chap was never seen again. Of course, Terence had no qualms about making the most of the opportunity."

"How sad," I said, perhaps missing the point of the story. "Do you happen to know his name?"

She raised one finger on her free hand and, with a cheerful expression, exclaimed, "Yes, I– Actually no. I don't remember."

"Of course." Grandfather shook his head, presumably unhappy

with the result of his enquiry. "What about more recently? Why did your husband join the Gargoyle Club in Soho? We were there last night, and it seems he was a regular."

For the first time since we'd arrived, Baroness Pritt appeared to disapprove of our presence and curled her lip. "We're both members, as it goes, but there's only one reason he went there. He was forever on the lookout for strumpets who were stupid enough to fall under his spell. I doubt he went a week of our marriage without turning on the charm for some young trollop. Now, I'm terribly sorry to interrupt this fascinating conversation, but I'm expecting company."

She emitted a lascivious cackle, and I think we all knew the sort of company to which she was referring. I secretly thought it only right for her to find love, considering that she was finally free from the constraints of her marriage – though I wouldn't have expressed such thoughts in front of my grandfather.

"I thank you for your time, madam," he murmured politely and then rose from the sofa in order to bow to her.

I was still a little mesmerised by the unashamedly larger-than-life character in our midst and hadn't taken the hint that it was time to leave.

"Christopher?"

"Oops, yes." I jumped to my feet. "Sorry… and thank you madam, as Grandfather said, for telling us about your horrible husband… may he rest in peace."

She let out another raucous laugh at my clumsy tribute, and the three of us moved to the door.

"I did have one more question, in fact." Lord Edgington chose his words carefully before spitting the next sentence out with crisp determination. "Where were you at the time your husband was killed?"

She examined him for the briefest of moments before a response exploded from her. "I was at home with the man I love. But I'll tell you this; if you find the person who murdered Terence, I'll reward him handsomely."

CHAPTER EIGHT

"She wasn't a great deal of help." Grandfather still seemed a little removed from reality. It was hard to know if it was due to the alcohol working its way through his body or the unusual case we were investigating. "Fancy telling a former police superintendent that you wish you'd killed your husband."

"I thought that the reward she offered was a particularly nice touch." I was still laughing at the bizarre interview we'd conducted. She certainly hadn't been intimidated by my grandfather's parting enquiry.

Halfway down the stairs, I was about to ask a question of my own when we heard a voice float up to us from the entrance.

"Good morning, Mr Fischer," the porter said. "The baroness told me you were coming. Go straight up."

I pulled grandfather into the doorway of an apartment to hide. This was a very poor plan, as whoever was coming would have seen us immediately. Instead, I tried to act calm and composed, as the man who I took to be the recently deceased Terence Pritt's estranged wife's lover approached.

"Hullo, chaps!" The nattily dressed fellow came straight up to us, and my subterfuge came to naught. "You're friends of Fabian, isn't that right? I saw you at the club last night."

"That's correct." Grandfather's eyes narrowed to inspect the young buck. "And you are?"

With a great smile on his face, the dark-haired dandy held out his hand. "Cyril Fischer." He had a grip like the metalwork vices at school. "I'm Ermentrude's gentleman caller. Used to have to pretend I wasn't, but now that her husband's kicked the bucket, we can do what we bally well like, eh?"

He did not seem particularly bright, and my grandfather was stunned into silence yet again.

"Yes, I suppose you can," I replied. Not knowing what else to say in such a situation, I finally decided upon, "Congratulations."

His smile stretched his cheeks even tighter. "Oh, how kind of you. Yes, Ermie and I are over the moon. Truly." He looked at Grandfather as though he expected the distinguished character to add his thoughts on the matter. When his silence continued, the young gent said, "Well, I should be off. I hope you liked the treasure hunt last night. I devised the clues myself, you know. Jolly difficult they were, though it turns out that a few of you were able to crack them. So bravo on that score."

There was another tense exchange of glances, as no one said anything. Grandfather continued to stare at this cheery fellow as if he were a visitor from Neptune or Italy, or somewhere equally far.

"Jolly good." Cyril Fischer attempted one last smile and then skipped past us and on up the stairs.

"Interesting," Grandfather said once we were back outside in Grosvenor Square.

Deep in thought, he didn't look where he was going and almost walked into the path of a Hackney cab. I pulled him back at the last moment, but he still didn't react. He merely waited for the road to clear and crossed over to the large garden in the centre of the square. There was a pretty fountain in the middle of the green, and a tennis court had recently been installed for the wealthy inhabitants of that fashionable district. A glance around at the expensive cars lining the streets was enough to reveal how expensive it must have been to live in that part of London, but the tennis court was a good clue, too.

"It's all coming together." Grandfather sat down on a bench beside the rose garden and rubbed his hands together with glee. He was in a mercurial mood that day, and even this positivity didn't last long. "Though, perhaps a little too easily. Everything keeps coming back to Fabian and his friends. It feels too perfect somehow, as though someone were guiding us through a maze."

"You mean you'd rather discover the solution for yourself?"

He looked up at me without moving his head. "Well, yes. Precisely."

I studied his face for a moment as he considered what we'd learnt about Terence Pritt. I suppose that my skills of reasoning and ratiocination must have been improving after all, as something of a revelation occurred to me. "You didn't believe that the baron was murdered at first, did you?"

Instead of denying my claim, he gave a half-hearted huff.

"You only brought me to the city this weekend because you realised I was bored at Cranley with nothing to do all winter."

He pretended to be glum. "Really, Christopher. Does that sound like something I would do?"

I let out a "Ha! Yes, it absolutely does. The truth is that you saw this investigation as a game for us to play together. You thought I might learn some *valuable lessons* along the way, but you never imagined for a second that Pritt had been murdered..." I paused and considered his feigned bemusement for a moment longer. "...until now."

This got the old goat excited. "Oh, you clever boy." He stood up so that my eyes were almost level with his. "And what was it, exactly, that brought about this epiphany? How did you know what I was thinking?"

I'll continue with our conversation in just one moment, but I'd like to call a brief interlude here to point out something rather important. I said that my towering grandfather's eyes were not so much higher than my own, which told me something I had been acutely unaware of until that very moment. I had grown a good few inches over the last year. I was taller!

Sorry about that. Where was I?

"Because there's nothing but circumstantial evidence," I replied. "Unpopular men must die every day without anyone crying murder. Men who seem healthy are constantly keeling over about the place. A friend of my father's collapsed one morning at breakfast when he was forty-three. It was only because of the treasure hunt – and your desire to be crowned champion – that you thought it would be a nice excursion on an otherwise dull weekend."

He clapped his hands together once again, but this time, he repeated the action several times to applaud my deduction. "Spot on, dear grandson! That is some truly marvellous intellection... for a beginner."

I tried not to be offended by the implication that I'd only recently learnt how to think.

"There's one thing I still don't understand," I told him. "What's changed? We still don't have any physical evidence of a crime. No one has singled out a particular motive or suspect, but I read it on your face as we emerged from the building. You genuinely believe the man was murdered."

He stroked his long white whiskers for a moment before conceding my point. "That is most astute, Christopher. Most astute." A spurt of energy carried him several yards away, but then he waved for me to follow him through the garden towards Claridge's. My stomach still hadn't recovered from lunch, and I was afraid for a moment that he planned on a spot of afternoon tea. It was always feast or famine with my grandfather and so I can't tell you how relieved I was when he stopped at the reception to use the phone.

"Connect me with the Yard, please," he said to the operator. She apparently didn't understand, as he had to clarify. "Scotland Yard, the headquarters of the Metropolitan Police." He shook his head in my direction and was soon connected to the internal switchboard. "Yes, hello. This is former Superintendent Edgington. I'd like to speak to Police Constable Simpkin in the Black Museum. He tends to be there at this time of day."

There was a pause as he waited for the correct line. I was terribly excited that he was speaking to the beating heart of the police force. I'd heard him mention P.C. Simpkin on a previous case, but all I knew about him was that he was a "good man" and a "very good researcher" like his father before him. To be perfectly honest, I'm surprised I remembered this much.

"Yes, hello? Simpkin? That's right. It's a pleasure to hear your voice."

I could only hear a buzz and crackle down the line whenever the other man spoke.

"I was terribly sorry to hear about your father. Did your mother get the flowers I sent?"

I leaned in closer to make sense of the response, but Grandfather didn't appreciate my presence and waved at me to wait outside. I felt like a naughty child and must have looked rather silly sitting on the front step of the most famous hotel in the capital, still wearing all my layers of clothing from the previous evening and feeling terribly sorry for myself.

"Come along, Christopher," Grandfather said as he came striding out through the huge double doors. "We've evidence to examine."

We'd left the Alfa Romeo in Soho, and so Grandfather had the doorman flag down a cab for us. I no longer had my map with me and can't tell you the names of any interesting landmarks we passed, or even the streets we travelled along. All I can say is that London is a truly gigantic place, and that my grandfather seemed to know every inch of it.

To my disappointment, however, we did not travel to New Scotland Yard as I'd been hoping but came to a stop in a rather nondescript commercial street in the north of the city. Waiting for us in front of a particularly unassuming building was a particularly unassuming man.

"Simpkin, my dear friend," Grandfather shouted once he'd paid the driver. "It's been too long."

P.C. Simpkin was a smiley, middle-aged fellow with a bulging waistline and approximately seventeen hairs left on his very shiny head. I'd been expecting a crack sleuth like my grandfather but tried to hide my true feelings on the matter.

"'Ello, 'ello, 'ello." At least he sounded like a policeman, but he wasn't even wearing his uniform. "You must be the grandson."

"You must be P.C. Simpkin."

"Simpkin by name, simple by nature..." he said with a smile, before adding, "Is something that people never say about me, and I'd prefer it if you could refrain from doing so."

He punched me on the shoulder, and I didn't know what to make of him. With his wide, naïve face and rather childlike phrasing, he certainly didn't leave much of an impression. And yet there was a flash of something in his eyes which told me that this persona was a carefully constructed smokescreen. Much as my grandfather liked to put suspects at ease by acting old and doddery, I believe that Simpkin employed a similar technique.

Having suitably bewildered me, the constable turned to his former boss. "It's been a while, Superintendent."

"How true, but it's wonderful to see you after all this time."

The two men fondly bashed one another about the shoulders.

"I 'eard a rumour that you'd given up the ghost. But I knew you weren't the type."

Grandfather gave me something of a shock just then by turning to offer me a compliment. "That's partly down to Christopher here. He had a hand in, shall we say, bringing me back to life."

He really looked proud of me at that moment, and we exchanged a warm glance before Simpkin got the wheels rolling once more on our investigation.

"After you, gov." He pointed at the unmarked building and my grandfather took the lead.

I followed after them, got about three steps inside and turned back the way I'd come when I realised that we'd entered a funeral parlour. I certainly had no interest in spending any longer than necessary around dead bodies, thank you very much!

CHAPTER NINE

"No chance. Beurggg!" I retched rather loudly, as Grandfather clamped his hand on my shoulder and pulled me towards the place where they kept the cadavers. "I mean it, Grandfather. Beurggg!"

"Oh, stop being such a coward. Seeing a corpse is no different from eating a piece of chicken at Sunday lunch. You do eat chicken, don't you?"

I failed to see the comparison, and the fact he'd mentioned food only served to turn my stomach more. Simpkin had a giggle at my expense. Sadly, Grandfather's grip was too strong to escape, and I was reluctantly towed backwards into a cold room at the rear of the building. A small bespectacled chap with the straightest side parting known to man was waiting for us inside. He sneezed repeatedly the whole time we were there.

I tried not to look too closely at the space we'd entered for fear of… well, where do I start? Everything! There was a selection of incredibly sharp tools arranged on a table, which I was trying not to notice. Drawings of various body parts and anatomical features decorated the wall but, worst of all, there were two long tables in the middle of the room with… with… Well, I'm sure you can imagine what they held.

"I'm not feeling very well." I ran to the corner, clutched my tummy and closed my eyes.

While I'd only had a brief look at him, it was true that Baron Terence Pritt had retained his youthful physique. There was only a small flannel placed over his loins to protect his dignity, and he had the muscular chest and broad shoulders of a much younger man. I caught a glimpse of his face too, though I'd rather I hadn't.

"Has anyone carried out a post-mortem?" Simpkin asked the undertaker.

"Of course. Doctor Wilson was here yesterday. I observed him myself," the man said between sternutations. He certainly didn't seem like the most hygienic sort of fellow and kept pulling a handkerchief from his pocket to anticipate sneezes that he then missed.

Grandfather hadn't said anything since we'd arrived, and so I took a peek through a crack in my eyelids to see what he was doing. He'd leaned in very close to examine the dead man's skin, and I immediately looked away again. Pritt's face was dark blue, as though someone had smacked him about the head.

"And what did the doctor make of the open wound here?" the junior officer asked, presumably pointing as he did so.

"Achoo!" was the only response the undertaker could provide before he wiped his nose and tried again. "He made very little of it. I had to assume that it happened when the unfortunate soul fell to the ground in the moments after the infarction. Though I may not be a doctor myself, I've seen a lot of dead bodies over the years. I can assure you it's quite common in cases such as this one."

Simpkin was carrying a small briefcase with him (I should probably have mentioned it before) and I heard him extract a file from within it and flick through some sheets of paper. Who needs eyes when our ears can do so much of the work for us?

"It says here that Baron Pritt was driving his car when he died. That's quite some bruise on his forehead."

The belligerent sort released three short sneezes in quick succession. Each one was in a slightly higher pitch than the last.

"Are you perfectly all right, man?" my grandfather enquired. "Is it contagious?"

The sniffly fellow ignored the interruption but responded to Simpkin's point. "Then he must have collapsed forward onto the wheel or dashboard. Doctor Wilson examined his heart and ruled out the possibility of foul play in this man's death."

Simpkin had lost his gentle tone and grew angrier still. "So how can you explain his face turning that colour? I've dealt with heart attacks before. This chap looks like he's been strangled."

I had another quick look at the corpse and instantly wished I hadn't. In fact, it was so repulsive that I wished I'd not left home that weekend. His face was as swollen as a Victoria plum.

"Pish posh," the prickly character sneezed once for each of these dismissive syllables. "I'm telling you now; he died of a heart attack. There's nothing more to it and he'll be buried tomorrow, whether you like it or not."

"By all accounts, that will be a quiet service," Grandfather contributed. "His brother hated him, and his wife is glad that he's dead.

Let's hope, for his sake, his parents are still around to pay their respects."

"That's neither here nor there." I could hear the funny little man pulling a sheet over our potential murder victim. "The funeral's been paid for, and we will do our job." He made a few pointed sneezes to usher the troublemakers out of the room, and I was only too glad to lead the way.

Back in the relatively fresh, corpse-free air of north London, my grandfather was in an oddly distracted mood. A far-off look had taken charge of him, and it was left to Simpkin to commence the analysis of their findings.

"You were right to inform me of this, Superintendent Edgington. I'll talk to my sergeant about investigating Baron Pritt a little more thoroughly. Let's see what the Met can turn up on the apparently extensive list of people who would have wanted him dead." As he spoke of the investigation, the shrewder side of Simpkin's personality emerged.

When he finally replied, Grandfather's voice was noticeably restrained. "I appreciate your help, Simpkin. I'll be in contact again before the week is out. You'll no doubt inform me of anything significant you discover before then."

The two men nodded and walked in opposite directions without another word. Grandfather and I followed the snaking high street south towards the city until we spotted a cab. At first, I thought we might have to take a growler pulled by two rather skinny nags but, at the last moment, a Beardmore Mk2 came flying in to collect us. It truly is 'The Rolls-Royce of taxicabs' and we travelled in style.

"What's the next step, Grandfather?" I injected my words with all the enthusiasm he lacked.

Sitting beside me in the back of the spacious black vehicle, he didn't respond. In fact, it was only when the driver demanded to know where we wanted to go that Grandfather showed some sign of life.

"Dean Street in Soho, if you please."

"We're going to get the car?" I asked, still trying to sound positive. "Do you have an idea to whom we should next speak?"

Grandfather had his hand to his chin and was leaning on the window rest. "We're going home, Christopher. You have school tomorrow, and I've some thinking to do."

"But, Grandfather, we've only just found proof that Pritt was murdered. We can't give up now. We must strike while the iron is–"

"I've made up my mind, boy. Please don't be so impertinent as to question my decision."

As he said this, something in me curled up and hid away. The trust that had been established between us suddenly diminished. He had never spoken to me so dismissively before, and I couldn't think what had changed.

I was tempted to shout and argue my case, but I could see it would do no good. He didn't say another word until we reached the Alfa Romeo.

Soho in the daytime is a very different proposition from the gloss and colour of Soho at night. I was disappointed to see that there were no Bright Young People loitering around the Gargoyle Club. No Jazz musicians or American dancers. I'd hoped that Pandora or Fabian would shout down to me from upstairs, but the only sign of life was a window cleaner plying his trade, and an old man in a bowler hat reading a paper on a public bench.

"There'll be plenty of time in your life to dance and be merry, Christopher. But if your last year at school is a disaster, your mother will blame me, and rightly so. You're under my care, and I was a fool to involve you in all that we've done this weekend." Even rarer than Grandfather speaking rudely to me (his presumably favourite grandson) was to hear him speak in less than glowing terms about himself.

"Very well," I said, though I thought the absolute opposite.

I took one last look at the upper floors of number sixty-nine Dean Street, and I could just make out the bright red chimney pots poking out from the terrace. I wondered if I would ever have an opportunity to dance up there in the moonlight again but kept such thoughts to myself. I got into the vehicle beside my grandfather, and he took us on a scenic route through the city to make up for the glum expressions we now wore.

We drove through Piccadilly Circus, its illuminated adverts for Bovril, Guinness and Schweppes Ginger Ale all shining in the early evening light, then along to Whitehall, where Big Ben was chiming just for me, before following the river south and out of the city.

When we left the towering metropolis behind, there was nothing to comment on but the silence between us. The further we drove from the city, the deeper the pain inside me grew. A magnetic attraction tugged upon my very being, so that it felt as though some essential part of me had been left behind.

Dusk was replaced by darkness and the headlights of Grandfather's zippy sports car showed us a world far removed from the immense, unfinished artwork within which we'd spent the weekend. There were trees and fields, and I spotted one single rabbit shooting across the road in front of us. By the time we got to Surrey, few other motorists accompanied us, and this lonely state seemed to emphasise the gulf that had formed between the old man and me.

"I know you better than you realise," I eventually found the courage to tell him when the silence had become oppressive. "For some reason, we both pretend otherwise, but the truth is that I'm starting to understand you at last."

"Oh, yes?" He raised one eyebrow but kept looking straight ahead.

"Yes. Even though I shut my eyes in the undertaker's–"

"I was meaning to speak to you about that," he interrupted. "You know, you really must learn to deal with such unpleasant scenes. I thought you would be used to them by now."

I ignored him and continued with my point. "Something unsettled you back there. I think perhaps you're disappointed. I think that you realise that our sneezy witness spoke a lot of sense and you've led us on a wild goose chase. Perhaps you were savouring another juicy investigation into which you might sink your detective's chops but, instead, we're left with nothing."

"A few hours ago, you were telling me the exact opposite." Just for once, he slowed the car a little. "Your skills of deduction have let you down this time, my boy. I'm not disappointed because I believe that Terence Pritt died a natural death. In fact, it's quite the contrary." His moustaches drooped, and he said something that I couldn't have anticipated. "Everything we've learnt this weekend points to the very real possibility that he was murdered, and I'm unsure whether I have the resources to identify his killer."

Perhaps it was the after effects of my culinary overindulgence, but my attitude was about to turn itself inside out for the third time that day. On hearing the tentative voice he'd used, I was suddenly desperate to comfort him. "You'll manage somehow, Grandfather. You always do."

He shook his head, and a look of despondency transformed his face. "Not this time, boy. London is a different beast from a house in the country or a boarding school. The police won't involve me, and I don't blame them. If Pritt's murder is solved, we'll have no hand in it. You can be sure of that."

With this statement delivered, my clam-like grandfather clamped his mouth shut and would answer no more questions for the rest of the journey. When we arrived at Cranley, I thought he had something significant that he wished to impart but, instead, he disappeared up to his rooms, and I was left to my own devices.

Whenever I found myself with a touch of the megrims, there was really only one place that would make me feel better about the world. The kitchen at Cranley is the heart of that great edifice and can always guarantee warmth, comfort and hopefully a biscuit or two. For a building with hundreds of rooms, it's amazing how often that cosy space below stairs is the only place with any life in it.

Delilah was terribly pleased to see me. She wagged her tail and walked around me in circles when I arrived, and she wasn't the only one. Well, the others didn't bark or rub themselves against me, but everyone was happy I was there. Once Todd had put the car away in my grandfather's barn-cum-automobile museum, he wanted to know every last detail of our adventure. Cook was busy preparing a (thankfully) light supper but listened in when she could. And several of the maids, and even Driscoll the gardener, were fascinated by my tale of fashionable names, treasure hunts and late-night parties.

"It's a different world," Todd exclaimed, and the look on his face was not so different from the one he wore when devouring his favourite adventure novels.

I wasn't used to being the centre of attention, even amongst people I considered friends, and I felt rather special for once. Delilah was the only one who looked less than fascinated. She curled up on the floor by my feet and did nothing but yawn all evening. There's no pleasing some dogs.

After we'd eaten, and my grandfather had officially retired for the night, the staff had a party of their own. It, somewhat inevitably, turned out that Todd was a wizard with a fiddle and, accompanied on the penny whistle by our elderly footman, Halfpenny, he kept us entertained all evening. I sipped at my lemonade and watched as Driscoll danced about the kitchen with his lovely new wife and Todd took a turn with the queue of maids who wished to woo him. Cook even managed to persuade Halfpenny to have a jig, and I laughed with joy and affection to see their cheerful faces. A new maid named Agnes asked me to dance, but I'd already had my heart broken twice in the last year (there was still no reply from the Lake District to my Christmas card). I decided that a third romantic disappointment in quick succession might cause irreparable damage.

Watching that happy scene made me realise that there really wasn't so great a difference between those famous carousers over in Soho and the staff of Cranley Hall. I had to imagine that there were celebrations such as this one taking place in homes all over our fine nation. It seemed quite obvious then that, regardless of one's background or station in life, the glee that comes with dancing and laughing with friends is a universal pursuit that all must enjoy.

My happiness was only limited by the fact I had school the next morning.

CHAPTER TEN

Oh, how dull the world of academia looked after my glowing weekend. Life at Oakton Academy for Boys felt like some sort of prolonged incarceration. Our classrooms were our prison cells, our teachers, gaolers. I was supposed to be concentrating on the important lessons of that week, whatever they might have been, but my head was full of the Bright Young People.

Every night when I slept in my dorm, I dreamed of Fabian, Pandora and Augustus. I imagined my life as a free man, passing my days in London, searching for the latest thrill, the next compulsive experience. But when I woke each morning, it was to return to a life of academic drudgery.

My friends could do little to help; they were trapped within the same sad system as I was. And while previous years at school may have had their rays of sunshine, our final months there offered not even a chink of light. My best friends Marmaduke and the three Williams were just as inured as I was. They were so stunted by our teachers' constant pressure that they didn't even think to ask me about the joys of my quickly fading weekend. We spent time between classes reading our notes, then went to bed at eight o'clock to be able to rise all the earlier and continue with our study the next day. I longed for the end of the week to arrive but held out little hope for what it might bring.

I could no longer rely on my grandfather to provide entertainment after he'd cooled on our time together so suddenly. I rather feared that, when I next saw him, he would have returned to past bad habits and would be locked away from the world, no longer accepting visitors. After the way he'd looked at me in the car on Sunday night, I seriously wondered whether I would have the ability to pull him out of any new patch of gloom he had entered.

So you can imagine what a surprise it was on Friday afternoon when a prefect brought a message to my chemistry class to say that there was a car waiting for me at the school entrance.

There were five minutes remaining before the end of the day, but my rather wonderful teacher seemed as curious as I was to discover who had the cheek to demand I leave at such a time. Along with the rest of my class, he accompanied me outside to marvel at an unexpected wonder.

I was as surprised as anyone to see a sporty silver Alvis 12/50 parked in front of the school. This was not one of the numerous specimens from my grandfather's car collection, and there were three people sitting inside, smiling out at me.

"Hurry up, Chrissy." Fabian Warwick, the libertine of fashionable London society, had driven all the way to my school in the back of beyond. "Time is of the essence."

"It's so nice to see you again," Pandora said, as she jumped from their vehicle to give me a hug. Every other boy there was quite speechless. I'm fairly sure this was her intention, as she took my hand and tugged me into the vehicle, laughing ever so prettily. "You can sit in the back with me."

As ever, Augustus could be relied upon to maintain a sober disposition in the face of frivolity. "Don't worry, chum. Your grandfather knows all about it."

"Don't do anything I would, Chrissy," Marmaduke shouted from the school steps, as his very smiley father arrived to collect him for the weekend. "I'll be off on an adventure of my own." He paused to regard my new friend's car. "Though yours looks more fun."

The three Williams still hadn't said anything and appeared to be drooling.

"I'll send you a postcard!" I stuck my head out of the window to yell.

Billy managed to find just enough co-ordination to wave goodbye, as Fabian spun the wheels of his car over the gravel drive. When we pulled off the school grounds, I was overcome with emotion.

"What on earth are you... I never imagined that you would... I'm quite tickled, really I..." I failed to complete even the simplest sentence.

"I was terribly bored with London, and so I suggested we escape for the afternoon." Despite reports to the contrary, Fabian was a comparatively sensible driver – as long as my grandfather was the point of comparison. "I like to get out to the country from time to time to remind myself of the joys of the city."

"We only left the capital a couple of hours ago," Augustus reminded him, as he sucked on a long cigarette and blew out the smoke into the cool afternoon.

Fabian nodded efficiently. "Yes, and that's plenty long enough for me. Have you seen this place? Nothing but leaves and acorns and the odd weasel." He pointed at a squirrel that was watching us pass.

"As ever, the boys are taking credit for my good idea." Pandora poked the driver in the seat in front of her. "I suggested we come down here to surprise you. And it was worth it just to see the look on your face." She pinched my cheek then, and I turned quite red.

"And don't worry about the costume, Chrissy." Augustus spoke most reassuringly and, had I been worried about any costumes, this would have quickly set my mind at ease.

"Costume? What costume?" Instead, I was quickly on edge.

"For the Wonderland Ball, of course." Much like my grandfather, when I failed to extract meaning from whatever he was saying, Fabian spoke as though I was very slow not to understand something of which I'd never previously been informed.

"That sounds... interesting," I replied, but in my head, I was screaming, *Help! Somebody, help! These mad people have kidnapped me, and they're almost certainly about to dress me up as a Cheshire Cat!*

"We'll have to wear our costumes to the hunt, but that just makes it more fun," he continued before Pandora's voice rose with great elation.

"Wait until you see what we chose for you to wear. You'll be the talk of London."

Yet again, her sweetness and positivity had soothed my fears. I'm sure I would have dressed as the Queen of Hearts if she had told me I looked handsome.

"I can't wait," I said, and I'm almost certain I meant it.

But first, before our night of fun, there was an evening of fun to enjoy. We had an early dinner in the plush, velvet basement of Café de Paris in the heart of the West End. A jazz band performed on the stage for us, as neatly uniformed waitresses delivered mouth-watering bites to our table. When dinner was complete, our plates were whipped away, and the restaurant transformed into a ballroom for all those beautiful creatures to dance away the night.

Fabian seemed to know every last person there by name, from the Prince of Wales's cousin – with whom he happened to cross paths in the toilet – to the bubbly girl who took our coats in the cloakroom. I decided that he should have been up on the stage rather than dancing in front of it. He was the pulse of every party and could make me cry with joy at his endless stories of famous figures and their unlikely misadventures.

Pandora split her time most democratically among her band of followers but looked at her fiancé with such tenderness that it was easy to tell whom she most adored. Though too shy to dance with us, and with his feet firmly on the ground, Augustus himself was simply indispensable. Without his steadying presence there, I don't think any one of us would have known what we were doing.

Dancing the hours away was only part of the plan, though, and the time soon came for us to leave. Fabian had smuggled in our costumes, and we retreated to the facilities to change before heading off into the night. We certainly received some suspicious looks as we rampaged out of the club and across Leicester Square in search of a cab. It was one of those airy, shimmering nights for which winter was invented, and I felt entirely exhilarated by every last moment of it.

"I still don't understand why you decided to pick up a silly schoolboy from the middle of nowhere and show him the town. What were you thinking?" I asked the whole group when we arrived at St James's Park, the starting point for that night's challenge.

They smiled at one another and, had it been a less generous bunch of characters, I might well have suspected them of cozening me!

It was Fabian, or rather, The Knave of Hearts, who finally answered the question. "You may not realise this yet, Christopher, but you're just about the only real person left in this city."

I already had spots of theatrical makeup on my cheek but managed to blush all the same. "You're clearly all quite mad." I was, thankfully, not dressed as the Cheshire Cat after all. They'd found me a fetching woollen suit and a bejewelled crown to play the White King.

Pandora (who was only ever going to be Alice) put one hand on my shoulder to confirm her friend's statement. "It's true, Chrissy. We think you're one of a kind."

I like to imagine that Augustus, our Mad Hatter for the evening, would have echoed the sentiment, but we were interrupted before he could.

"Ladies and Gentlemen, Kings and Queens, Dodos and Mock Turtles, may I have your attention?" Cyril Fischer, the man I'd met at Baroness Pritt's apartment the previous Sunday, was standing on a park bench in front of the lake, shouting to the assembled menagerie. "I'm sorry to tell you that we have dispensed with this evening's treasure hunt."

Boos and whistles of disappointment rang out around the park and over towards Buckingham Palace, but Cyril calmed everyone down by raising his hands in appeasement. "Easy there, children. If you give me just one moment, I'll explain what new thrill I have cooked up for you all." He had a strangely undulating voice and spoke as though there were several silver spoons and a cake knife still wedged in his mouth. "In place of the treasure hunt, we're going to play a little game of Hare and Hounds."

The revelation sparked a buzz of anticipation and I glanced about at the group of competitors. It was hard to recognise many people because of the elaborate costumes that most of them wore, but I spotted the young reporter, Peggy Craddock making notes of everything that was said. Her boss, Leopold Twelvetrees, was there too. He was lurking a little way from the main group, clearly desperate to win this time.

"My lovely assistant, Marjorie, here has a pile of envelopes with your names upon them. Inside, you will discover your role for the evening. If you are a hare, you will also find a list of destinations to visit, which you must leave your mark upon with chalk. If you are a hound, you will be chasing after your designated hare and attempting to stop them before they can reach the three famous landmarks on your papers. Each pair has a different itinerary, and the winner is the first hare to reach the final destination without being caught. Is everything clear?" Cyril waited for an answer, which Fabian was, of course, happy to provide.

"No, sorry, old man. Could you start again from the beginning?"

"What a wit you are, Mr Warwick." The foppish caller shook his head but winked encouragingly at my friend.

Throughout the time he'd been explaining the rules of the game, a tall, lithe man dressed as a lion had been looking in my direction. He was on the far side of the group, but I was sure he was staring straight at me. I didn't think too much of it at the time as, just then, Marjorie appeared with our envelopes. I was about to discover whether I would be a hunter or the prey.

"Hare!" I said, disappointed by the very inevitability of it all. "I suppose that means I'll have to run across the city all night. If there's one thing I hate, it's running... and swimming. Actually, I tried climbing once, and that was even worse."

My friends were in hysterics by this point, and I decided not to go into my distaste for cycling.

Pandora held up her paper. "I'm a hound."

"Me too." Augustus sounded rather cheerful for once.

"Hare," Fabian said with a note of despair. "Looks like you won't be the only one out of breath tonight, Chrissy."

We didn't have time to go into any more detail than this, as Cyril was about to start the race. "Hares, you will depart on my first whistle. Hounds, you'll depart on my second whistle, giving your targets a three-minute head-start. You may travel by any means of transport except cars and taxis, as that would simply be cheating. And so, if everyone is ready..." He held one hand in the air and then brought it swishing down in one clean motion. "Go!"

CHAPTER ELEVEN

I ran.

I ran with all my puff and energy and didn't stop until I'd reached Charing Cross Underground. The first stop on my list explained that I would have to *Visit the two lost princes*, which I thought a pretty straightforward clue, even for me. I paused to look at the snaking Tube map on the wall of the station and soon found that The Tower of London was straight along on the District Railway line and that I could get off at Mark Lane.

So far, so simple, but I was gripped by the idea that I was being hunted. I paid my fare and shot down the stairs to be swallowed up by the subterranean tunnels, like Orpheus descending into Hades. It made me a little claustrophobic, and I realised that this was the first time in my life that I had boarded a train – or any form of transportation, for that matter – by myself. The late-returning commuters suddenly looked grim and dangerous to me, and I tried to appear calm so as not to catch anyone's attention. The fact that I was dressed as a fictional king didn't help on that score.

I watched the tunnel behind me as I waited for the next train to arrive. Even the slightest delay could mean that I would be thwarted before the race had begun. Luckily, the Tube rolled into view, and I got on without incident. I saw a glamourous unicorn lady and a man dressed as a lobster stroll onto the platform as we pulled away, but I couldn't tell whether they were hares or hounds.

It was oddly serene to sit in that comfortable carriage with businessmen reading the Financial Times, and I rather wished I'd had a book with me as we whistled under London in the darkness. The occasional spark of the wheels on the tracks added some drama to the occasion, but I was otherwise quite peaceful. I even managed to put thoughts of my hound from my mind, for the six stops to my destination at least.

On arrival, I scanned the platform to ensure I had not been followed before getting off the train.

"Hurry up there, son," the station attendant bellowed. "Doors closing!"

I jumped down at the last moment and my exertions commenced once more. Running up all those stairs made me wonder whether any game was worth so much effort. I emerged into the frosty night, panting, though relieved that my costume was so well insulated.

The Tower of London was only a few minutes' walk – or, in my case, a five-minute exhausted stumble away. I passed Tower Hill, where so many doomed men had been hanged over the centuries, and approached the great stone fort. The White Tower itself was closed at that time of night, but I could access the outer ward to leave my mark. Cyril had thought of everything, and there was a piece of clean, white chalk in the envelope. Somewhat solemnly, as though paying my respects, I left my initials on the flagstones in front of the Bloody Tower where the two princes had met their fate.

Leaving that ancient site behind brought the danger back to me. My heart beat out a steady thud in my chest, which seemed to echo about my body and up to my ears. I was certain that my pursuer would appear at any moment, but I needed a moment to read the next clue.

"*Go to where the Lord Chamberlain's Men once trod the boards,*" I said aloud, and a rather grumpy road sweeper mumbled under his breath in a deep Scottish accent.

"Bloody bairns dressing up like idiots. *Bright Young People*? More like Dim Immature Upstarts if you ask me!"

I'm not very good at responding to criticism, and so I laughed and said, "Oh, that's very witty. I don't suppose you know where William Shakespeare's theatre once stood?"

He clearly hadn't been expecting a response and looked a little apologetic for his barb. "Maybe I do. What's in it for–"

"I'll give you two bob," I interrupted, as there was no time for a protracted negotiation.

"The Globe Theatre," he recited, "rebuilt, after a fire, in June 1614, closed by the Puritans of the Long Parliament during the First Civil War of 1642."

I was genuinely impressed by his knowledge. "How marvellous. You certainly know your stuff."

He gave a good-humoured sniff and wiped his nose on the back of a filthy sleeve. "As it happens, I'm something of an aficionado of history."

"That's wonderful, truly wonderful. I must admit it's one of my less strong subjects at school, but I do find it fascinating since a new teacher took over last term." I extracted the coin from my purse and held it out to him. "So, whereabouts was Shakespeare's theatre then?"

I followed his ever so helpful instructions and walked across Tower Bridge and along the southern bank of the river. As I crossed the relentless waters of Old Father Thames, I had the feeling once more that someone was running me close. I pulled my white suit jacket tighter against the cold and quickened my step, but my heartbeat had become quite earsplitting.

I soon found myself at an inconsequential spot beside a noisy pub called The Globe. The picture of a circular, Elizabethan theatre on a hanging wooden sign seemed to confirm that I had come to the right place. But, as I withdrew my chalk, I hesitated. There was something deeply sinister about the darkened doorways and grim shadows of that dingy street. In the moment before a hand clasped my shoulder, I had a sense of how it must feel to be an antelope pursued across the plains of the Serengeti.

"I've got you!" a voice bellowed, and I tried to jump backwards, but it was too late. The lionish figure I'd seen at the park loomed over me and I screamed like a baby boy.

The man wore a mask, a thick mane and a long beige cashmere overcoat, but it wasn't his costume that frightened me so much as the intensity of his stare. All of a sudden, I knew that Baron Terence Pritt's killer stood before me, and that I didn't stand a–

"Christopher, do calm down." I recognised that voice. "Why on earth are you so startled? It's just a game." Removing his mask, my pursuer looked quite mystified by my behaviour. I was not about to be cut to pieces by a savage killer, after all.

Just at that moment, two boisterous lads crashed out of the pub and gave the lion-man and the white king a bewildered look.

"Are you all right there, boy?" one of them asked in a thick northern accent. "This old fella giving you trouble?"

I probably blushed then, as The Marquess of Edgington, Lord of Cranley Hall, stepped out of the shadows to reply. "I most certainly am not. This boy is my grandson and I have successfully chased him across the capital in a game of Hares and Hounds."

The two young men looked at one another and the first chap let out a long breath. "Well, there's nowt so queer as folk." With a shrug, he put his arm around his friend, and they wandered drunkenly away.

I decided that this was the moment that I should take off my crown and hit my grandfather gently about the arm with it. "You terrified me."

"Well, you have my apologies, but this clearly isn't the game for you. I've been waiting for you here for ten minutes already. How could you be so slow?"

"Waiting for me?" My voice rose, and I sounded like a strangled parrot. "That's cheating. You skipped the first clue and jumped ahead to the second."

His snow-white moustache bristled in the glow of a pink-hued streetlight. "I certainly did not cheat. I merely made an adjustment for your age and relative vigour."

"That sounds like cheating to me."

"And you sound like a sore loser."

We held each other's gaze, and I allowed the standoff to simmer for a good five seconds before I burst out laughing. "Oh, Grandfather. I accept defeat. It's lovely to see you, and I'm awfully glad to know that I wasn't being chased by a maniac. I genuinely thought that Jack the Ripper had returned from the annals of the past to continue his campaign of violence."

He squeezed my shoulder more affectionately now. "You too, my boy. And I apologise for alarming you." He seemed to hesitate over his words for a moment. "Though, please don't mention Jack the Ripper. It may seem like long-forgotten history to you, but speaking as a bobby from those dark days, I can tell you that I still have nightmares about the wickedness that he enacted."

I had another brief laugh, and we headed off to investigate our last clue together. "*Where Kings are crowned, married and laid to rest.*"

"How infuriatingly easy," Grandfather complained. "They might just as well have given us the postal district and sub-sector."

I wasn't as confident as my wise old forefather and felt I should confirm my intuition. "So that would be… Westminster Abbey?"

"Yes, Christopher. That is correct." At least I'd made him smile. "Off we go."

We soon discovered that everyone in the game had the same final clue and that several pairs of competitors had already finished when we arrived.

"Oh, Chrissy," Pandora called from the steps of the church. "Don't tell me you were nabbed?"

"Sadly so." I thought about bringing up the unfairness of my grandfather's hunting strategy but concluded that it was best to let that particular dog have a few more winks.

His claws raised to the heavens, a decidedly sheepish lobster was standing next to my friend. I had to conclude that she had caught her prey; it was hardly surprising considering the oversized costume he wore. I was glad that I hadn't had to run about in such a bulky ensemble.

"No sign of the boys yet," Pandora explained. "I thought that Augustus would romp home, but apparently he's fallen at one of the hurdles." She enjoyed her own metaphor immensely and tittered, as our leader Cyril called for everyone's attention.

"I know that we're still missing some of the others, but it's rather cold tonight and we have a ball to attend." There were some cheers of approval at this, and he waited to have our attention again before continuing his announcement.

I noticed a flash, like distant lightning, and turned to see the hardworking reporter, Peggy Craddock, taking a photo of the group. Cyril was drawing out his announcement, and there were calls for him to hurry up.

"And so, the winner of the first ever cross-London Hare and Hounds pursuit is…" He paused once more and, before he could finish the sentence, a harrowing scream rang out from the direction of Parliament Square.

Cyril tried once more to reveal the name, but halfway through the sentence, police whistles started blowing. I heard the heavy-soled shoes of bluebottle policemen pounding across the pavement and people running closer to see what had occurred. Grandfather looked troubled by the development and traversed the crowd to investigate. I found myself involuntarily following him, but Pandora stayed behind, that angelic smile never leaving her face.

"Head back into Parliament and use the phone there to call it in," I heard a sergeant say to his junior officer. "This could be political. We don't want to make a hash of things."

My grandfather had already passed through the thick concentration of people and on to the triangle of grass behind St Margaret's. I had almost reached him when I saw a young man dressed as a playing card go hurtling forward.

"No…" Fabian screamed, apparently able to make sense of this unusual scene in a way that I couldn't. "Please tell me he'll be all right."

My grandfather had knelt down beside one of the constables and was examining a small heap that was laid out in front of him upon the ground. He nodded to himself gravely and then rose to stop Fabian getting any closer.

"Tell me he's fine." The poor chap was on the point of tears. "Tell me this is just a joke and he'll be–"

"You know I can't do that." Lord Edgington seized our new friend by the wrists and looked into his eyes to calm him down. "Augustus has been shot through the heart. I'm afraid he's quite dead."

CHAPTER TWELVE

I'm sure I will never forget the wail of agony that cut the night when we broke the tragic news to Pandora. Is there any pain so great as that felt by parted lovers? If so, it would have been hard to convince my dear Lady Pandora of such a possibility. Still dressed as that curious heroine of Victorian literature, she collapsed to her knees on the grass, and Fabian tried to comfort her as best he could.

I also felt like crying and was struggling to make sense of what had happened. I'd been witness to more than my fair share of murder cases over the last year but, unlike some of the earlier victims (mentioning no names) it was hard to imagine that anyone could do such a thing to a kind-hearted fellow like Augustus Harred.

With the initial formalities concluded, and an inordinate number of officers spilling out of two Model T vans, I saw that my grandfather was alert to the scene. I watched as his eyes danced about the faces of those present and noticed several young chaps from the Gargoyle Club who had stayed to be of help. There were loiterers too; people with no connection to the dead man who wanted to take home some exciting titbit to their families. To be able to say, *I saw a murder victim. He was lying dead not two hundred yards from the Houses of Parliament.*

The police moved to control the excited crowd and would let no one close to the body. I decided that, as I was now rather keen on the idea of my detective skills one day matching my famous grandfather's, I should copy his example and observe what was unfolding. The primary protagonists were still comforting one another. Fabian had stayed strong for Pandora's sake and answered any questions the police put to him in short, sharp sentences. I hadn't seen him so controlled before. He had to fight to hold in his usual eccentricities, but he managed it for the sake of propriety and his beloved friend.

Cyril lingered at the edge of the action, and I found his continuing presence there a little odd. From what I'd seen, he was not a close confidante of anyone in Fabian's gang, though they clearly knew one another. And yet, from the look of him, he was quite devastated by the series of events that had occurred. Having abandoned the other competitors, he was a haunted figure, peering in from the outside. A few minutes later, his inamorata Baroness Pritt appeared, and I didn't see them again that night.

I watched my grandfather and had the definite impression that he was waiting for something to happen. Rather than approach the scene or introduce himself to the officers on duty, he was content to keep his distance, and I eventually understood why.

"Chief Inspector Darrington," he called when the top man arrived.

He waited for the senior officer to notice him and then negotiated with the closest constable for permission to pass. I was eager to see how the two men would react to one another. It had been many years since my grandfather retired, and I was unsure whether they would shake hands, punch one another boyishly on the arm or offer a cold nod. Instead, the chief inspector stood up to his full height and saluted his former colleague.

"Superintendent Edgington, what an honour to have you here."

"The honour's all mine, Chief Inspector." Grandfather offered a casual salute in return and acted as though no time had passed since their last case together. "I was here when the corpse was discovered and happen to know the deceased. I would appreciate it if you could keep me abreast of your findings."

I really thought that Darrington would object, but the man was evidently one of my grandfather's admirers, and we were lucky he'd been put in charge of the case. "Of course, sir. I'd appreciate any help you can give on the matter."

The chief inspector had a stern face and a military air about him. I had to imagine that he had done something important during the Great War, like liberating a French village or capturing a platoon of murderous Germans. This had little bearing on his relationship with my grandfather, though, and it was clear that he was awestruck. Perhaps he'd been transported back to a time when he was a new officer, and it was Superintendent Edgington who gave the orders.

He turned to walk towards the scene of the crime, but my grandfather dallied for a moment to point past the line of uniformed officers. "The young boy dressed as a chess piece; he's my assistant."

Darrington nodded to his underlings, and they broke their chain to let me through.

"This is Christopher," Grandfather explained. "I've been training him for a life of detection." I wasn't expecting him to reveal this so openly. He'd certainly never said the words to me before. "Someone will need to keep an eye on all the miscreants in our family when I'm gone, and so I've chosen my grandson."

Darrington seized my hand and gave it a violent shake. "It's a pleasure, young man. Your grandfather is a fine teacher. Tougher than a chest of boot leather and a fine teacher. Though I'm sure you don't need me to tell you that."

Grandfather snickered under his breath. "I like to think I've mellowed a little in my dotage."

The chief inspector let out a note of disbelief as, even after this short reunion, it was plain that Lord Edgington's mind was as sharp as it had ever been. With his lion mask and mane discarded, Grandfather looked like any other plain-clothes officer, and we took the last steps over to see Augustus.

"You say you know the man?" Darrington asked.

My grandfather was examining the position of the corpse and did not immediately answer. "That's right. A recent acquaintance and we'd spent no great time together, but he certainly seemed like a stand-up fellow."

It was tragic to see my friend lying there motionless, the spark gone from his eyes. He was positioned half on his side with one leg trapped beneath the other as though he were trying to run away. His lips were open a fraction, and I wondered if he'd uttered Pandora's name one last time before dying.

The very idea brought a tear to my eye, and I thought I might have to turn away. It was not just that Augustus was young. After all, I had witnessed the murder of one of my brother's friends, born a decade later. No, what struck me so acutely was the wasted potential he'd possessed. He would never develop his style as an artist. No great Parisian gallery was likely to exhibit his work. He was simply one of the many thousands of undiscovered geniuses whose name would slide into obscurity.

"He was a wonderful painter," I felt I should mention. "I visited his studio at the Gargoyle Club last weekend, and he was incredibly talented."

"The Gargoyle?" the rather severe policeman confirmed. "So he's one of these Bright Young People we keep getting calls about, is he? Racing across the city at all hours of the night, breaking the speed limit without fail. In my day, playing a hand of cards was enough of a diversion. I don't hold with all this modernity."

I noticed Grandfather wince as his former subordinate mentioned speeding. "Oh, quite."

"And I suppose that explains the costumes." Darrington waved one arm about the scene at the remaining Wonderlanders. "Did the Mad Hatter have an enemy in the books? Perhaps we should be interviewing the Queen of Hearts or…" He clearly didn't know a great deal about Lewis Carroll's masterpiece.

"Time," Grandfather finished the sentence for him. "In 'Alice's Adventures in Wonderland', the Hatter has an argument with Time. Though I don't think that will help us catch Augustus's killer. On the other hand, if you happen to have a murder investigation kit at hand, it could prove very useful."

Darrington shouted something to one of the men, who returned forthwith carrying the small black bag that the renowned detective had requested.

My grandfather knelt in front of the body and, upon extracting a pair of gloves and tweezers to avoid contaminating any evidence, looked set to rifle the man's pockets but paused to glance up at the supervising officer.

"May I?" he asked just in time.

"Of course, Superintendent." Darrington spoke with a tone of great humility.

With permission granted, the onetime bloodhound of Scotland Yard commenced a thorough search of the dead body. He extracted a passport and a slim leather wallet but found little of interest inside, and the rest of the pockets were empty.

"That's odd. Why would he carry a passport?" Darrington asked when no one had commented upon it.

Grandfather flicked through the pages and found stamps from various countries on the continent. France, Belgium, Germany and Luxembourg were all well represented. "Identification, I suppose." He tapped the document against his gloved hand before adding, "Perhaps people mistook him for a younger man."

"He's clutching something," I said, pointing to the dead chap's right hand. I could just make out a small metal object peeking through his fingers.

"Well observed, my boy." Grandfather looked over his shoulder at me with a smile before carefully prising the item free.

"A cufflink!" Darrington exclaimed with some astonishment.

"Yes. And there's a monogram on the back." Lord Edgington held up the mother of pearl cufflink to the light of a distant streetlamp and attempted to read the two letters. "It says, *S.M.* If I'm not mistaken. Tell me, James, what do you make of that?" He spoke to his colleague in much the same tone as when lecturing me.

Darrington bent to examine the inscription. "S.M. could be anyone. We'll have to look into his family and acquaintances. What's more interesting is the fact it ended up in his hand. Might it not have been torn from the killer's sleeve in a tussle?"

Grandfather's moustaches wavered upon his lip as he considered the possibility. "I think the chances are slim. It's the sort of thing that happens in ha'penny novels, of course, but it would be a challenge to catch hold of a cufflink and even harder to pull it clean from a man's shirt."

"So we can conclude that the killer wanted us to find it." A thought occurred to me then, but I refused to say it out loud. It was my grandfather's three final words that gave me the idea. "…a man's shirt." Very few women wore cufflinks. Perhaps the killer thought that, by leaving such an item in Augustus's hand, we would assume a man was responsible for the crime.

Although I did not voice these points, the expression on Grandfather's face told me he knew just what I was thinking.

"It's a genuine possibility that the killer wanted to shift the blame." He ran the nail of one thumb over his cheek, as though attempting to shave off the short white bristles. "Perhaps S.M. is a person in Augustus's orbit who fits many of the criteria of what we might look for in a culprit. But I'm telling you now, if that is the case, they will not be to blame."

"Fascinating," Darrington responded – much as a child would be impressed by a wise old uncle. "We'll send it to a chap I know at Scotland Yard. He's a sort of scientist, I suppose. Fingerprints, bullet casings, the tiniest thread of cotton on a victim's clothes – if there's something to find, he'll find it."

"'Every contact leaves a trace,'" Grandfather replied under his breath, then looked back at his former colleague. "Jolly good. You must tell him to investigate the hallmark on the cufflink, too. The back is made of white gold and, if I'm not mistaken, that is not a British stamp. An ornate crown in a circle – I've not seen one quite like it before. I imagine that Spilsbury, the Home Office pathologist, will want to examine the body. The government will be eager to rule out any political connection."

"Good thinking, sir." Darrington looked even more impressed by my stately grandfather's conclusions. He took the neatly bagged cufflink and placed it in his breast pocket. "However, I think there is a more pressing question to address. Do you have any thoughts on who might have wanted the man dead?"

I looked across the lawn to where Pandora was sitting. She had her back against the church wall and her legs crossed. In her blue pinafore dress and long white socks, she looked like a broken-hearted schoolgirl, and I felt terribly sorry for her. I noticed that she was resting her head on good old Fabian, and I realised how difficult it would be for me to consider my new friends' guilt in the case. It's awfully hard to investigate a murder when the suspects are all such nice chaps.

"We've only just begun," my grandfather stole these words from the tip of my tongue. "Most people have skeletons buried about their properties if you make the effort to investigate. There's plenty of time to discover an impoverished relative or a jilted lover from Augustus's past. However, I believe that Terence Pritt's death of an apparent heart attack just one week ago bears re-examining. There may well be a connection."

"Of course, sir. I'll get my best men onto it right away." Darrington hesitated then, as though worried he would lose his mentor's esteem. "You have my thanks, Lord Edgington. Though I'm afraid I can't allow you to investigate the case in any official capacity." His voice had grown gruffer, but he now broke into a cautious smile. "Though I can assure you that none of my officers will stand in your way if you wish to assist us informally. We will share information as soon as we have anything, and perhaps you'd be so good as to return the courtesy."

Grandfather took one last look at the deceased and then rose to standing. "Thank you, old friend. That is exactly what I wanted to hear."

CHAPTER THIRTEEN

I could see that my grandfather would have loved to spend the night interviewing witnesses and looking for clues, but it was already past twelve, and the temperature had dropped some distance below freezing point.

"Which car did you bring?" I asked, in order to speed things along.

"The Silver Ghost cabriolet. Why do you ask?"

"Because we're going to drive Pandora and Fabian home."

He regarded me in that strangely detached manner of his, but then nodded as Peggy Craddock arrived with a question.

"Lord Edgington, do you have anything to tell the readers of The Chronicle concerning the events that occurred here tonight?"

Grandfather didn't move but used that penetrative stare of his to study the smart young woman, who was always at the ready to deal with breaking news. With this examination over, he adopted a polite demeanour, bowed a little and said, "Perhaps another day."

"And do you have any theories about who could be to blame for the killing?"

His smile became positively serene. "Plenty, thank you. Good night," and strode off to see to our friends.

Pandora and Fabian took no persuading and trundled behind us most despondently on the short journey to where Grandfather had parked his car on Birdcage Walk. Upon seeing the Rolls Royce, the young lady was moved to tears once more. Her crying soon gave way to fluted laughter and, by the time she was able to explain this unexpected reaction, a tragic smile shaped her face.

"I'm sorry, you must think me a loon, but... well, Augustus said he would buy himself a Silver Ghost when he made his fortune as an artist. And it's just occurred to me what a ridiculous world this is." Her laugh became distorted and eventually quite unrecognisable as she collapsed onto the running board of Grandfather's impressive automobile.

Fabian had already got into the car on the far side, and so it was down to me to comfort her. Considering the number of dead bodies I'd come across, I'd spent surprisingly little time consoling the bereaved.

"Don't think of it like that." I had to rack my brain for something to say. "Think of Augustus up in heaven, instead. I'm sure he's driving around in a winged chariot by now. He'll be off to a painting class with Da Vinci, Van Gogh and Monet. Mozart will be there to accompany them on a heavenly organ and–"

"Oh, you are sweet, Chrissy." I was terribly glad she interrupted me just then, as I had no idea what to say next.

She hugged me tightly and, with a distressed smile, climbed into the back seat. I got in on the passenger side and, once the car was running, Grandfather whispered, "As far as I know, Claude Monet is still alive. But it was a noble speech nonetheless."

Perhaps unsurprisingly, it turned out that Lady Pandora lived really not so far away in Mayfair. Stafford House couldn't have been closer to Saint James's Palace and was a vast, neo-classical affair with columns all over it. It made her neighbour's abode look rather meagre, in fact.

Pandora must have noticed the gormless look on my face, as she commented in a shy voice. "Yes, it is a little grand, isn't it? I've been thinking of moving somewhere smaller, but Mummy and Daddy did so love it, and one must think of the staff." She sounded most apologetic and gave me a kiss on the cheek, then dashed lightly up the stairs like… well, Alice in Wonderland, obviously.

"I can walk from here," Fabian told us, his exuberance now extinguished like a birthday candle.

"Nonsense," I replied, and Grandfather drove off before the distraught chap could escape.

I was rather surprised to discover that Fabian's own lodgings were just a five-minute drive but a million miles away from his friend's. He directed us to a remarkably ordinary tenement near Victoria Station. From the outside, at least, it was hard to imagine a man of significant character and charm living in such humble accommodation.

He came to stand at Grandfather's window and, his face still scarred with sorrow, nodded solemnly as he spoke. "I truly appreciate your friendship this evening, Lord Edgington. I'm not sure how Pandora and I would have fared without you."

"You're welcome, my boy," Grandfather replied, his tone softening slightly for the first time since we'd discovered the body. "Though you mustn't thank me until I catch Augustus's killer."

For a moment, as though we were far from the hubbub of the city, there was silence. The noise of cars and buses on that normally busy road faded out, and I could hear the two men's breathing.

"It's reassuring that you'll even try."

"And Fabian?" Grandfather paused for a moment as a delivery van rumbled past to fight back the calm. "I will find his killer; I promise you that."

Fabian nodded once more and stood back on the pavement to let us drive away. I watched him in the side mirror for some seconds as he looked up at his building and shook his head a little. I wondered if he was still thinking about Augustus's death or the very idea that he could be home at such an early hour on a Friday night.

"That was inspired thinking, Christopher," Grandfather said with a click of his fingers. "Suggesting that we drive them home in order to inspect their residences really was a clever move. Who would have thought that the notorious Fabian Warwick would live in an apartment overlooking the railway tracks?"

I hadn't actually thought of this before. I'd really only wanted to take them home as I wished to be kind. Of course, I wasn't about to tell my grandfather that.

Instead, I giggled gingerly and said, "Right-ho! Inspired, indeed." I had to swallow just then, as I was sure he'd see through my acting. "Should we stay at Claridge's tonight, or would you prefer The Savoy?"

"I'd prefer to go home to my own bed. If you don't mind. The drive will help me consider the facts of the case. And, besides, Delilah will be missing me."

We navigated the maze of streets, which the naturalised Londoner seemed to know as well as any cabman. By the time we found the route home on the King's Road, it was long past my bedtime, but I didn't fall asleep. Augustus's death had slapped me awake like a wet flannel. I had so many questions and no real understanding of what could have happened or how it might be connected to Baron Pritt's murder. I hadn't even put the two events together until Grandfather had mentioned the possibility to the chief inspector, but it must have been the same killer.

"It does seem likely," he confirmed, and I was no longer impressed that he had read my body language and mood so precisely that he could predict what I was thinking. Oh, fine. Maybe I was just a tad.

"But as far as I can tell, Baron Pritt and Augustus didn't know one another," I countered, as much to myself as my elderly companion.

"Or did they? We know that Pritt was on the treasure hunt when he died. And it said in the paper that he was a member of the Gargoyle Club. Who's to say he wasn't friends with the whole lot of them? Pandora, Fabian, even his wife's lover, Cyril Fischer? There'll be a link to find there. We just don't know what it is yet."

I wasn't going to make any further ill-conceived predictions, so I shut my mouth and watched the dim scenery roll past the car.

"It is a puzzle, though. I'll grant you that. And quite different from the cases we've investigated before. At this moment, it seems that anyone in London could be the killer, but we will whittle that number down. It may take some time, but you can be sure that we'll finish with just a few possible names for our potential culprit. That's the way of these things."

His words kicked the dust from a previously unexplored thought. "The treasure hunt." I sounded rather joyful, considering everything that had happened. "That's the linking factor, don't you think?"

"It certainly connects the two cases, yes." He clearly couldn't always read my mind, or he would have known what I was implying. "But why would you–"

"No, I mean that's what will help us find the killer. Surely, whoever murdered Baron Pritt and Augustus Harred would have been there for the two games. Cyril Fischer should have a list of the people who attended both."

He didn't respond to this immediately but pursed his lips and mulled over the possibility. "Though not a perfect method of elimination, by any means, it is a point that we must consider. Of course, we were at the hunt last Saturday without registering for it."

"So was the reporter, Peggy Craddock," I reminded him.

"Quite right, my boy. In fact, almost anyone could have swanned over if they'd known where to meet."

I thought he'd disproven my hypothesis entirely, but a further idea sprang from my mouth. "That's just it, though. Not everyone would have known where to meet. We had to call Albert in Oxford to get the information, and he called his friend at the Gargoyle. In fact, that wonderful club is at the heart of the matter too. Everyone we've met over the last two weekends has been connected to the place."

There was a long silence then, and I was worried what judgement he would devise. "Christopher, you'll be happy to know that I am not going to remove my hands from the wheel to applaud you, but you surely deserve it."

"Thank you, Grandfather. I aim to please." A truer word was never spoken.

Another rash of silence broke out as I examined the facts once more. A gang of wealthy young people in London, playing games in the dead of night, had been connected to two murders. A killer was on the loose at the highest level of society. Perhaps it would only be a matter of time before he struck again.

"It truly is a puzzle," he said. "There are so many tiny details that could be significant at this moment. Facts and statistics that, with the help of the hardworking men and women of the Metropolitan Police, we will have to analyse with sober heads. From the bullet in his heart, and the passport he carried, to that curiously placed cufflink you discovered, there is so much to be deciphered. And one thing is already preying on my mind."

As a loyal grandson and an even better disciple, I promptly asked the question he required. "What's that, Grandfather?"

"Why did the murder occur in that exact spot?"

He didn't normally like people answering one question with another, but I suppose that's what I'd requested. I was about to prod him onwards when he rephrased the point.

"Why did the killer lure Augustus to Westminster rather than some deserted part of the city?"

I hadn't considered how Augustus had ended up beside the Abbey before now. "What makes you think he was lured there? Perhaps he followed the list of clues, as we all did."

"It's possible, yes, but then the timing would be wrong. After all, nobody remembered hearing a gunshot, and that makes me think that the murder took place before the organisers arrived in Westminster. At that time of night, the area isn't busy, though the police are never far away."

I'm always ready with an answer to such conundrums. "Perhaps Cyril and the others mistook the sound for a car backfiring." And yet my answers are normally wrong.

"No, that can't be it. From the look of his body when I first saw him, I believe Augustus had been dead for some time. I can only conclude that, as he was a hound, he followed his hare in that direction when the game began. But why did the killer murder him there? So close to Parliament and the Abbey. What could it mean?"

I thought about that chaotic scene when the first police officers arrived, and someone had stumbled across the body.

"Broad Sanctuary," I said, remembering the white street sign upon a lamppost. "That's the name of the piece of land where he was found."

"That's correct. Westminster Abbey was a place of sanctuary in the Middle Ages. Debtors and criminals could escape there and seek refuge from punishment. I believe there was a fort built on that very spot to protect them."

"So might that be significant? Could Augustus have been running towards the church to escape his pursuer?"

"Anything is possible, my boy." He sighed a weary sigh as we crossed Putney Bridge to leave the city. "And tomorrow, we will investigate the matter in earnest."

Vol. XXXI

[393]

The London Chronicle.

Issue No. 1224

FEBRUARY 13th, 1926

Bright Young Thing Murdered in Westminster

Acclaimed painter found dead mere yards from Westminster Abbey.
Bright Young Person shot through the heart by unknown assailant. Full story **page 2.**

February Fashion for the London Lady	The Widows, Orphans and Old Age Contributory Pensions Act Comes of Age	Anyone for Tennis in February? Don't mind if I do!
Full article page 17.	Full article page 7.	Full article page 12.

CHAPTER FOURTEEN

I was very much hoping that we would enjoy a leisurely breakfast the next morning. I can't tell you how much I fancied a helping of Cook's bacon, potato and rollmop hash. Sadly, one man and his dog had other ideas.

Delilah had clearly been feeling left out as she not only woke me up at some ungodly hour with her cold little nose, but she also proceeded to jump up on my bed and bark at me until I submitted. I knew there was no use arguing with the persistent creature, and so I pulled some clothes on and lumbered downstairs.

In the stately breakfast room of Cranley Hall, I discovered not the delicious morning feast I'd been savouring, but my grandfather, already immaculate in his favoured grey morning suit and top hat. He was tapping his cane on the floor and looked quite impatient.

"Why on earth haven't you packed?" he enquired.

In reply, I could only stand there like a punch-drunk boxer, waiting to hit the mat.

"Never mind that now. Get dressed, and we can call in to see my tailor on Saville Row. It's about time you dressed like a civilised human being rather than a nineteenth century Parisian urchin."

I looked down at my pyjamas and, I must confess, they were a little grubby. When I didn't say anything, he barked again.

"Chop, chop. I'll see you in the car."

My Cranley-family instinct kicked in, and I was about to turn on my heel and do as I'd been told, when a voice in my head said, *Resist, Christopher! Resist!* and a response burst out of me. "Not without breakfast!" The phrase emerged as an anguished scream. Clearly taken aback, Grandfather pulled his neck in, and I thought he might chastise me again.

I cut him off before he could. "You made me skip breakfast once and I still haven't forgiven you for it. So, instead, I will go to the kitchen to find something to eat, and you will have to wait an extra five (to twenty) minutes for me."

I didn't give him the opportunity to reply but brushed my hands off and marched from the room. He must have been rather proud of the backbone I'd shown as, when I was a little way along the endless east-wing corridor, I heard the sound of applause coming from the breakfast room and Grandfather shouting, "Bravo, Christopher. It's good to see you standing up for yourself."

There was no sign of Cook in the kitchen and so young Agnes, the maid, put together a package for me to take on our journey. I was too hungry to wait and opened the canvas parcel as soon as I was out of the kitchen. I hadn't eaten anything since last night's early supper and would swear under oath that a ham sandwich and a Chelsea bun have never tasted so exquisite.

I returned to my room to get changed, threw a few shirts and whatnots into a bag, then hurried (at a leisurely pace) down to the car. I was greatly cheered to see that Todd and Delilah would be coming to the city with us, though I was a little surprised to find Cook in the passenger seat.

"Morning, Master Christopher," she sang self-consciously.

"Good morning, Henrietta. I trust you are well." I replied with a respectful nod of the head, but it was Grandfather I needed to quiz. "You do know that I have school on Monday?" The haughty fellow was already installed in the back of the vehicle. "We're only going to be away one night. Surely the chef at Claridge's would be acceptable?"

He looked almost as abashed as poor Cook. "I told you, Christopher, I did not like the way in which the butler at the hotel spoke to me last weekend. As a result, I'd prefer to have my own trusted members of staff with me." He held the door open, and I climbed aboard. "Besides, I'm never going back to that hovel again. It's clearly gone downhill since its heyday."

I decided not to point out how ridiculous such a criticism of the finest hotel in London truly was. There would be plenty more opportunities to argue with him that weekend, and I needed to conserve my energy.

"Off we go, Todd!" he shouted, with an uncharacteristic whoop. Delilah emitted a very much characteristic bark of agreement, and our journey got underway.

"Who should we interview first?" I asked, once Todd was piloting the Silver Ghost through the forests of Surrey on our way to the metropolis.

"You tell me, my boy."

I'd been considering this question since we left London the night before but was fairly sure I'd be wrong no matter what I might say.

"Well… I think we should work through our suspects from the victim outwards, just as we did with Baron Pritt. We'll speak to Augustus's fiancée first, then his friends, and then acquaintances and so on and so forth. What do you say?"

I could see that it would be a day of surprises; he was about to agree with me once more! "A fine idea."

"But?"

"There are no buts – though I do wish you would use full sentences. I approve of your plan. We will start with Lady Pandora Elles and move through Harred's coterie one by one." He stopped talking, and I was sure he still wanted to contradict me in some respect, but it never came.

I was much more comfortable idling along in the back of the car with Todd at the wheel in place of my manic grandfather. It was like taking a punt along the river, or a carriage through the park, and I might well have nodded off if I hadn't had such a perplexing case to occupy my mind.

We arrived at St James's and mounted the steps to Pandora's own private palace. It was a beautifully crisp winter's day, and I could see how much Grandfather was anticipating a nice, old-fashioned interrogation.

"Delilah, dear girl," he said to his most loyal assistant. "You are to wait here. I'm sure that some soft-hearted footman will be only too happy to take care of you."

Delilah let out three disgruntled barks and turned away from him.

"You can say what you like, but you're lucky that I brought you in the first place. You know my feelings on the topic of dogs in the city."

Having arrived at an impasse, Grandfather rang the doorbell and we awaited admittance.

"I should probably have mentioned that Pandora inherited the Stafford Estate from her father, the Duke of Elles. If you think Cranley is grand, wait until you see what's beyond these walls."

When the enormous front gate opened, we were greeted by a corridor of impeccably liveried staff. I had to wonder whether they'd been waiting there on the off chance that someone would come a calling, or my grandfather had rung ahead to warn them.

"Lady Pandora will see you in the Japanese Salon," a permanently bowed footman revealed, and two other strapping young servants motioned for us to follow them. Delilah ignored her master's instructions and strolled right inside.

Coming from such a ridiculously wealthy family, I was used to grand houses and fine furnishings, but Stafford House was something altogether more impressive. Once inside the main building, gilt and gold glittered from floor to ceiling, and our every step was cushioned by thick woollen carpets. The house possessed a level of opulence with which few in Britain could compare.

We ascended the immense staircase that made up two sides of the central hall. Overhead, twenty bronze Atlantes supported an ornate lantern roof with golden reliefs dotting its elegant ceiling, like stars in the night sky. To be quite honest, even His Lordship, the Most Honourable Marquess of Edgington, seemed impressed.

We finally discovered the Japanese Salon, which was – much as it sounded – a salon decorated in a Japanese style. It was all white with little decoration and a few simple chairs about the place. Only joking. It was full to the brim with priceless Eastern antiquities and even a couple of Samurai suits that made me want to turn around and run back downstairs.

The ceiling was hung with a thousand tiny lanterns that looked as though they were floating there of their own volition. On the four walls, a golden mural was punctuated with grand paintings of willow trees and crane-like birds (which might also have been storks, herons or flamingos). And at the far end from where we had entered, a full-size red dragon stood on guard duty. Despite all this grandeur, the most breathtaking feature in the room was sitting quietly on a low sofa, sipping a nice cup of tea.

Pandora was no longer Alice in Wonderland. She had grown up overnight and looked more of an adult than she had at any moment since we'd first met. She wore no makeup or elaborate dress, and sat perfectly upright, as though waiting to be called for some horrible appointment – or perhaps an exam.

"Lady Pandora," my grandfather said, once the twin footmen had presented us, "thank you for receiving me at short notice."

She managed to smile. "Of course, Lord Edgington. You know how grateful I am for everything that you've done for me. You're welcome here at any time."

Delilah was apparently even more welcome. Pandora opened her arms wide, and our sunshine-haired canine bounded over for a hug.

I might just as well stop my report of the interview here as everything that unlucky woman said made me convinced that she was the most pure and innocent human being to walk the earth in nearly two millennia. No matter what Grandfather might do to transform me into a detached, rational detective, I was quite certain that I would never look at a charming woman like Pandora and think, *yes, she probably shot her own fiancé through the heart.*

"We're terribly sorry to disturb you, my dear girl," he began, "but I must ask you some questions about Augustus while any significant memories are fresh in your mind."

The woman was in agony at the loss of her once-future husband and could only nod in reply. Her eyes were quite pink from crying – and there were no onions or citrus fruit about to explain it.

"I would like you to provide me with a brief sketch…" Apparently eager to avoid a pun, he searched for a better word. "…or rather, a précis of Augustus's life. Exactly who he was, how you met, what drew you to him, those sorts of things."

Her voice high and nervous, she began her answer at a fair clip. "We met on a train, of all places. I was travelling home from a holiday to Strasbourg two summers ago, and he was already there in my carriage when I boarded. You know, it took him the whole journey to Calais to find the courage to talk to me. I could tell that was what he wanted from the moment I sat down. He was awfully sweet and respectful, and I honestly believe I'd fallen in love with him before he said a single word."

"He was some years older than you, is that correct?"

"Oh, yes, but what does age mean today? People like you and Baron Pritt are given that same awful label in the papers as I am. *Bright Young People* they call us, regardless of age. Augustus was only ten years older than me, and I'm twenty-four now, not some dizzy novice."

We were separated from Lady Pandora by a low table which was decorated with intricate carvings. Grandfather presumably felt this was impeding his ability to communicate with our witness, and so he moved to sit next to her. He placed one hand in hers, and I thought this was awfully kind of the old softy, until I realised it was just another of his tactics to set a witness off guard.

"What a lovely story, my dear. And you're right that age need not be an impediment to love, life or even jumping from a hydrogen balloon." He turned to wink at me when he said this. "I know that Augustus was a fine painter, but what did he do prior to his artistic endeavours?"

She looked a little vague then, as though a cloud of mist had swept into the room. "I think he tried a few different careers, never settling on one thing until he dedicated himself to painting. He said he'd always done it as a hobby, but that no one had told him how good he was until he met me."

"Ahh... How lucky he was to have found two things that help make sense of one's life: a metier to which to devote oneself, and an inamorata with whom to share it." I could see that these romantic reminiscences were not the sort of evidence that my grandfather wanted, and he pressed her for more. "Though, I must ask you, where was he born? Do you know anything of his family?"

She shook her head sadly. "His parents both died when he was young. There was an aunt with whom he was close, but he didn't like to talk about his past and I couldn't stand upsetting him. Oh, and he did mention a cousin on the continent somewhere. He was coming back from visiting her when we met."

"That's very good, Lady Pa–"

"Please don't call me that." She suddenly became more insistent. "I have no time for titles. You are my friend, and you must call me Pandora."

"Of course, Pandora. And I was very sorry to hear of your parents' passing so close together."

"Thank you." A fragile tone took possession of her voice, though it wouldn't crack entirely. "They'd been ill with various issues for some time, but it still broke my heart when the doctors could do nothing for them. I suppose that was something else which brought Auggie and me together; we were orphans, the pair of us. Wandering alone until we found one another on a French train."

Grandfather managed a smile and patted the young lady's porcelain hand. "I'm afraid I must ask whether you know of any rivals or foes that Augustus had."

She shook her head. "No, nothing like that. Everyone just adored him."

"Then what about financial issues? Did he have any debts? Or perhaps someone owed him money?"

"No, that's impossible. He wasn't wealthy, and he always wanted to stand on his own two feet, but he had a little money in reserve. In fact, he'd received a new commission this week, which was more than he'd ever earned before." She looked terribly embarrassed then and glanced about the grand parlour in which we sat. "It's not as though I'm short of a pound or two. He could have always come to me if he was in trouble. My daddy used to say that money is one thing that is truly not worth dying for."

As she spoke, a team of her esquires – or whatever they were – appeared with trays of petit fours and hot drinks, which they placed on the table and began to serve. They were far smarter than our crooked old footman at Cranley. They wore breeches, gold-buttoned three-quarter length coats and appeared to have been chosen for the job based on the natural curliness of their short, blonde hair. The group of men were so similar, in fact, that I wondered if someone had created them in a laboratory, like Frankenstein's monster.

"True, very true," Grandfather said, once we were sipping coffee (disgusting, I should have asked for a sweet tea!) and nibbling on tiny, delicate pastries with golden swirls on the top. How the other half live, eh? Well… *the other* other half.

"What about the war?" I asked, dropping crumbs all over the sofa upon which I was perched. "Do you know where Augustus served?" I remembered the faint scar on one side of his face and had to assume he'd been on the front line.

Pandora's face creased in sadness once more. "He would never talk about his experiences. I know he saw fighting, and I believe it affected him more than he would say. Occasionally, he'd tell me stories from when he was a child. They were full of glee and excitement, and I think the war tore all that away from him. I think it changed him beyond recognition."

She raced to clarify her words. "Which isn't to say that I didn't love the man he became with every fibre of my being, but any hint that he might be unhappy drove me to distraction. And so I suppose I noticed such things more than most people would have."

The three of us consumed our refreshments in silence for some seconds, and I regarded her carefully. As much as it was our job to analyse the truth of what she was saying and come to cold, scientific conclusions, I couldn't strike upon the first reason why she would lie about such things. Everything she told me chimed with my limited knowledge of Augustus. Her description of his reticent personality and poetic soul could have been lifted from my very own thoughts. So it's hardly surprising that I failed to fathom a single reason she might have had for murdering her fiancé. It certainly couldn't be for his money as, compared to Pandora, the Queen of Sheba, he didn't have any.

Evidently, these hypotheses were playing out across my slightly sticky features, as Grandfather shook his head in my direction and prepared to ask a key question.

"You're aware, I'm sure, that the industrial magnate Baron Terence Pritt died last weekend whilst engaged in one of the treasure hunts that Fabian had organised."

"Yes, of course. I saw his car. I had to stop the hunt to check that he was all right. His Bentley wasn't damaged, but by the time I reached him, he was already dead."

Grandfather weighed her words before responding. "That's very interesting. At what time, precisely, did he die?"

"Oh..." She looked up at the finely decorated wooden ceiling beyond the illuminated golden lanterns. "It was after I'd found the second clue. We'd driven all the way to Richmond, and he'd gone off the road near one of the park gates."

"And do you know if there was any connection between Augustus and Baron Pritt?"

Her eyes flicked quickly between Delilah and me, as though she were looking for corroboration that Lord Edgington had discovered a link between the two men's deaths. "Are you suggesting that Terence Pritt was murdered?"

Grandfather sat back in his seat and stroked one finger along his rough sideburn. "It's a possibility that we must examine."

Pandora opened her eyes wider, as though she'd woken up from a strange dream. "Well, everyone knew Pritty – that's what we all called him at the club. He was loud and brash and always had an eye for young ladies."

"And what about Augustus?" Grandfather leaned a little closer to her. "Did the two men have any dealings?"

"No... or rather, certainly not to my knowledge. I don't remember them ever speaking to one another."

"I see... Thank you, Pandora." His intensity fizzled away, and I believe he was about to end the interview when she spoke again.

"But you should speak to Fabian rather than me."

"Really? And why is that?"

"Because he's Terence Pritt's nephew, by marriage at least. Fabian's family is practically penniless. It was Pritt who kept him in the lifestyle he's come to enjoy."

CHAPTER FIFTEEN

"Well, that was a relief," I said with a sigh, as we left the gorgeous mansion. "I couldn't stand the thought of Pandora being involved in her fiancé's death, and she clearly isn't."

Delilah was reluctant to depart and so my grandfather had to carry her. He remained quiet for a moment but couldn't hold in his thoughts. "Do you genuinely not think that she might–"

"No, I don't," I told him quite resolutely.

"But don't you remember what she said when–"

"Shh!"

"And there's always the chance that she and–"

"Enough, Grandfather. I refuse to hear another negative word said against her. Lady Pandora Elles is not a killer." Though I spoke with great confidence, as soon as the words were out of my mouth, I wished that I'd taken the time to listen to what the old devil had to say. I would spend the rest of the morning wondering whether I'd missed some key scrap of evidence and the young lady's guilt was plain for all (but me) to see.

Todd had taken Cook to the Ritz to start work on our meals for the weekend – though it seemed unlikely we'd be spending much time there – and so we walked down to The Mall to wait for him.

"Very well, I will leave you in the dark on my suspicions but let me ask you one thing." I believe he was genuinely seeking my permission and so I nodded for him to continue. "Do you know the ancient Greek myth of Pandora?" He waited for my inevitable ignorance to shine through.

"I know she had a box."

"Actually, if you go back to the original texts, it was a jar."

"Of course it was!"

"Either way, the story goes that, once opened, the vessel she possessed would pour forth sin upon our prelapsarian world. Pandora herself had been designed by the gods of Mount Olympus to be a beautiful evil that no man could resist."

"So you're saying that our Pandora might not be so dissimilar?"

He made me wait for his answer. "No, not at all. I'm merely

pointing out that, for millennia, right back to Pandora and Eve and countless other figures in the legends and parables we tell, women have been used as scapegoats for the sins of man and all mankind."

"Oh, of course. I see now." I really didn't.

"Here's Todd." Grandfather raised his hand to catch our driver's attention.

He came to a stop, and we climbed inside the white and silver-grey cabriolet to drive on towards Pimlico. My experienced companion discussed some old cases in which women had been made to take the blame for various dastardly men's crimes, but I didn't see the relevance and turned over the facts of the two murders in my head. It didn't take long, which is lucky as there wasn't far to drive. We soon pulled up outside Fabian's rather grim tenement and Todd drove off to look for somewhere less dirty to park. Delilah didn't like the look of the place and stayed behind in the car. She really was a most perceptive canine.

We knocked on the front door and waited for the porter to grant us entry.

"You'll be waiting a while if you expect someone to let ya in, guvnor," an old man sitting on the pavement told us.

"Oh yes, and why is that?" It was hard to imagine my lordly grandfather working with the rougher elements in society during his days in the police. He sometimes sounded so *posh* that it was almost as though he was doing an impression of what he thought poor people expected the rich to sound like.

"Because there ain't no porter in this building. You'll have to let yourselfs in."

"Ah," Grandfather replied. "How foolish of me."

I felt sorry for the poor old chap sitting on the cold ground like that, so I took out my purse and selected the shiniest half-crown piece I possessed. "There you are, my good man." Now I sounded like my grandfather. "For your troubles."

He looked vexed for some reason. "I'm not a beggar, ya cheeky little…"

I dashed inside the building before he could throw the coin at me.

A series of locked post boxes in the entrance hall revealed that Fabian lived on the top floor of the building. There was no lift, and the staircase was carpeted with thick, velvety dust. It was quite the loneliest looking place I'd ever visited. Raised voices and violent coughs emanated from every apartment we passed. I felt as though we'd travelled back through time and found ourselves in a Charles Dickens novel.

Grandfather did not seem perturbed and took the staircases and squalor in his stride. When we reached the third floor, he approached the first apartment we came to and knocked.

Once again, there was no answer. He knocked twice more, and I was about to suggest we try the handle when it pulled away from us.

"Yes?" Fabian peeked through the gap in the door and his half-opened eyelids.

"We'd like to talk to you about Augustus." Grandfather had donned his police helmet (metaphorically at least) and showed none of the tenderness he had demonstrated when interviewing Pandora.

Fabian looked hazy on the matter, but then reality seemed to come back to him. He shook his head as though he wished to clear away his bad thoughts. "Come in if you feel you must."

He turned on the balls of his feet and walked down the long corridor without ceremony. He wore a red silk dressing gown that flowed out behind him like a cape. I was reminded of just how magnetic I had found him at the first treasure hunt we'd attended.

He had disappeared into the bright room at the end of the narrow space before we'd even crossed the threshold. Unlike the landing where we'd been waiting, the interior of that apartment was unexpectedly well kept. The walls of the corridor were lined with mahogany panels that you might find in a gentleman's club, and unlighted chandeliers hung from the ceiling. I assumed that the whole place would be just as classically decorated, which shows how wrong I generally am.

My grandfather navigated the hallway somewhat hesitantly and stuck his head through the far door in an experimental manner which seemed to say, *is this right? Am I allowed to enter?* He would receive no response and so we lingered in the doorway.

What a sight the room was. A line of huge, leaded windows let in daylight from the acres of clear sky above Victoria Station, but the decoration of the spacious salon was what most impressed me. There were a series of disparate sculptures placed like chess pieces around the room. A figure of Hercules glared across a sofa at Jesus Christ, while a wooden carving of Shakespeare seemed to be in league with Florence Nightingale in the far corner. Each one had been restyled with wigs, glasses and makeup, and it was hard to imagine them being accepted back at whichever museum or stately home they had been pilfered from.

On the wall beside the window, buckets of paint had been haphazardly splashed about to make the most fantastic mess, and the red velvet curtains had heart, spade, club and diamond-shaped holes cut out of them. Lengths of chiffon fell like waterfalls, and the ceiling was painted with a five-word slogan in varying shades of pink. It bore several exclamation marks in place of the interrogative punctuation it required, and the words, *What are we doing HERE!!!* just made me feel nonplussed.

"Come along, gentlemen," Fabian called, as he lit a rather fat cigar with a book of matches from the Gargoyle. "There's nothing to fear. Come right in."

He was sitting on a golden throne with his back to the window so that the light flowed in around him like a swarm of insects drawn to a flame. The back of this impressively large chair was padded with red velvet and featured carvings of various regal symbols. It would have looked far more at home at Pandora's house, and yet it was perfectly suited to the king we had come to visit.

Passing one of the statues, with trepidation plain on his face, Grandfather was out of his element. There was a ring of seats positioned in reverence to the great Fabian Warwick, and I was about to sit down on a chaise longue when I noticed it was already occupied. A strangely faunlike man and woman, wearing little but their underwear, were asleep upon it.

Fabian laughed, and the sound bounced back to us off the walls. "Don't worry about them. They'll be sleeping for hours." He pointed for me to sit down with the glowing end of his newly lit cigar and, being far too polite to refuse, I managed to squeeze in next to the sleepers' feet.

With his bright green eyes blazing, our host looked down at us from the high seat. His intense beauty was hard to describe. It was both affected and masculine. In everything he did, he was strong yet tender. Lily-cheeked but with jet-black hair that swooped across his forehead

112

like a young lady's fashionable hat, he was a study in contrasts.

Lord Edgington tried to show that he was not intimidated by the madhouse we had entered and began his interrogation.

"Thank you for seeing us, Mr Warwick, I was–"

Fabian emitted a close copy of the laugh he'd previously released. "'Mr Warwick?' So I take it you're here in a professional capacity."

Grandfather took in an indignant breath through his nostrils and held it for some seconds before replying. "As I told you last night, I'm going to find the killer of your friend Augustus. As you were at the scene of the murder and knew the deceased, it's only natural I should want to talk to you."

"And it's only natural that I should be prickly and uncooperative. Let battle commence!"

CHAPTER SIXTEEN

Lord Edgington fell silent for a moment to strike some fear into our suspect. When that didn't work, he started in on his questioning. "I'd like to commence by asking you what it is, precisely, that you do?"

"*Do?*" Fabian sounded bewildered by this. "Does anyone really *do* anything these days? I've always thought it was far more important to *be*."

Now I was the confused one. "So then… what do you actually be? Or rather… What are you?" I pronounced the words with more than a hint of wonder.

I was happy to see that I'd caused him to think over his answer. "Well… I suppose you might say that Fabian Warwick exists to illuminate the dark age which we inhabit. I am a firefly, a lighthouse, a gas lamp burning brightly in the night."

"Oh, yes. I see." I am a compulsive white liar and was clearly no closer to understanding who this unique character was.

Luckily for everyone, my grandfather was on hand to clarify. "I believe what Mr Warwick here is suggesting is that he is a shiftless layabout, happy to fritter away his wealth on wild parties and even wilder outfits."

"Oh, Lord Edgington. You sound as though you don't approve."

"Far from it," the old man replied with an unforeseeable snort. "I was not so very different when I was your age. Just like you, I attended gatherings of the great minds of the day. I even crossed paths with Oscar Wilde on occasion."

I was surprised how critical he sounded, and his voice would only grow sterner. "You and your friends appear to believe that drinking, dancing and the pursuit of pleasure are new inventions. I can assure you that such hedonism has existed for millennia. The one distinction between your generation and my own is that we conducted our merrymaking behind the closed doors of our country estates, far from the prying eyes of Fleet Street journalists."

Fabian Warwick raised one hand to his mouth in a mock yawn. He was no doubt used to hearing such tirades. "No, you're wrong there. The one difference between my generation and every other is that ours

115

will forever be held up against those great men who came before us. I was too young to die in a French field and the world will never forgive me for it." He paused to suck on his cigar like a baby with a bottle, before blowing the smoke up to the graffito-scarred ceiling. "Wasn't this supposed to be an interview? That would be far more entertaining than a lecture."

Grandfather adjusted his position and snapped back a reply. "Fine. Tell me about Augustus. Had you known him for long?"

Under his dressing gown, Fabian wore spotted silk pyjamas, a pair of pointed leather slippers (which I'm fairly sure he'd stolen from a genie) and no socks. He crossed one bare ankle over the other and huffed out a response. "Not so very long. We started palling around together after he moved down here a couple of years ago. I knew Pandy from my days at Oxford."

"Where did he live before?"

"Oh, somewhere northerly. Newcastle, Edinburgh, Camden Town. You know, one of those places. But don't ask me anything more, as I never did discover what dear Augustus had done with his life. He was almost thirty-five, you know, and a bit of a dark horse in some ways."

"Don't you think it's strange that you'd been friends with a man for two years and still knew so little about him?"

A magical smile enlightened Fabian's visage. "No, I think it's wonderful. What fun would there be in having friends if we knew every last thing about them?"

Grandfather ran one hand through his long silver hair as though he were trying to untangle a knot. "Are you in love with Lady Pandora Elles?"

The question shot out of him like a volley of artillery fire and cut straight through our suspect. "Gosh, what a question." He soon recovered and let out a brief giggle. "No, I am not in love with Pandora. She is rich, beautiful and everything a man could look for in a wife, which means she is entirely wrong for *someone like me.*"

I felt his use of this phrase implied something that I was too young to understand. I didn't raise my hand to ask him what he meant, though, because Grandfather moved the conversation on to the next topic.

"I see. A man such as yourself would have no interest in marrying into money. I'm sure you adore living next to a train station and relying on your relatives for donations."

"I didn't say I don't like money. In fact, I love it." His eyes sparkled as though he were gazing into a pot of gold. "It's the pursuit of money I find dull. And I'd also rather avoid the marriage plot if I can help it."

Grandfather blinked ever so slowly then. He was enjoying the confrontation. "Which brings me back to my first question: what do you hope to achieve in this life? How do you expect to keep yourself if not by doing something or at least marrying someone who can?"

Fabian tipped his head back and looked at the slogan painted above him as though it would provide an answer.

When no response came, Lord Edgington continued his questioning. "I happen to believe that it was Baron Pritt who was funding your lifestyle. And, as he's now dead, I was wondering whether you had considered another route to secure a living. After all, Lady Pandora is quite wealthy."

"Oh, so it's only Augustus I've murdered. Are you certain you don't wish to blame me for my uncle's death while you're at it?"

Grandfather leaned forward in his chair and placed his hands together with a slightly diabolical gleam in his eyes. "I'm sure I could think up a scenario in which you murdered both of them if you so desire."

"No, I do not." The old detective had got under Fabian's skin at last. He stood up from his throne and went prowling about the place like a lion in search of a snack. "If you must know, I never asked my uncle for money. I would have come to London and made my living as a starving writer if it weren't for him. But he insisted I introduce him about town and paid me handsomely for the trouble."

"So you were the one who first brought him to the Gargoyle Club?"

"I might have been. What of it? Why are you so interested in my miserly uncle, anyway? The man's dead and few will miss him."

Grandfather paused to think. "I'm terribly sorry, but I'm struggling to understand one point. You have no interest in earning money, though you're happy when people give it to you. You don't wish to marry the richest debutante in the country, and your uncle was both miserly and your benefactor."

"That sounds about right." Fabian clutched the high golden back of his throne; the lion had become a hawk. "You see, he kept me on

117

an awfully short leash. He rented me an apartment in quite the least fashionable quarter imaginable and barely provided enough for me to decorate it to my taste. A man cannot live on net curtains and chintz alone!" He was clearly passionate about the topic of home furnishing. "Uncle Terence was a swine through and through. No! Worse than that, he was a vampire. He sucked the blood and joy from me, all so that he could come to my club, drink with my friends and tag along on my adventures."

"It sounds as though you didn't particularly like him." Grandfather surprised me by changing the topic just when he had the advantage. "Tell me, why did you decide to stop organising the treasure hunts?"

Our suspect seemed relieved but maintained his aggressive tone. "Because I thought it would be far more pleasant to participate in one than sit in the cold, waiting for everyone else to have fun without me."

"And why did you allow Cyril Fischer to take charge?"

"Because I am a martyr!" Fabian blew a channel of smoke up towards his long fringe. He suddenly reminded me of my soppy brother, which slightly undermined my belief in him as a modern-day hero of London Town.

Grandfather remained calm. I never failed to be amazed at how patient he could be. "Would you care to expand?"

"Yes, I would." Fabian violently stubbed his cigar out on the back of his chair and cleared his throat. "People are forever begging favours off me, and this time it was my aunt's turn."

"Baroness Pritt?"

"Yes, Auntie Ermie! She said that her little toy, Cyril, was having trouble making friends. She wondered whether I could include him somehow in the colourful world of Fabian Warwick, *enfant terrible.*"

The sleeping man next to me stretched one leg out, so that I was forced to shuffle along the sofa. Any further and I'd have been on the floor.

"You know, my boy. I can tell you from experience that it is never a good idea to read what journalists write about you in the papers. Either you will object, and there's nothing you can do to change it, or, worse still, you'll like what they say and start to believe their hyperbole."

It occurred to me then that this wasn't so much an interview as an opportunity for two planet-sized personalities to dance about in front of one another. As it happened, I was rather upset about the death of our friend and took this moment to return us to more pressing issues.

"Why did you arrive so long after everyone else last night?"

The two titans turned to look at me.

"What do you mean?" they both intoned at the precise same moment.

"Fabian, you were the last to arrive in Westminster. Pandora and most of the others had already been there for some time. You even managed to take longer than me, and I can assure you that I do not know London very well."

Fabian's jaw opened just a crack and, in a strange reversal of their previous roles, he glanced at my grandfather as though he would be able to help. "I... I evidently adopted a different strategy from everyone else. Rather than attempt to be quicker than my hound, I loitered in the shadows at each point on my journey to make sure he hadn't caught up with me."

"By whom were you pursued?" my grandfather asked.

"I can't say for certain. But he wasn't very good at it. He was dressed as a jabberwocky – a big dragony sort of creature – and could barely run after me with the weight of his costume."

"How convenient," the sly old chap purred.

"And what is that supposed to mean?" Fabian leapt forward. He was a wounded animal now. I'd lost track of which one.

"I mean that you're the connection between Baron Terence Pritt and Augustus Harred; two men who just happened to die one week apart at the same treasure hunt that you devised and helped organise. Don't you think that's a coincidence?" I'd rarely seen my grandfather show such anger in an interview.

"That's just the thing. I didn't organise the hunt last night, as you well know. I'm as much in the dark about any of this as you are."

Grandfather rose imperiously, his eyes forever trained on his prey. "We'll see about that. And if, as you say, I am in the dark at this moment, it certainly won't be for long."

With no warning to his devoted grandson, he moved to leave. I remained behind, tentatively hoping that someone would tell me what to do next. He didn't even stop in the doorway to deliver a witty closing line. So, finally, I removed the sleeping man's foot from my lap, made my apologies and coolly attempted to scurry after my grandfather.

"Chrissy, wait," Fabian shouted, as I was about to leave the flat.

I heard him passing through the room like a gust of wind. The door burst open at the end of the corridor, but he came to a stop as soon as he laid eyes on me.

"I shouldn't have been so flippant." His voice seemed to emerge from somewhere deep within him. "I know you came here to help and, if I'd been honest, I would have told you..."

When he couldn't get the words out, I prompted him to keep going. "Yes?"

"I *should* have told you that I'd noticed something strange about Augustus." He glanced at the floor as though he was too shy or ashamed to keep going, but then the words spilled out of him. "It wasn't just that he was secretive about his past, as your grandfather already seems to know. I felt that Augustus was hiding something."

Magnetically tugged towards him once more, I took a step closer without knowing why. "What was it?"

He searched for his words, then took a deep breath before replying. "I can't say for certain, but there were times when it felt that he would do anything he could to avoid talking about the life he'd lived before he moved to London. Whole merry conversations would come to a halt with absolutely no warning. On more than one occasion, I saw him fighting tooth and nail not to be pinned down on a topic."

He shook his head and let out a half laugh. "Please, don't misunderstand me, Augustus was the nicest chap you could hope to meet, but I occasionally realised, after we'd had a night out together and all sorts of wild adventures, that I hadn't scratched the surface of who he really was. And that made me wonder..."

His voice trailed off again, but this time I thought I knew what he wanted to say. "You wondered if he had done something terrible in his past?"

He would not utter an answer; there was no need. He gave a reluctant smile and a near invisible nod of his head, and I gasped far more melodramatically than the moment warranted.

CHAPTER SEVENTEEN

My head spun as a list of crimes (from littering to mass murder) reeled itself off in my brain. It was hard to imagine what Augustus might have wished to conceal and so, out on the landing, I told my grandfather what I had discovered.

"Well, then our trip here wasn't entirely wasted." He was clearly still fuming at his run-in with our flamboyant suspect. "The rapscallion! If he had information to share, he should have told me."

I was terribly confused and, while I know that may not sound unusual, it felt different this time. "Grandfather..." This was as much as I managed to articulate as we wandered down the drab staircase of Fabian Warwick's apartment building.

"Infuriating tyke," he continued under his breath, apparently still disturbed by events.

We reached the ground floor, and I found my voice again. "I'm sure I'm being awfully dim but... I thought you rather liked Fabian. Do you really believe he's the killer?"

He stopped in front of the post boxes of every last person in the building. There must have been sixty of them, which meant there were sixty families, couples or lonely individuals squashed together in that grim edifice. The names were all quite different from most of the people I knew. I noticed a Jack Smith, a Norman Butler and a Peter Mason, and I was certain that none of them had rich benefactors to pay for fine clothes and interior decoration.

Grandfather finished scanning the names and finally replied. "No, of course I don't. I actually find him quite amusing. And while it's possible that he would have decided to murder his unpalatable uncle, I have failed to land upon a strong motive for his involvement in Augustus's death. Though none of that changes the fact he's an impertinent imp."

I was even more mystified now than before I'd asked the question.

Todd was already waiting for us in the car when we exited the building – predicting the future being another of our chauffeur's apparent skills. Delilah jumped from the open seat and came running over, but someone else found us first.

"Lord Edgington," a young woman shouted from further along the pavement. "Peggy Craddock, London Chronicle. I was hoping we could have that interview you promised?"

Grandfather smiled. I sometimes wondered if he was as easily charmed by pretty young ladies as I was. "I don't believe I promised any such thing, but I appreciate your sense of enterprise."

"So you'll talk to me then?" Her tightly curled hair was most expressive as it whipped about her shoulders. I had to wonder how she had known we would be in that part of town just then.

"What would you like to know?"

She clicked her fingers together with glee and poked about in her coat to find a pen. She had a lot of pockets and struggled to find the right one but was even more excited when she did. "Do you believe that the killings over the last two weekends are linked?"

Grandfather looked surprised by the question but soon recovered. "If you are referring to the tragic death of Baron Pritt, then I think you will find the man died of a heart attack. Now ask me a more sensible question or you won't get another try." If I hadn't known for certain that he was lying, I never would have believed it.

She cursed herself silently and took a deep breath before making a second attempt. "Do you believe the violence we have seen can be put down to the destructive influence of the so-called *Bright Young People's* loose morals?"

Grandfather managed to huff, roll his eyes and shake his head at the same time. I think it's fair to assume that he was not impressed. "No, I certainly do not. And as for the *Bright Young People,* I believe it was your own paper who invented that lazy moniker. Just as your paper loves to criticise anyone who doesn't agree with your ill-minded proprietor's way of thinking. Now, I believe you've wasted enough of my time. There are more important matters to which I must attend."

He folded his arms – to make it abundantly clear that he disapproved of her questioning – and rapidly turned to leave. I gave her an apologetic look and ran to catch him.

"Please!" she shouted, but Grandfather was almost at the Rolls. "I need this job. You have to help me."

He was about to step into the vehicle but froze where he stood.

"I mean it, Lord Edgington. I will lose my job if I don't find something interesting to say about the murder. Mr Twelvetrees called me into his office this morning. Me! A junior reporter on the social desk and he called me in to see him first thing. Sadly, it was not because he wanted to compliment me on my work. He said I have forty-eight hours to secure a scoop for The Chronicle or I'll be out of a job. He says I'll be the last female reporter he ever hires if I don't discover a major development in the case."

That not so steely chap breathed out a frustrated breath and turned around. "Very well, Miss Craddock, I will give you the time it takes to get to Victoria Embankment to ask your questions... but not a moment longer."

She replied with a blank stare, and he sighed once more and gestured to his car. "The automobile, Miss Craddock. Please climb aboard."

In her neat tweed skirt and jacket, she motored over to our motorcar and did as instructed. Despite the roomy Rolls Royce's red leather interior being designed for five people, it was something of a squeeze with the three of us on the back seat. Matters only deteriorated when Delilah hopped in after me and lay across our laps. Miss Craddock didn't seem to mind, though, and patted the dear creature's head as she asked her questions.

Todd pulled away from the kerb. He was apparently far more knowledgeable about the day's itinerary than I was.

"Here we go then," she said, clearly anticipating the opportunity. "Harred was a newly fashionable artist, who had been linked to commissions from several well-known figures. Do you believe the murder could be connected to one of the famous British families? And, in particular, to Harred's fiancée, Lady Pandora Elles?"

This was an awfully long query, and I was quite lost by the end of it.

"No, I do not." Grandfather didn't have any such problem. "Next question."

I must say, it was rather nice to see him on the receiving end of an interrogation for once.

"This is the fifth murder in London this year. Would you say that the capital is spiralling back towards the dark days of violence for which the last century was known?"

Grandfather at least took a moment to reflect before answering. "No, I would not."

His frosty responses were clearly flustering the young lady, and her tone became more insistent. "Do you believe the killer will strike again?"

The former officer glanced out of the window at the buildings that were flashing past us. "I have no reason to believe that is the case, but I cannot rule out such a possibility entirely."

It was a step too far, and the reporter emitted a groan. "Really, Lord Edgington, I'm trying to ask serious questions here. The least you could do is give me an inkling of your thoughts on this strange case. Our readers are hungry for information. We've had to print an extra run of papers this morning, as everyone is desperate to discover the truth of the Bright Young Thing murdered on the steps of Westminster Abbey."

Turning back to her, Grandfather tutted. "But Augustus Harred was not murdered on the steps of Westminster Abbey. He was murdered on a small patch of grass nearby. Such inaccuracies and sensationalism are part of the reason I have no faith in your profession!" He did not spare the young lady's feelings, and the words roared out of him. "And just so that it's clear, I'd like to point out that the least I can do is to stop the car and throw you out right here."

She looked as though she might cry. "I appreciate that, Lord Edgington. I really do, but..." Her voice faltered as she gave the fruitless task one last go. "There must be something you can tell me that the people of London would be interested in reading."

Appeased by the question, Grandfather smiled. "As you expressed it in such a manner, as opposed to framing your every enquiry in lurid terms, then, yes. Perhaps your readers would like to know my suspicions that the victim was shot at point blank range with what I can only assume was a revolver."

Her previously positive expression now muted, she scribbled his words down in some indecipherable shorthand. "Was there anything else?"

My mentor looked past the journalist to where I was sitting. He made an infinitesimal shake of the head to remind me not to divulge too many secrets. "Nothing I am at liberty to reveal to the press." She let out a half-squeal of disappointment before he pressed on with another thought. "And yet, if you wish to hear my professional opinion on the matter, it did not appear to be a simple case of a botched robbery or an unhappy accident. Harred still had his wallet and passport, for one thing. Furthermore, most casual thieves in London don't carry guns and, were they to attempt such a crime, it would not be in Westminster, mere yards from the headquarters of the Metropolitan Police."

She had perked up enormously by now. "May I quote you on that?"

He debated with himself for a few seconds before tipping his head to one side and acquiescing. "Oh, very well. But if you attribute a single word to me that I haven't said, I will be suing The Chronicle for every penny it possesses."

She made another short squeak, but this time it was a sound of pure elation. Delilah looked up at her, perhaps thinking that the young lady spoke a little dog.

"Now, Miss Craddock," Grandfather continued, placing the flats of his two hands together. "I have a question for you." The old fox had known all along it would come to this. I felt that poor Peggy had fallen into his trap and not the other way around. "Tell me exactly what happened on the night that Baron Pritt died."

She truly was an encyclopaedia of emotions, and her face now showed a hint of doubt. "There's not an awful lot to tell after the altercation."

"The altercation?" Grandfather's eyebrows rose like hydrogen balloons.

"Yes, with Cyril Fischer. I assumed you knew all about it. If you'd happened to read last Saturday's social pages, you certainly would."

"Cyril Fischer and Terence Pritt had an altercation before the baron died?" I asked in a far too dramatic tone, as though I were a supporting character in some tawdry piece of theatre. I really wished that I'd grown out of such habits.

"That's right. Pritt arrived late and was already quite drunk from the look of things. When he spotted his wife's lover there, he lost his temper and pulled the man from the crowd. He didn't seem to mind who saw him, and they continued the argument even when they noticed me there."

"Did it come to blows?" I was transfixed by her account and, no doubt just like her readers, was desperate to discover more.

"Practically. Though Mr. Fischer looked mortified at the idea. You see, Pritt made a big scene, telling anyone within earshot that his wife had been stolen from him by a house-breaking skipjack. He raised his fists and danced about a little as the others crowded around him in a circle. It was quite exciting, I can tell you, though I think the Baron was merely putting on a show. Even between the threats, he couldn't help laughing. He kept demanding satisfaction, but Cyril wouldn't be drawn into a fight. Instead, he apologised to his rival and confessed his undying love for the baroness, who swooned accordingly."

"Baroness Pritt was at the treasure hunt?" Grandfather looked surprised yet again.

"That's right. She's been a regular participant since she left her husband last year."

This was enough evidence for me to conclude that the baroness had chased the baron down and forced him to crash, only for her lover Cyril to finish the job with his bare hands. She could definitely link the two murders and, considering the state in which her husband's body was found, this surely made her a likely killer.

"You *do* think the killings are connected, don't you?" Miss Craddock asked, a look of not just interest but delight on her attractively sharp face.

Grandfather had left us. He was still there in the car, of course, but his mind was far away. He stared at the back of Todd's head and would not respond for some thirty seconds as the ramifications of this new evidence played out in his brain.

"I think..." he began, his voice still hollow. "I think... I think we've arrived at our destination."

Our chauffeur parked the car in front of a tall building, but I didn't take much notice of where we were.

"Thank you, Lord Edgington." Happy with what she'd gained from their exchange of information, Miss Craddock smiled an appreciative smile. "I've no doubt our paths will cross again before long."

"Indeed, Miss Craddock. And may I be the first to wish you the best of luck in your job?"

She held out her hand to him and he shook it gently. "Sincerely, thank you. You don't know what a help you've been."

I helped her onto the pavement, and she walked off in the direction of the newspaper offices on Fleet Street with a glint in her eye. I was no longer quite so confident that she was the innocent I'd taken her to be.

CHAPTER EIGHTEEN

While Grandfather gave Todd more instructions, I took in the rather imposing building I was standing before. The construction had a somewhat fairy-tale-like appearance, with two turreted towers on either side of it and an immense granite base. Bands of red brick and Portland stone decorated the higher floors, and I found myself in quiet awe of our new surroundings.

"What do you think of that?" Grandfather asked, a proud note in his voice.

"Scotland Yard," was all I could murmur in reply as, in my head, I was recalling all the wonderful stories I'd read that were connected to that famous location.

"It's *New* Scotland Yard, in fact." Grandfather is a stickler for accuracy. "Come along, Christopher."

I couldn't believe my luck. "Can we go inside?"

He was already a few steps away when Delilah barked a similar question.

"No. You stay here... and this time I mean it."

I must have looked terribly glum as I sat down on Todd's running board and waited for him to return.

"Not you, Christopher. The dog!"

I got to my feet and happily scampered after him through the discreet entrance, where a small plaque on the wall was the only thing to reveal the significance of that uniquely famous address.

"How can I help you gentlemen?" a young constable standing behind the front desk enquired. As soon as he said the words, an older, tubbier sergeant gave him a quick elbow and whispered something into his ear. The superior did not appear to be a fan of my grandfather, but the young chap clearly was. "Oh, my stars... Lord Edgington... What an honour." He came out from behind the desk to shake the old superintendent's hand. "That's the only word for it. Really, it is. I became a policeman after my old dad used to tell me stories of what you achieved here all those years ago."

He was still shaking Grandfather's hand, and the sergeant was still glaring, when Lord Edgington replied. "It's always a pleasure to meet young officers. I'm here to see P.C. Simpkin."

"Yes, sir. Right away, sir." Still moved by the encounter, the uniformed constable looked one way and then another, uncertain what to do next.

"Simpkin ain't on duty today, Edgington," the older chap said.

"Which is why I'd like to go to the Museum to see if he is there." Grandfather could have lived to be a thousand and not been caught out by such an obviously grumpy character as Sergeant *not important enough in this story to deserve a surname*.

The constable looked at his superior for assistance.

"The Black Museum, boy. He's talking about the Black Museum."

His eyes grew just as wide as mine at that moment. Everyone had heard of the Black Museum. It was the room in Scotland Yard where they kept artefacts from some of the most notorious crimes of the last fifty years. It was normally only open to serving officers, and I was struggling to believe that I'd be allowed to set foot in such a remarkable – though admittedly terrifying – place.

"Yes, of course. The Black Museum." The hesitant young chap reminded me of me. "Would you like me to show you the way or…"

"I think I'll manage," my grandfather replied in a rising tone. "But I appreciate your help, P.C.…?"

"Penge, sir. P.C. Frederick Penge."

"Very good, constable."

Penge seemed thrilled by this and nodded over and over as we followed the corridor deeper into the building. The sergeant was less enthusiastic and sent a mumbled shout after us. It might have been *"Traitor!"* or perhaps it was, *"See you a bit later."* I can't say for certain.

The two men's responses were a perfect dichotomy of the way in which people tended to react to my esteemed grandfather. They either loved him or wanted to see him locked away somewhere (preferably on an island in the middle of the Atlantic Ocean).

I was slightly disappointed to discover that the bowels of Scotland Yard looked an awful lot like the bowels of the bank where my father worked. A series of dimly lit hallways took us to a staircase, which we descended in order to navigate yet another series of dimly lit hallways. It was not the hub of adventure that I had been expecting. The most interesting thing we saw on our tour of the building was an elderly cleaner, who was mopping the floor as we passed. He was only remarkable for the fact he wore an eye patch, like a pirate. This was still not enough to make up for the dull grey décor and the smell of disinfectant.

"Ah, here we are," Grandfather said, just as I was beginning to wonder whether he really knew where we were going. "Are you ready?" Smiling widely, he pushed the door open and stepped inside.

The room I now peered into was a large office. There were a couple of officers working at a table and an inspector standing at a blackboard with a piece of chalk at the ready.

"Ummm... Can I be of any help?" the inspector asked, just as Grandfather realised his mistake and ducked back out again.

"My apologies. It has been some time since I last visited," he said through the closing door, then turned to continue down the corridor. "The Black Museum must be the next room along."

He shuffled forward, looking a touch embarrassed, then knocked on the neighbouring door. When there was no response, I swung it open to step into the past.

"Incredible," I intoned, truly impressed by the breadth of items on display. There were death masks from wicked criminals, long since hanged, and the ropes which did the job suspended in one corner. I spotted a glass case that was full to the brim with guns of every imaginable description, from flintlock duelling pistols to modern automatic weapons. There were swords, axes and even a set of knuckledusters, while police notices on dangerous criminals, complicated schematics of crime scenes and old photos lined the walls. It was hard to imagine a type of criminality known to man that couldn't be solved based on the information contained in that subterranean space.

"'Ello, 'ello," a voice said, stepping out from a hidden door with the sound of a toilet flushing nearby. "I thought I might see you here today."

"Simpkin!" Grandfather was sincerely thrilled to see his old colleague once again. "Just the man I need. I trust that you've caught up with the details of the murder in Westminster last night."

"Of course, Superintendent. I take it upon myself to keep abreast of developments in even the most insignificant cases; and that one was a whopper!"

"Jolly good, man." Grandfather walked closer to get on with the inquiry, but I was still admiring the work that had gone into preserving so much information there for future generations of Metropolitan Police officers.

Simpkin was watching me as my eyes darted about from one object to the next. There was a violin fixed to the wall high above me that particularly caught my interest.

"Do you know what that is, young Master Christopher?"

I was unable to respond with much more than a vaguely negative sound.

"What you're looking at there is the violin that once belonged to Charles Peace."

The name didn't mean anything to me, but Grandfather certainly remembered it. "Ah, yes. I can still recall the day he was arrested. He was already somewhat infamous when he was brought in for a string of daring robberies in Blackheath. I was still a young copper at the time, but I'll never forget Peace."

The two men stared up at the instrument as though looking back on happier days. I appeared to have missed a key fact of the case.

"And so... the violin?"

"Yes, the violin." They continued staring until my grandfather finally explained. "Peace used to walk about wealthy neighbourhoods in the day, playing the violin for coins and sizing up the best houses. At night, he'd come back and rob them. He was finally caught after one of my colleagues – a chap by the name of Robinson – spotted him and gave chase. Peace shot the poor bobby in the arm, but P.C. Robinson wouldn't relinquish his quarry, and the scourge of Blackheath was apprehended. A week later, we discovered he was wanted for murder in Manchester."

I must have betrayed my amazement at the story as Simpkin laughed and said, "That's right. The cheeky so-and-so seemed like a nice ordinary sort of fellow, but he'd got a criminal record as long as my mum's nightie. He'd shot his neighbour to death, and it wasn't his first killing."

"Still, it was a different class of criminal we had back in those days," Grandfather continued, nostalgia thick in his voice. "Peace even attempted to jump off the train on the way to his trial. Luckily, he knocked himself unconscious and was recaptured. But he gave us

130

a run for our money, that's for certain."

They laughed once more, before Simpkin added a rather mournful coda to the case. "He couldn't escape the gallows forever, mind. Much like that fellow, in fact." He pointed up to one of the death masks on a shelf above a cabinet filled with bottles of poison. "Do you know who that is?"

I looked up at the disgusting figure. His head was shaved, his eyes closed, but there was an unmistakable air of malevolence about him. I shook my own head and waited to be appalled.

"That's Frederick Bailey Deeming. A true face of evil if ever there was one. He killed his whole family. Some people believe he was Jack the Ripper himself."

Lord Edgington shuddered then, and the fear carried over to me.

Simpkin, meanwhile, was clearly immune to such emotion and had a good laugh at our expense. "Oh, yes. We've got some real monsters down here. There's the Stratton Brothers' masks, the very badge and button from the Badge and Button Murder, and this may be the deadliest item of all." He walked over to a case where a photograph of a young man with cropped black hair was pinned above a letter written on government-headed notepaper. There was also a silver fountain pen, and this is what Simpkin wanted to show me. "It's not always guns and knives that do the most damage. Lord Marchant cost the lives of hundreds of British troops when he gave away secrets to the Germans and spread false information during the war. He may not have shot nor stabbed nobody, but he met the same fate as all them other murderers nonetheless."

Grandfather made a low utterance of pure disgust. "Yes, I remember it well. Septimus was a viscount until he met his fate before the firing squad on Tower Hill. Some crimes are unforgivable." I was feeling a little queasy by now, and so it was lucky that he took pity on me and changed the subject. "Simpkin here knows more about London's criminals over the decades than any other officer on the force. His father helped establish this museum as a resource for future recruits, and he's continued that legacy."

It was a good thing that former Superintendent Edgington held no truck with phrenology or physiognomy, as Simpkin had one of the most fatuous-looking faces of any man I'd met. He had small features and far too much cheek, forehead and chin in which to house them. If I had never heard him speak, I might well have wondered what such a mooning simpleton was doing in a place like Scotland Yard.

"Back to the murder last night," he said, suddenly turning serious. "Curious matter, if you ask me. I wasn't on duty – I play darts on a Friday – but a number of interesting features stand out."

Grandfather nodded in encouragement, and Simpkin closed his eyes to reel off the details like some idiot savant.

"I volunteered to look over the files first thing this morning, and I can tell you that my colleagues have done a thorough job. Chief Inspector Darrington will make sure of that. They started by examining links between the dead man and the other figures on the scene. There were far too many to draw any conclusions, of course. Which is to be expected with toffs; no offence, Superintendent."

"None taken. In the English aristocracy, everyone is connected to everyone. Please continue."

"Then they tried to rule out some of the suspects by looking at which pairs of hares and hounds in the game were together and when. As the partners were assigned quite randomly, this seemed like a good bet, but unfortunately, none of the targets were captured after their first clue, which means the killer would have had time to murder Augustus Harred and then go on to the second location on his list."

Grandfather had placed two fingers to his face and was pinching his lips together contemplatively but took this moment to interrupt his subordinate's steady flow of facts. "What about the chalk markings left on the ground at each point in the game? Did anyone think to inspect them?"

Simpkin nodded with his eyes still closed. "They did indeed, and all marks that should have been there were indeed present. However, it was only this morning that we had the manpower to investigate this. The culprit could quite easily have gone in the night to add whichever mark he had skipped. And remember, it was only the hares who had to leave proof of where they had been, so it wouldn't help verify the whereabouts of the hounds."

"Interesting. Though much as I'd expected. What else did they uncover?"

"Well…" Simpkin paused and walked over to a desk, which held several perfectly stacked piles of paper. He thumbed through one with incredible speed before finding the sheet he sought. "This is a list of all the hares and hounds contrasted against the known attendees from the night that Baron Pritt died. I took the liberty of calling at the Gargoyle Club this morning to obtain the information."

I scanned the names and didn't find any one of them particularly surprising.

Fabian Warwick
Cyril Fischer
Marjorie Price
Lady Pandora Elles
Baroness Ermentrude Pritt

I hadn't spotted the baroness at the start of the game, but she kept popping up wherever Cyril went, so it wasn't too much of a shock.

Simpkin drew our attention to another issue with the list. "Of course, the fact that they weren't participating in the treasure hunt doesn't prove they weren't involved in the murders. There were bound to be hangers-on at these things."

It was that time of day when I surprised everyone by making a salient point. "I'm not so sure about that. On the one hand, the killer would have wanted to stay anonymous. But, if they were planning a murder, they would have needed to make sure that they were involved in the action. Last night, for example, we must assume that Augustus was murdered by the man he was pursuing in the game. Otherwise, there would have been an extra hare without a hound."

"An excellent point, Master Christopher, and that was another point which I sought to confirm in Soho this morning. I spoke to this Marjorie Price, who works at the club and helped organise the event. She says that Augustus Harred was originally paired with a young lady called Paulette Greggs. When the event started, Miss Greggs ran off and completed the three clues without being caught. In fact, she would have been the winner if the body hadn't been found. But that's mainly because there was no one chasing her."

"Harred's clues!" Grandfather boomed out unexpectedly. He clapped his hands together in irritation before continuing. "They weren't on his person when we found his body. The killer must have removed them."

"So someone interfered with the game," I said, to underline the obvious. "But why?"

Grandfather looked at me with a mix of curiosity and confidence. "As we said last night, Chrissy, the killer wished to isolate Augustus in order to murder him. We have to assume that he had access to the club where the game was planned. He could have inserted his own sheet of clues for his prey to follow then merely laid in wait."

"They found a costume abandoned close to the scene of the crime," Simpkin added. "The mask and coat of the White Rabbit!" He said this as though it were of great importance, and I hoped once more that this would rule out Pandora and Fabian as they already had costumes and wouldn't require a further disguise.

"You mean he was lured to his death?" Grandfather asked, picking up on the literary reference which I had ignored.

"It could be." Simpkin considered the possibility and then pointed his finger approvingly in his old boss's direction. "It could well be."

Grandfather let out a joyful punch of sound and began to pace. "This is more like it, Simpkin. This is more like it, indeed." As they'd both uttered such repetitive phrases, I thought, perhaps, it was my turn, but my grandfather continued. "Yes, we're on to something now. And what about the victim? What have the police discovered about Augustus Harred?"

"I was reviewing that myself before you got here. He certainly has no criminal record, as you would expect, but he doesn't have much else either."

"In what sense?"

"Well, when two officers set out to locate Harred's family to inform them of his death this morning, they ran into a brick wall."

"You mean his parents are deceased?"

"Pandora told us that he was an orphan," I added, but Simpkin batted the comment away with a quick hand.

"I don't mean that they're dead. I mean that there's no record of them."

Grandfather's face fell, and he tensed the muscles in his arms. "How is such a thing possible?"

"It could be a mistake. Of course it could," Simpkin increased his pace as he hurried to get the words out. "Perhaps the family lived abroad, or a file was lost, but Harred is a rare surname in Britain. I mean, it's extremely rare, perhaps even extinct. I worked with the pair of constables for two hours in the records room here, and we couldn't find a single mention of any Harreds. Our dead man didn't exist."

CHAPTER NINETEEN

Though they were wildly different from one another in many ways, I did spot one similarity between P.C. Simpkin and my illustrious grandfather. They both liked to do things for the sake of suspense. If I'd been telling someone all the information I'd discovered on a case, I'm fairly certain that I would have started with the fact that the man whose murder we were investigating did not appear to be a real person. Instead, Simpkin had regurgitated a number of less significant facts in order to build tension before the grand reveal. Perhaps all police officers were like that, but I somehow doubted it.

"It doesn't make any sense," the more experienced dramatist declared with a theatrical explosion of fingers into the air. "Pandora was about to marry the man. He can't just be a ghost?"

"Perhaps she doesn't realise that he lied about his past." Thoughts from that morning's interview at Stafford House went flashing through my brain. "She even spoke of his reticence to discuss the Great War. She surely wouldn't have mentioned such things if she was keeping his secret."

Grandfather's expression remained dubious. "His passport was official. I have no doubt about that. I've seen good forgeries before, but this was the real thing.

"The cufflink," I suddenly remembered. "Simpkin, have you found anything to explain the maker's mark?"

The constable shook his head. "Not yet, but it's the weekend. If the goldsmiths were open, I'd go down myself. Instead, we'll have to wait for Darrington's expert to tell us what he knows. Same goes for the bullet; such a range of knowledge is beyond me."

Grandfather jerked back to life after a sustained period of reflection. "What about Spilsbury? Has he looked at the body yet?"

Simpkin glanced about the rows of cabinets, as though he were afraid the great Sir Bernard Spilsbury, Britain's foremost pathologist, could be hiding in the museum. "My contacts can only get me so far, and you know what Spilsbury is like. He only trusts himself and works alone. I won't know what he's discovered until he releases his report."

Grandfather punched a fist into his open hand to express his aggravation but swiftly complimented his subordinate. "Good show all the same, Simpkin. We'll be at the Ritz if you discover anything new."

"Very well, sir. I will do my best to keep you informed."

The jolly fellow's positivity seemed to cheer the frustrated detective. "I know you will, Simpkin." He contemplated the man for a short spell and then said, "Christopher, you could do a lot worse than to learn from Simpkin here. If he can't find out a fact on a case, it probably isn't worth knowing. That Simpkin hasn't made it to chief inspector yet is the real mystery."

Our inside man just laughed. "Don't tell anyone, sir, but I wouldn't let them promote me if they tried. If I was an inspector, I wouldn't have the time to run down here after hours and learn about old cases. And where would the fun be in that?"

"Where indeed?" Grandfather replied. "Where indeed?"

They enjoyed some more nostalgic grinning before I decided to pull my supervising officer out of the basement and back into the light.

"Now what?" I asked once we were standing on the pavement and Todd was pulling the Rolls Royce up alongside us.

"How many times must I ask, Christopher? Would you please use full–"

"Fine. Now what are we going to do, my beloved grandfather?"

He tipped his head back and looked at me through narrowed eyes. "There's no need to be sarcastic." He didn't answer my question directly but turned to the road and whistled. "Delilah, with me. Todd, drive the car to the hotel and, as soon as lunch is over, you may have the afternoon to yourself. Find a matinee to enjoy or take a young lady dancing. I'll drive the car if needs be."

"Very good, M'Lord. Thank you." Todd couldn't believe his luck and drove off before Grandfather could change his mind.

"So, what are we doing next?" I asked with just a hint of a whine in my voice.

Delilah had come to stand next to us and enjoyed an affectionate pat on the head from her master.

"What do you think?" he paused to give me time not to answer. "We're going for a walk in the park."

We cut through the twin buildings of New Scotland Yard and made our way to St James's Park, where the game had started the night before. We emerged by the lake and caught a glimpse of those impressively large pelicans sunning themselves under the... umm... gloomy grey skies. You'd think that such exotic birds would get tired of the British climate and fly back home, but apparently not. Perhaps the fish in Britain are tastier than the ones abroad. After all, we did invent fish and chips. That has to count for something!

Delilah went dashing off down the path in search of a squirrel to chase, and Grandfather was resolutely silent. I wondered if he was turning over the conundrum of why pelicans don't fly home and whether it's something to do with Britain's–

"Don't be ridiculous, boy. Their wings are clipped," he barked, which put paid to that theory. "If you must know, I'm considering the facts of the case."

I wasn't going to just stand by (or walk by, as the case may be) and tolerate such rudeness. "What do you mean, 'If you must know'? I didn't say anything."

"Yes, but you were wondering what I was thinking and, to me, that is almost as noisy." He seemed quite ruffled, even for him. Instead of arguing, I decided to see whether I could help set his mind at ease.

"Is there something you'd like to tell me, Grandfather?"

He let out a long, tuneless whistle. "Yes, there is."

"Well, I am all ears. Please unload your burden upon me. (I sometimes think it's all I'm good for anyway.)" I didn't actually say this last sentence, though I imagine he knew I was thinking it.

He sighed a pitiful sigh and finally disclosed his concerns. "For a moment, back at the museum, I thought we were getting closer to the killer. But we've been investigating Augustus's death for half a day, and I don't feel we know a single thing for certain."

"You seemed most energised when we learnt about the White Rabbit costume," I reminded him, but he was determined to be miserable and could find no positivity in my response.

"Yes but, unless the police turn up some unlikely fingerprints, we can't know for certain that the killer wore it. In fact, it's not much of a clue even then. I enjoyed its symbolism more than anything else. With even our victim disappearing out from under us, what chance do we stand of catching the culprit?"

As my mother often tells me, and I have no doubt mentioned

139

before, I am a pleaser. It was my first instinct to keep babbling on until I found something that would reassure him of his brilliance. The problem with this, of course, is that the ideas that I spontaneously pull out of my head don't tend to be very good. So, instead, I shut my mouth and had a good old bout of cogitation.

I weighed up all the evidence we had uncovered, and then weighed it up once more, as I've never been particularly adept with weights. I considered the various players in our orbit, from Baron Terence Pritt through to the execrable Leopold Twelvetrees, Fabian, Cyril, Miss Craddock and even lovely Pandora. And all the time that I was thinking, my grandfather had a worried expression on his face.

"You don't seem yourself. What is it?" he asked when he could take it no more. "I can't read what's going on in your precious little head, and I don't like it one bit."

"I'm thinking," I explained.

"Ah, that must be it."

Undeterred, I knew that there was something on the tip of my brain, but I couldn't quite transfer it to my tongue. "Cyril Fischer!" I began, as I was somehow certain that the crime was connected to Baroness Pritt's fancy man. "He'll have the answers we require."

"Why would you say that?" As he asked this question, Delilah ran up to us with a pinecone in her mouth for her master to throw. He duly obliged.

The answer came to me as I spoke. "Because… because he's our likely suspect."

"Oh, is he?"

"That's right." I was becoming more confident now, and the words flowed out of me, much in the way a master musician can create the most beautiful combinations of notes when improvising a tune. "The fact is, though he may not be the at centre of the group, we've come across Cyril at every turn. He was there at the treasure hunts and in the Gargoyle on the night we attended. He didn't have a costume of his own, as he was organising the game, and so he could have had the White Rabbit disguise stashed in a bush in the park."

I peered around at our environs as though I might still be able to spot his hiding place.

"So you're saying he had the opportunity?" Grandfather's words emerged in a low, steady tone, as though he were saying a prayer. "Continue."

"Well… don't forget what Peggy Craddock told us. Cyril argued with Terence Pritt just before he died."

"Yes, his relationship with the baroness certainly gives him the motive to murder her husband, but what about Augustus? Why would Cyril have wanted him dead?"

This was more difficult to answer, and I found myself, quite literally, scratching my head. "Ummm… perhaps he was jealous."

"Jealous?" Grandfather had an incredible talent for investing a single word with lashings of incredulity.

"Yes. Of Pandora and her friends. We heard from Fabian that his aunt had asked them to play nicely with her *petit ami*. That must have wounded his pride."

We reached The Mall, and he came to a halt. "You know, Christopher, that is a well-considered and realistic solution to the mystery."

His compliment only served to make me suspicious. "And what would you say the probability is of it being correct?"

He sucked his cheeks in and glanced up at the steely sky. "Oh, I'd say… yes… approximately one in twenty. But–"

I had to pause to perform a mathematical equation before I could sufficiently show my outrage. "A five per cent chance that I've come to the right conclusion? Thank you so much for your confidence."

"Really, boy, try to concentrate on the positives. You may be wide of the mark with your theory, but you are approaching the case in the right manner. And, perhaps more importantly, you've given me an idea."

By this point, it had been hours since my ambulatory breakfast and I could think of nothing but food. "Have I given you an idea of where to have lunch?"

"Don't worry about that." he replied with a dismissive shake of the head before realising how glum I looked and humouring me. "We're on our way to the Ritz. As it happens, the idea you have inspired is where we should go for dinner. I will reserve a table at the Gargoyle Club."

This was finally something that I could feel pleased about. Not only had Grandfather praised my analysis of the case, but I was guaranteed at least two more meals that day. Such things were never certain when the great Lord Edgington was involved, and it cheered me up no end.

CHAPTER TWENTY

We walked in a swift fashion through St James's and up to the Ritz, with its illuminated arcade that funnelled us towards a much-needed repast. I had to hope that Cook had been alerted to our imminent arrival and that whatever feast she had planned for us would be waiting. Though not always guaranteed to produce dishes that are instantly recognisable, good old Henrietta's food is generally quite tasty.

Rather than eating in the suite my grandfather had reserved for us, we consumed our lunch alongside the other diners in the exquisite restaurant. On the one hand, this was magnificent as I got to enjoy the stunning frescos on the walls of the charming room and marvel at the ceiling, which was painted to look like the sky on a fine day. What I enjoyed slightly less about it, however, was the fact that everyone kept staring at us. They clearly thought it strange that the famous (and famously eccentric) Lord Edgington would bring his own staff to attend him at one of the finest hotels in London.

To be perfectly honest, I didn't blame them for their bemused looks and searching glances. Whenever the haughty French waiters came near our table, Grandfather would shoo them away, much as one would a cat trespassing on a neatly trimmed lawn. The only person allowed within a five-yard radius of our spot by the window was Todd who, dressed in his footman's livery, delivered us dish after dish from Cook's repertoire.

After a potato and pigs' trotter potage, the next course was all winter vegetables. Stuffed pumpkin, stoved leeks, cardoon fritters and salsify certainly helped tantalise my appetite for the real thing. The main course of Huntingdon fidget pie, with baked black pudding, was just what I needed. It was most amusing to see the other guests in their finery, delicately picking oysters from their shells and sucking down caviar. I, meanwhile, buried my face in that delicious pastry of apples, bacon and onion all glued together in a cider gravy – though I politely declined the accompanying liver and laverbread gelatine.

"You don't know what you're missing, my boy," Grandfather informed me as he tipped the revolting mixture down his throat.

"I know it's not as good as this pie," I replied. "Though I may enjoy the finer things in life as much as the next grandson of a marquess, give me a hunk of meat pie, and I'm in very heaven."

I was so transfixed by the meal that I didn't say a word for some time after this. All I could think about was getting as much of that mouth-watering nourishment inside me in the shortest time possible (without choking). And when I sat back in my seat with my stomach bulging, exhausted from the effort – as though I'd spent the last hour running laps of the school field – I realised that my companion hadn't spoken either.

"Is everything all right, Grandfather?" I enquired, studying his face before I dared say a word.

"Yes, boy. Now hush." He spoke in a small, hard voice, as if someone had just insulted his sense of dress or told him that amethyst-topped canes were no longer in fashion. His jaw was set, his brow creased, and he looked as though he were concentrating incredibly hard.

With the main meal polished off, and dessert soon to arrive, I listened to the conversations at the neighbouring tables. The funny thing about restaurants is that people speak just as loudly as if they were alone at home, all the while expecting their fellow diners to ignore their grand pronouncements. I heard one couple, sitting barely three feet away from me, discuss their plans to tell their respective spouses of their undying love for one another. They were both desperate for the truth to come out, though the man decided it would be a good idea to delay the announcement until after his son's fourth birthday. The rotter!

A shrivelled-up character over to my left was miserable after she'd had to fire her long-serving lady's maid because the poor thing had lost an earring. "How am I supposed to find a new maid, may I ask? I'll be weeks dressing myself and where's the justice in that? The damn woman should have found her own replacement before getting herself dismissed!"

Her companion appeared to be dozing off into his chateaubriand and had to slap his own cheeks to stay awake. "Yes, dear. Of course, dear. It's exactly as you said."

"The Bolsheviks!" came the call from a dyspeptic chap on Grandfather's side of the table. "That's who'll be behind it."

"I'm sorry, Daddy," the young lady beside him began in a lazy drawl. She was dressed in a floral fabric that looked an awful lot like

144

the curtains from my dormitory at school. "What are you blaming the Bolsheviks for now?"

He snorted loudly. "This business in Westminster last night. Man shot dead practically in front of the police. By the sound of things, they don't have a clue who's responsible, but I have."

"The Bolsheviks?" There was a slight laugh in her voice, and I immediately liked her.

"Absolutely!" Every word he shouted was furious. "Never trust a Russian, that's what I say. Not with all this revolution they go in for. It's not to be tolerated, I tell you. Not to be tolerated."

I was rather enjoying their discussion until Grandfather clapped his hands together to get my attention. "I've heard enough. We can go."

I stared at him, then at my empty plate, and then at the man who was rambling on about Bolsheviks – not that he could help me. "But… But I haven't had dessert yet."

Grandfather had already crushed his napkin into a ball and was about to leave the table. "There's no time for that, my boy. We've a murder to solve."

It was at this very moment that Todd appeared from whichever kitchen had been reserved for the exclusive use of Lord Edgington's staff. He was carrying a silver salver with an oval dish set atop. I recognised it as the one in which Cook made her apple and rhubarb crumble. If such a sight didn't change my grandfather's mind, nothing could.

"Crumble!" I said in little more than a miaow.

"Hmmm…" He was clearly overwhelmed by the strength of my argument (and the ever so tempting smell of dessert wafting over to him). "Very well. We can stay for one piece, but no more."

In no way was this a problem for me. I would simply take twice as large a serving as normal, thus avoiding the need for a second helping. Todd reappeared with a jug of thick custard, and I drowned my dessert like Poseidon attacking a ship of sailors who had displeased him. I may have let out a wicked laugh as I watched the bowl fill.

"Grandfather, why are we here?" I asked with my mouth full. "We obviously came for a reason."

He was eating with all his usual grace and looked appalled at the speed with which I was consuming my prize. "I don't know what you mean."

I wouldn't let him get away with such blatant untruths. "Admit it. You came here to eavesdrop."

He finished a spoonful of his sweet and tutted at me. "I do not 'eavesdrop' Christopher. I merely overheard some relevant information."

I'd touched a nerve and couldn't help smiling. "Oh, that's much better. So what exactly did you 'overhear'?"

"I've confirmed what I suspected."

I drew a sharp breath and, in far too loud a whisper, asked, "Was it really the Bolsheviks?"

The father at the other table threw his hands in the air, as if to say, *See! I told you the Bolsheviks were to blame.*

Grandfather shook his head ever so slowly. "No, Christopher, I do not believe that the Russians were behind Augustus's death. I came here to confirm that no one in the higher echelons of London society has the faintest idea what went on in Westminster yesterday. Sometimes the social grapevine can catch hold of information to which a detective may not be privy. In this case, however, the views I have encountered here today are presumptive and ill-informed."

He directed this comment towards the man who was now boring his daughter with his predictions of the imminent Soviet infiltration of Great Britain.

With our meal concluded, Grandfather ushered me up to our suite where he had another surprise for me.

"You said that we had a murder to solve!" I complained, as his tailor took my measurements in front of a wide window overlooking Green Park.

"There is always time to dress smartly, Christopher." He was busy admiring his own patented ensemble in the long mirrors of his dressing room.

"I sometimes doubt that you go about things in the most efficient manner possible," I told him, though the same could not be said for his tailor. The short, balding man worked swiftly with a tape measure, notebook and pencil.

He soon had the information he needed. "The items will be available on time, as requested, Lord Edgington," he said as he packed his equipment away. The little bag he carried, full of pins, tapes and scissors, rather reminded me of the detective's kit for investigating murders that Grandfather had called for the previous night.

I felt confident that, as soon as we were alone, Lord Edgington would spring into action and whisk us across town on the next stage of the investigation.

"Why on earth are you wearing that?" I asked, when he appeared from the bedroom in a velvet-trimmed dressing gown, checked pyjamas and a sleeping cap.

He looked at me as though I was being entirely unreasonable. "I need time to consider the case and I do my best thinking when I'm at my most comfortable... with my eyes closed."

He never failed to surprise me. "You plan to have a nap?"

My grandfather really wasn't one to admit to such a thing. Instead, he turned his nose up and, with a swish of his gown, went back to his room to contemplate sheep jumping over fences. I, on the other hand, was more than ready to continue with the investigation. I felt like chasing after criminals and breaking down people's doors to get to the truth.

As such excitement did not appear to be on the cards, I retreated to the nineteenth century. I sat on the sofa with Delilah at my feet and spent the next hour reading Charles Dickens's unfinished novel, 'The Mystery of Edwin Drood'. Perhaps I should have given the details of the case to my grandfather for him to solve as, sadly, Dickens left no notes on who the killer would turn out to be, and we will never know the fate of poor Edwin for certain.

I read several chapters and was just nodding off when Grandfather reappeared, dressed for a night out. "Come along, come along. No dawdling. We have a murder to solve."

I was tempted to point out that his urgency had not precluded an afternoon nap, but I was sure he'd have a clever retort up his sleeve. So, instead, I changed into the only smart jacket I had brought with me and dashed from the room.

CHAPTER TWENTY-ONE

There was a message waiting for us in the foyer of the hotel. Chief Inspector Darrington had phoned with some vital new information, and it certainly made Grandfather think.

"German!" he said, with the exclamation mark most audible in his voice. "The hallmark on the cufflink that they found in Augustus's hand was the sun and crown common to German goldsmiths."

"What could it possibly mean?" I asked so that he could look clever.

He tapped the elegantly written note on his hand before answering. "Perhaps it's nothing. Perhaps it was planted there to suggest some connection to the continent and send us on an erroneous tangent. Although…" He didn't finish this thought but dashed from the hotel.

I dutifully trundled after him. "I did a little thinking while you were…" I concluded it would be wise not to say *sleeping*. "… ruminating on the case, and I've decided that you were right in the park earlier. The chances of us catching the killer are growing slimmer by the hour."

"Oh, yes? And why do you say that?"

The doorman had flagged down a black cab and opened the back door for us to climb in.

"Well, for one thing, we have no way of eliminating any of our suspects. But even more significantly, we have no way of saying whether one of our suspects is actually the killer. Terence Pritt and Augustus Harred could have been murdered by nearly anyone in the city. Except for the coincidence of their both being on a treasure hunt at the time, there's nothing to say we're looking for one culprit."

"It's a fair point but not persuasive enough to make me doubt our process. After all, this is not the first case I've investigated in which evidence is lacking and our suspects are too numerous to mention."

"Very well. What about the sheer range of possibilities that we don't have the time to investigate for ourselves?"

"Driver, take us to number sixty-nine Dean Street, please," Grandfather called into the front of the taxi, and we set off along Piccadilly. He turned back to me and, with a deferential tip of his top hat, conceded my point. "You are absolutely correct, my boy. We cannot possibly investigate the countless threads we have uncovered. We haven't the manpower to look into Baron Pritt's business dealings, or the time to interview his various acquaintances who could well hold vital information on his death."

"Precisely. How do we know that he wasn't murdered because of the chemical formula he stole?"

"We don't." He did not sound disheartened by this. "But there are two things which I believe you have overlooked. To begin with, though *we* may not have such time or resources at our disposal, the Metropolitan Police certainly do. As you yourself can attest, I made sure to alert my two closest allies to our investigation and dropped certain hints to Chief Inspector Darrington to ensure that he would look into those elements of the case to which we are unable."

I suppose this made sense, but he seemed less eager to explain the second of his two points. "And?"

"How many times do I have to remind you, Christopher? It is an Englishman's duty to speak in full sentences!"

I rolled my eyes as he was being excessively pernickety, even for him. "And what was your second point?"

"And second…" He smiled most broadly then. "…as you explained to me some time ago, so much of what we have discovered revolves around the Gargoyle Club, to which we are currently en route."

We zipped across Piccadilly Circus, where Eros looked down at me forlornly from his plinth, and I considered Grandfather's point. "You're right… or rather, I'm right! The main link between Pritt and Augustus is the club."

"That's correct. All our suspects, without exception, are members. I think it's fair to say that, if the Gargoyle doesn't hold the key to our investigation, a visit should, at the very least, shed some light on the major players involved."

"That's wonderful," I declared before a thought occurred to me. "Is this what you realised back at the hotel when you were… lying comfortably in bed?"

He hummed a little then, as he considered the truth of my statement. "Well… No, not at all. In fact, you were right. I'd had too much wine with lunch and fell fast asleep. But when I woke up, I knew what we had to do. So, in a very real way, my plan had its desired effect."

My grandfather was the only man I'd met who considered himself as much a genius asleep as awake.

We made it to Soho with the sun having set over London and the bright lights of the theatres on Shaftesbury Avenue shining up into the dramatic black sky. We'd gone weeks without rain – which is nearly unheard of in Britain in the winter – but, as we stepped from the cab on Dean Street, the clouds turned on their taps and the first drops fell to earth.

Grandfather held his hand out and inspected the marks on his white gloves as though they were another clue for him to investigate. The taxicab drove away, and he looked up at the townhouse where the Gargoyle Club was located. "It may be a long night, Christopher, but by the time we leave here, I hope to know an awful lot more about our two victims and their killer."

It was early to be heading to a club, but there were already plenty of people milling about on the pavement. On the steps up to the property, a young man was waiting for his paramour, who arrived in a car shortly after us. They kissed discreetly, and it reminded me of how happy we'd all been the last time we'd visited – a gang of friends with no worries or cares.

The well-dressed couple followed my grandfather and me into the rickety metal lift. I must confess that I crossed my fingers as the old thing shuddered upwards. I was terrified that it would go crashing straight back down again. We rode in silence with none of the laughs or nerves that had consumed me the last time I'd visited. I felt almost as though it were an entirely different place. The walls, carpets and decoration looked the same, but something had changed. It's hard to know whether it was the knowledge of Augustus's death, the absence of his charming fiancée or simply the time of day. All I can say for certain is that, when the lift reached its destination and we politely shuffled out, I knew that I was there as a detective, not a guest.

The young man knocked on the door to the club and Grandfather nodded to me. Though it was only a fleeting gesture, it spoke libraries. He was saying, *Boy, tonight is the culmination of this case. The events we witness beyond this threshold could mean life or death. The slightest missed piece of evidence could be the difference between a wicked man paying for his crimes and going free. But, most importantly, I want you to know that, whatever happens, I respect you as my assistant and–*

"Christopher?" he said, to break into my thoughts.

I may have been daydreaming for just the briefest of moments and, when I looked around, I realised that the young couple had gone in ahead of us. An eager doorman beckoned me forward to explain the concept of a door, and Grandfather wore a concerned expression.

"Oh, you are open," I mumbled, to cover my faux pas. "Jolly good."

I stepped into the club and was once more immersed in the world of the Bright Young People. Though the majority of such luminous characters would now be dining at Simpson's-in-the-Strand or The Ivy, I could feel their energy pulsing through the place as the band practised upstairs and the first guests of the evening arrived.

"We'd like to speak to Cyril Fischer before we dine, please," Grandfather told a man with a face like an axe head who was standing behind a small lectern, observing the comings and goings of the club.

He examined us, as if to check we were worthy of such information, before silently pointing to a closed door on the other side of the staircase. Grandfather merely nodded in reply and walked across the entrance hall.

"Thank you," I felt obliged to say, as I thought it awfully rude that everyone was being so quiet.

My aged companion knocked on the plain black door and we entered a surprisingly spacious office. There was a green baize table and a row of bookshelves covering the wall with countless large files upon them.

"Lord Edgington, what-ho!" Cyril attempted to sound like his usual cheerful self, but it was evident that he was uncomfortable with our unannounced intrusion.

If I had noticed this, then you can be sure that my grandfather had too. Without being invited, he sat down in a hard leather chair and gazed mutely at our suspect.

Poor Cyril pulled at the cuffs on his shirt as though they were stifling him, but Grandfather still said nothing. I waited. Cyril waited. But the only reaction Grandfather made was to cross one leg over the other and inspect Baroness Terence's lover from another angle.

"Do you work here at the club?" I asked, when I could no longer endure the tingling silence that had built up around us.

"In a sense." Cyril was evidently relieved that some form of conversation had been initiated. "David, the owner, is a friend of mine and encourages all sorts of creative endeavours. He lent the studio to Augus-" He cut the word short as though even mentioning the dead man's name could incriminate him.

I gave my grandfather another chance to contribute, but he kept his peace.

"And what is your creative endeavour?" I narrowed my eyes to terrify the chap. I don't think it worked, but at least my question stumped him.

"Oh... ufffff... that's a difficult one. I used to enjoy singing when I was a child, but–" He stopped himself once more. "Oh, you mean here, don't you? Well, for the last few months, I've been helping to organise the treasure hunts and parties. It was my idea to have the Wonderland Ball last night at the Cavendish Hotel... That didn't quite go to plan, but we're having another to celebrate Carnival tomorrow night. You know the type of thing, Venetian masks, harlequins and the like."

He was a strange sort of man. Older than I'd imagined when we'd first crossed paths, he was closer to forty than twenty, and there was a nervousness about him which, in the realm of a party or a bar, could have been dismissed as excitability. Perhaps it was the murder that had unsettled him, but I concluded there was something a little odd about Cyril Fischer.

"You argued with Baron Pritt shortly before he died, isn't that right?" I stuck the knife in when he wasn't expecting it, and his knees surged up under the table, like he'd received a shock from a bare wire.

"Baron Pritt?" he repeated in an innocent tone. "I thought you were here to talk to me about Augustus. Baron Pritt had a heart attack. Well, that's what Ermie told me, at any rate."

With my grandfather's presence no longer a factor, I was enjoying playing the part of the lead detective. "Your sweetheart, Ermentrude Pritt? The estranged wife of Terence Pritt? Yes, it's funny that you should argue with a man who accused you of stealing his lawful spouse minutes before his car was wrapped around a lamppost."

"Actually, the newspaper said that he missed another car and went off the road. There was no lamppost involved." Fear had been building up within him, but all my hard work was undone because I simply hadn't stuck to the facts.

"Right... thank you for the information. Ummm... Where was I?"

I looked at my grandfather for assistance, but the superlative Lord Edgington either had his mind on other matters or had nodded off with his eyes open.

"I believe you were hinting at my involvement in the death of Baron Pritt." Cyril really was ever so helpful.

"That's right." I brought my fist crashing down on the desk and made him jump with fright once more. "It's too much of a coincidence for two people to have died on the treasure hunt over two consecutive weekends. So what could be the connection between the death of a wealthy aggregates magnate and a penniless painter?"

Cyril raised one nervous hand to answer. "I believe they both knew Fabian–"

"You!" I screamed with another thump of my fist. I thought that he might burst into tears this time. "You couldn't marry your rich lover with her husband still alive, so you drove him off the road. You hoped that the car crash would kill him, but that didn't work, so you improvised a solution. We should know; we've seen the body."

"You have?" His voice came out like a hamster's.

"Pritt's face had turned blue, as though someone had strangled him." I paused to allow the revelation to have its effect. "Did you stop your car to finish him off and then continue on with the treasure hunt as though nothing had happened?"

"No..." His voice rose half an octave, and his eyes were as wide as Tube tunnels. "I didn't even see the crash. Ask anyone."

"Obviously, you made sure there were no witnesses. I'm not suggesting you're an idiot... just a killer."

I glanced at grandfather then, as I thought my interrogation was going exceptionally well. He was surely phenomenally proud of me but looked rather distant and did not give me the encouragement for which I'd hoped.

"Fine. If you believe that, tell me why I would have killed my friend Augustus?" Cyril sounded rather like a child. A singsong melody had entered his voice as though he was hoping to taunt me.

"Because..." Oh, he'd got me there. I'd felt so confident that he was about to confess to his every evil deed and didn't have an answer prepared. It would all come to nought, unless... "Because you don't have any friends." This was an infantile response to an infantile question, and I regretted the words as soon as I said them.

"I beg your pardon?"

It was too late now. I had to keep going. "We heard from Fabian Warwick that his aunt, your lover, Baroness Pritt, asked Fabian to include you in the treasure hunts because you found it difficult to make friends. Perhaps you killed Augustus in order to become Fabian's closest compeer." I had no idea what I was talking about. I should have stayed back at the Ritz with Delilah.

"She did what?" Cyril apparently hadn't known anything about this before and was more than a little hurt. "I thought they genuinely liked me." He gazed down at his hands in abject sorrow. "How typically pathetic."

He stamped his feet and pulled open a drawer. All the jolly cheer he normally exuded had dissolved and, with one aggressive finger pointing across the table at me, he used his free hand to tip a bottle of gin down his throat.

"I'll give you some advice, young man; trust no one but yourself." He wiped his mouth on his sleeve, then went to drink once more. "Friends, family, sweethearts: they're all the same. The only person you can trust in this life is yours truly."

I felt dreadfully guilty for making him so sad. I know you're supposed to have a thick skin to be a detective but robbing that bubbly chap of his vim made me feel as though I'd punched a nice, smiley penguin in the face. I considered explaining how difficult I'd found it at school until I'd made friends with the three Williams but, before I could comfort him, he put his head down on the table and started to cry.

CHAPTER TWENTY-TWO

Just when I thought things couldn't possibly get any more awkward, the man was really bawling!

I looked about for a handkerchief or what have you. In fact, I was about to rip a page from one of the files on the desk when my grandfather finally spoke and saved me from myself.

"How old are you, Cyril?"

Our suspect didn't have the strength to raise his head. "I'm thirty-five years old and I haven't got any friends." He really was a bit of a moaner.

"You're old enough to have fought in the war, then. Where did you fight?"

The soppy chap angled his head just enough to be able to see his inquisitor – the good one, not the idiot who went on about crashing cars into imaginary lampposts and killing people in order to make new friends. "I was part of the first wave of conscription. I served right through the war. It would be easier for me to name the places where I didn't fight."

"Which countries?"

"France for much of the war, but Belgium too."

Grandfather continued in the same neutral tone throughout. Unlike Cyril, he showed no emotion, no fear. "And on into Germany, one assumes."

Puzzled by the old man's line of questioning, our suspect straightened his back and regarded us both more keenly. "That's correct."

"And your surname – Fischer – that's German too, isn't it?"

"Yes. My grandfather was German, much like our current king's. What exactly are you implying?"

My own grandfather's hand formed a fist beneath the desk, and I could tell he had slipped up. His question had put Cyril on the defensive.

He lightened his tone to cover his gaffe. "Oh, nothing. Nothing at all. You'll forgive an old man for prying. I simply adore finding out about people. My son Maitland fought in the Battle of Ypres. Who knows, you might have crossed paths with him."

Cyril kept his eyes on my grandfather for a moment before

157

replying. "Yes, it's possible. There were an awful lot of men there and an awful lot of them died." He shook his head as if to dismiss whatever doubts had lingered. Though his eyes were a little pink, he soon returned to his usual blithe demeanour.

I couldn't imagine for one moment why Grandfather was discussing such matters. The cufflink in Augustus's hand was said to have come from Germany, but I didn't see any other connection.

I observed a change in the old man as he returned to more probing questions. "Tell me about the treasure hunts. You said that you've been helping with them for some time, and yet Fabian was in charge last Friday when Baron Pritt died. Is that correct?"

"Precisely. Fabian wanted to run the first one of the year. I suppose he was eager to show me how they should be done, but I'd spent the winter coming up with ideas for clues, routes and themes." His gently frivolous tone coated his voice, and he let out a lilting laugh. "Such fun! Really it is."

Grandfather clapped his hands together and joined in with the laughter as though he were just as silly as our suspect. "That's wonderful. My grandson and I certainly enjoyed ourselves, didn't we, Christopher?"

He had to nudge me to answer as I was still trying to decipher his strange switch in mood. "Did we? Oh, yes. That's right, we did."

"But I've been wondering how the killer could have changed the clues that Augustus received last night." He shifted attitude once more and delivered the question with the force of a dagger to the gut.

Trapped within the detective's gaze, Cyril couldn't answer and reached for the gin bottle to steady his nerves. "I… How can you be certain that's the case? I certainly wouldn't have changed them."

"Trust me, Cyril, they were altered. From the state in which the body was found, the police can determine when the murder took place. It's clear that Augustus went straight from St James's Park to Westminster. So I'd like you to tell me how the clues were swapped."

The slight chap straightened his cravat and took a deep breath. "It must have been here during the day. I prepared everything myself yesterday morning and left the packs with each competitor's name stamped upon them on my desk."

"Did you lock the door?" I asked, but he didn't look away from

Lord Edgington.

"No, I never do. Anyone could have come in and tampered with the clues. Though I can't imagine why they would."

"Think back to yesterday." Grandfather leaned forward in his chair. "Who had the opportunity to swap Augustus's clue sheet?"

"Well... Marjorie works here in the restaurant during the day and was in charge of transporting the clues to the park last night. She's been awfully helpful over the last few weeks but, as far as I know, she had very little to do with Baron Pritt or Augustus."

"Come on, man. You can do better than that. Did you notice anyone here whom you might not have expected to see? Anyone out of the ordinary?"

Cyril let out a long breath this time and considered the question. "The place isn't busy during the day, especially in the week. I expect there'll be a list of any non-members who visited. Give me just a moment and I'll see what I can find."

"That's fantastic, thank you." Grandfather's voice became exceedingly polite, and I wondered if he'd achieved exactly what he'd set out to do when we entered the office. "If you could also provide a full list of all the members, I would be very grateful."

We sat quietly as Cyril nipped from the room, but my grandfather started speaking at great speed as soon as we were alone. "Excellent work, Christopher. You had the poor man at sixes and sevens. It was the perfect prelude before I swooped in with more significant questions of my own."

This sounded like a compliment disguised as an insult but was probably quite the opposite.

"That's all well and good, Grandfather. But why did you ask him about the war and Belgium and all those things in the first place?"

"Germany, boy, not Belgium. I'm not the slightest bit interested in Belgium. Though, I did once have a friend who–"

"Grandfather, concentrate!" These two words served to slap him back to more important matters. "Cyril will be back any moment and I must know…" I had spoken more truth than I realised as, before I finished the sentence, the door had swung open, and Cyril returned with two books in his hands. "…I must know who decorated this lovely room." This was the only thing I could think of to disguise our covert discussion.

I'm not sure that my ruse had any effect as, if anything, Cyril looked at me more suspiciously. It really wasn't a very interesting room, and I would not require the designer's calling card.

"Yes, it's quite lovely," Grandfather added to convince him and, amazingly, it seemed to work.

Cyril shrugged and sat down at the desk to show us the members' list. "I believe this will be up to date."

Turning the book around for us to read, I noticed any number of famous names from the world of literature, politics, theatre and even film. Dotted in amongst them were our two victims and every last suspect. Fabian and his aunt and uncle had been the first to join, soon after the club opened at the beginning of 1925. Leopold Twelvetrees was the newest of the lot, having paid his dues just one week earlier, and I was surprised to see that Cyril himself was only a few names higher up the list. He'd joined the club in January, despite his claims of having worked there for months.

When my grandfather looked satisfied with his study, our interviewee presented the next piece of evidence. "This is the guest book, and here's the entry from Friday." He placed it before us. "Several of them are guests of current members, plus there are a number of tradesmen who come regularly. Our doorman, Michel, informs me that there are a few names which he cannot identify, and he's put a star by each."

A long column written in incredibly small letters filled the page. I skipped over most of the names and sought out the stars. Near the bottom, one name in particular stood out.

Samantha Unwin
The Marquess of Cranley
Alec Waugh
*Lionel Davidson
*Arthur Poundtree
Edwin Alsop
*Peggy Craddock
Tommy Hines

160

CHAPTER TWENTY-THREE

"We've found the killer," I said, hardly able to believe it.

We'd moved to our table in the restaurant and my grandfather was observing the world around us, rather than paying attention to me.

"It's the only thing that makes sense and it explains so much." My every word was dripping with disbelief, and yet I'd never felt more confident of a theory in one of our investigations before. "Peggy Craddock was there at the two killings and had the opportunity to lead Augustus to Westminster, where she pulled out a pistol and shot him dead." I took a gulp of breath, as I'd forgotten to do so until then. "It all makes sense. She must have been hanging around Fabian and his friends for months. And it helps to explain the severe lack of evidence we've found on anyone else."

"Oh, yes?" Grandfather finally replied, with very little interest in his voice.

"Most certainly. Now all we have to determine is why she did it."

"Did what?" His eyes broke from the other diners, and he cast his troubled gaze upon me.

"Killed Baron Pritt and Augustus Harred."

"Who killed them?"

I was beginning to wonder whether he'd been drinking pure ethanol at lunch in place of wine.

"The reporter Peggy Craddock. She was on the list that Cyril showed us. She was here at the club yesterday and must have changed Augustus's clues."

"Don't be ridiculous boy, why would she have done that?" He spoke as though I was the one acting abnormally.

"Because… because… Well, I don't actually know at the moment. But now we're sure of the killer, we can find the reason."

He gave me his full attention at last. "Really boy, you've clearly learnt nothing from me if you think that it's acceptable to conduct a murder inquiry in such a fashion. You don't start with the killer and then find the evidence unless you catch him covered in blood with a weapon in his hands. And, even then, you should never jump to the most obvious conclusion."

"But she was here," I tried one last time, barely managing a squeak of sound.

"Yes, I know she was. I saw her myself."

It took me a moment to realise what he was saying. "You mean... you mean you knew that she came to the club?" I needed a few more seconds to realise the implications of this. "Wait just one moment. What were you doing here?"

"Didn't you notice my name on Cyril's list? I came to enquire about joining." He hesitated, and I knew there was more to it. "Which gave me the opportunity to switch the clue sheets."

I stared at him in astonishment. "You swapped Augustus's clues to help the killer–"

"Don't be ridiculous. I paired your sheet with my own to ensure that I would be the one chasing you. I thought it would be more enjoyable that way."

"And what was Peggy Craddock doing here?"

"What do you think, boy? She's a reporter for the social column of a popular newspaper. She was loitering in the hope of discovering some juicy titbit of gossip. Failing that, I got the impression that she bribes the doorman for information about where the treasure hunts will take place. He probably singled her out on the list to distance himself from accusations of impropriety."

I really thought I'd found our culprit and wasn't ready to give up so easily. "Will you at least accept that Miss Craddock is a suspect?"

"Everyone is a suspect, Christopher," he said, as he attempted to get the apparently blinkered waiter's attention.

"Yes, I know that. All I mean is that she should be included on our list. She is the only person we know who had the opportunity to interfere with Augustus's clues."

The zippy chap in black and white had finally spotted him and Grandfather mimed the drink which he still didn't possess. "Except for me."

"Well, obviously you didn't do it."

"And nearly everyone in this room," he continued.

"Yes, obviously everyone..." I didn't finish that thought as I realised what he was implying. "Ah... I see. Club members can come and go as they please, and no one would have thought to make a note of their names. You may have a point."

Since we'd entered the restaurant, I'd spotted a number of famous faces that I'd previously seen on the London stage and in my father's newspapers. I'm afraid I couldn't name a single one of them. And that was the problem with this investigation; my grandfather expected me to be able to formulate theories as well as he could. This was only the second weekend in my life that I'd spent in London, and he was at a major advantage. With Peggy Craddock apparently dismissed as a potential killer, I found myself wishing that we were investigating a murder at my school again. At least I knew everyone's names back at Oakton Academy.

"Don't be so hard on yourself, boy," Grandfather consoled me, as the pianist in the corner played some light, breezy music which made everyone in the room smile. "You deserve to take a break from our inquiry. It's time to enjoy ourselves."

I didn't believe him for one second. "So you're not concerned that we still don't know who our second victim was, why he died, or who killed him?"

He attempted a smile, which made him look as though he'd eaten something unpleasant. "That's right. I'm only here to have a good time."

Rather than trying to prove him wrong, I looked about at the congregation of thrill-seekers. Whatever time it was by this point, it was late enough to start drinking, and nearly everyone had a cocktail in their hands. I noticed the American dancers from the previous weekend were there, dining alongside two grand dames of London. Leopold Twelvetrees was present too and appeared to have been drinking since lunchtime at the very least. There were girls in long beaded dresses who looked like they'd stepped out of a revue on Shaftesbury Avenue. A table of young men with paint flecks all over their clothes talked about nothing but love and art all night, and Baroness Pritt soon appeared with poor Cyril trapped under her arm.

Free from the need to identify a killer in a city of... well, I don't know how many people, but there were a lot of them! I was able to luxuriate once more in the pulsating atmosphere of the Gargoyle Club. The harder the gigantic piano player hit those keys, the looser my muscles became, and it made me feel like dancing. When the food arrived, I enjoyed it, of course, but I barely noticed what we ate (pumpkin soup, a filet mignon steak with a peppery cheddar sauce and apple crumble for dessert). It was the people I found so compelling, and that electric sensation that comes when you take an array of personalities, from all backgrounds and walks of life, and you throw them together in one place.

My grandfather clearly felt it too, as he started singing along to the piece of music that was playing.

> **"I'm Burlington Bertie. I rise at ten-thirty.**
> **And saunter along like a toff.**
> **I walk down the Strand with my gloves on my hand.**
> **Then I walk down again with them off."**

The people at the next table heard him and joined in with the verse. The song soon carried around the room like that until the whole restaurant was united in raucous noise. I was surprised to see the rather spectre-like figure of Mr Twelvetrees rise from his table and dance about joyfully with his arms in the air.

The portly piano player must have caught some notes of my grandfather's song floating over to him, as he leaned back from his instrument to shout, "Sing up, Your Lordship!"

I was sure that the stern figure who sat beside me would be loath to make a display of himself, but then, my grandfather is a man of contradictions. Though he could be deathly serious when it suited him, I should have learnt long ago that he could never resist a song.

He stood up from the table and, with a few neat sidesteps, mounted the small stage.

> **"I'm all airs and graces, correct easy paces,**
> **Without food so long, I've forgot where my face is!"**

His stentorious voice could be heard in every corner of the room, even over the chorus of support that his performance drew. Perhaps not wanting to be outdone, or simply so merry from the pink cocktails he was drinking that he didn't know any better, Twelvetrees joined him on the stage for the end of the chorus, and the two men stood arm in arm, swaying together like two swells strolling through Piccadilly Arcade.

"I'm Bert, Bert, I haven't a shirt.
But my people are well off, you know.
Nearly everyone knows me
from Smith to Lord Rosebr'y,
I'm Burlington Bertie from Bow."

When the song was complete and the entire room erupted with whoops and cheers, the two men embraced one another as old friends.

"That was simply marvellous," Twelvetrees guffawed.

"Perhaps we missed our calling on the stage." My grandfather was unable to hide his pleasure at all the attention he received, and I think he even blushed a little.

"Absolutely! We could call ourselves, 'The Two Singing Gents." Twelvetrees nudged him in the side. "It's never too late to try."

The old chaps laughed again and joined in with the crowd's applause. And that is how the scene was set when Fabian Warwick and a barely recognisable Lady Pandora Elles appeared at the door to the restaurant.

CHAPTER TWENTY-FOUR

Those who spotted the featured names from that morning's edition of The Chronicle fell quieter. This, in turn, led to a whole lot of murmurs and swivelling heads. Fabian stood proudly in his rightful domain, bedecked in a black trench coat with a leopard-skin stole about his neck. He would not be intimidated by the judgemental gaze of fashionable London and strutted over to the bar.

But it was Pandora whose eyes I met. The poor creature looked like a pencil sketch of her usually colourful self. She was dressed all in white, and I imagined her for a moment as Miss Havisham, doomed to live out her days as a fiancée but never a bride. She wore a silk shawl around her shoulders, as though attempting to hide some small part of herself, and her expression was one of pure tragedy.

I was desperate to go to her, but I was an imposter in her world. I was just a novelty – a mascot that the gang had taken out for the night – and I was under no illusions as to my importance there. Yet my heart felt as though it would leave my body if I didn't run to her, comfort her, tell her that life could still be wonderful.

Before I could decide what to do, Fabian seized a bottle of cognac from behind the bar and, raising it above his head, announced, "I've come here to drink and dance. If anyone here is brave enough, you're welcome to join me upstairs."

He nodded to me on the far side of the stage, then stalked back to the exit. As I remained glued in place, like a photograph in an album, he collected his heartbroken friend and the pair of them disappeared from sight.

"They'll be fine, Chrissy," my grandfather insisted, as he sat back down, and Twelvetrees came to join us. A waiter whipped a chair from another table and brought a round of drinks. I ended up with a lemon cocktail that our guest informed me was somewhere between a John Collins and a gimlet. It managed to be both excessively alcoholic and far too bitter for my liking and, after the first few painful sips, I stopped pretending to drink it.

"I'm terribly sorry about last weekend," the newspaper man said, once he was settled with his back to the stage. I noticed that he wasn't sweating anymore and had more colour in his cheeks than when we'd first met him. "I should never have got involved in all that nonsense with the treasure hunt. I'm too competitive by far."

Grandfather smiled. "Oh, there's no harm done, man. We all get carried away from time to time. Was it worth the effort? Have sales picked up?"

Twelvetrees raised both eyebrows as he took a gulp of his drink. "Yes, they certainly have. We had a stellar week, in fact. Though one imagines that was more to do with the public's interest in suspicious deaths than any foolishness on my part."

He let out a throaty laugh and slapped his leg. I would never have imagined such warmth from the man after the way he'd previously acted. I may have been getting ahead of myself, but I found him rather good company.

Grandfather had another question to ask. "And what about Miss Craddock?"

"I beg your pardon?"

"Peggy Craddock, your reporter on the scene. Did she get to keep her job? She told me that you were on the point of sacking her."

"Oh, of course, Peggy. I was never going to sack her." He sounded bemused by the idea. "I don't know where young folk get these ideas. I may have raised my voice a little that night, but I'm loyal to my employees. It's an important lesson I've learnt in life. I've already told her she'll be promoted after what she's achieved. A female head of the social desk makes a lot of sense, in fact."

A wry look briefly crossed my grandfather's countenance as he realised that Miss Craddock had diddled us. "She's a wise one; there's no doubt about it. And you'd be wise to keep hold of her."

"Well, I didn't get to where I am today without a little wisdom." The magnate in our midst gave me a wink then and threw a nut into his mouth from the bowl in front of him. "Speaking of which, I looked into Pritt a little this week, in case I could turn up anything for the paper. I have people to do such things for me, but I didn't want to go stirring the hornets' nest if there's no fire and only smoke."

I'd never heard such a mix of metaphors, but I think I grasped his basic point.

My grandfather's curiosity was most definitely aroused. "Oh,

168

really. And what did you discover?"

He had a quick glance about, which I deemed a little theatrical. Who could possibly hear anything in such a noisy place?

"That patent he stole – the concrete or whatever it was. It belonged to a young chemist named Stefan Müller. Müller worked at Pritt's metalworks and was known to be quite the rising star. He pioneered a number of projects, but his biggest discovery was that the waste slag which the factory produced could be mixed with aggregates to create a superior road covering."

Grandfather nodded. "That's right. I've read a little on the science behind it, but what happened to the man?"

Twelvetrees sat back in his seat. "That's just it. Nobody knows. His family was German and, when the war broke out, he went to fight for the Kaiser. There's no record of him ever returning."

Grandfather ran one hand through his long, silver hair and considered this piece of news. I'm not so slow that I couldn't match Stefan Müller with the initials they'd found on the cufflink in Augustus's hand. For the first time that week, it no longer felt as though we were stumbling about in the dark. We finally had something categorical to link the two murders.

"It's a fascinating discovery," Grandfather said in little more than a fascinated murmur. "Are you going to publish it?"

Twelvetrees threw his hand in the air, nearly spilling his drink. "Pah! Not a chance. Newspapers can't go printing unsubstantiated claims about a dead peer. And it's not as if it proves Pritt was murdered."

I thought Grandfather was about to respond, but he appeared to change his mind at the last second and turned to me instead. "Christopher, I'm going to talk some more to Leopold. Listening to two old men blithering on won't be very interesting for a young chap like you. Why don't you explore the club?"

I considered my options but ended up nodding my consent. To be perfectly honest, I was uncertain whether it was the best idea. Not only would my grandfather have the chance to discover more of our first victim's secrets, it was also dreadfully irresponsible of him to allow his seventeen-year-old grandson to wander about in a nightclub filled with alcohol, loose women and jazz music! Still, I wasn't going to tell him that and left them to their conversation.

As the older members of the club were finishing their dinner in the restaurant, the real Bright Young Things were arriving in droves. Well, in fours at least, as that was the number the lift could hold. It was hard to tell whether there was a themed ball on that night, or members of the Gargoyle Club were merely prone to wearing outlandish attire. There was a woman dressed as Charlie Chaplin, complete with a cane and pencilled-on moustache. A man in several feather boas was singing sea shanties on the staircase, and a pair of twin brothers were wearing identical outfits which were sewn together at the waist. I didn't know what to make of any of them.

As promised, I found Fabian on the dance floor, but there was no sign of Pandora. Saying that Fabian Warwick was the centre of attention is like pointing out that water is wet or the sky in London is grey. Every last fragment of mirror on the walls seemed to be directed at him alone so that, in place of a décor scheme, we had one thousand Fabians. Having shed his coat and furs, he looked as though he had dressed for a spot of exercise in the sixteenth century. In tight shorts and a flouncy, frilled shirt, he threw his limbs in every direction and swapped dance partners with every new bar of the jangling music that the band of four produced.

I could have watched him forever, though in my mind I was still considering what part he had played in the two murders and whether he himself could be connected in some way to Stefan Müller. After all, beyond his connection to the Pritt family, we knew very little of his upbringing. Perhaps he was a younger brother of the wronged scientist and had sought revenge for–

Before I could come to the end of this winding path of hypothesis, I was tugged into the centre of the action.

"Dance, Christopher," Fabian commanded.

At first, I just stood there, trying to discern the rhythm and flow of the music.

"Close your eyes if it helps. But just dance, you little wonder."

I was a dreadfully malleable sort of boy and did exactly as he instructed. With my eyes closed, I could feel the music travel through my body. I marked the beat of the big bass drum coming from the drummer's trap set and enjoyed the roll of the snare within me. I didn't have to tell my muscles to do anything; they worked of their own accord. My feet shuffled, my hips swayed and then, as if a spell had been cast, I was dancing.

My whole body felt extremely light, and I wondered quite how much impact a few sips of lemon cocktail could have on a boy of seventeen. With my eyes clasped shut, I could imagine myself floating above the heads of all those unusual people and jigging around the room, like an angel possessed by the force of the music.

"Not tonight, Chrissy," a voice in my head whispered, and I saw Augustus as clear as day. He spoke in his usual controlled manner but wore a half-frown that made me stop dancing and open my eyes. That magic space, which was filled with life and joy, suddenly seemed terribly unfeeling. Our friend had died that very weekend – his body was still on Spilsbury's cutting table – and I couldn't accept that no one would mourn him.

Fabian had his arms around two girls with short fringes and even shorter skirts and didn't see me leaving. I slipped back through a parade of couples dancing closely together and few people paid me any attention. With the scowl on my face and my truly mismatched clothes, I was a surplus part – no one would notice that I'd gone.

I wandered the halls of the Gargoyle for some time, peeking in at different worlds to which I didn't quite belong. In one lounge, a group was discussing modern writers like Virginia Woolf and James Joyce. I'm sure that, if I'd mentioned my love of Charles Dickens, they'd have found me terribly old fashioned. Another room hosted a pack of cheery youngsters who were stacking bricks, one on top of the other, like children trying to see how high they could go. I longed to join in with that joyful scene, but I knew that, had I asked to participate, I would only have brought the mood down.

I came across salons decorated in historical and geographical themes from Elizabethan to Amazonian. It was rather tempting to find an empty space in which to lie down, but I could still see Augustus wherever I went. He was not a ghost or a vision, but simply a reminder of what I had come there to do. I could hear his calm, steady voice and I knew I had to keep searching for something to set the world right once more.

CHAPTER TWENTY-FIVE

It was perhaps inevitable that I would float up to the roof terrace and all the way to Augustus's studio. How else can one feel better about a man's passing than to find proof that he hasn't really gone anywhere? In Augustus's case, he would live on as long as one single portrait hangs in a gallery, or even stashed away in a cupboard somewhere.

On entering his messy, paint-dappled space, I remembered just how much life there was in the paintings he'd created. Even the unfinished ones promised so much – their free, curving lines forever waiting for someone to add more detail.

I studied a large canvas with a barely present, yet recognisably male form, transmitted in ten daring strokes. It was a portrait of a lithe yet imposing figure in half-profile, and even though it was incomplete, it was already a masterpiece.

"That was his big commission," another soft voice informed me. This time, it was not in my head, and I turned to see Pandora. "It was supposed to make him famous, but now it will never be finished."

"I'm sorry," was all I could think to say, as I went to crouch next to her.

She was sitting on the floor surrounded by frames. Her white dress had spread out around her, and she sipped at a grasshopper, which she occasionally held up to the dim bulb above our heads to cast a faint, green light upon her blonde curls.

"Hello, Chrissy." She emitted a sad laugh and put her head back against the wall. "I have no idea why I came tonight. Fabian convinced me that it would make me feel better, and no one says no to Mr Warwick. To be perfectly honest, I think I only came to put his mind at ease. He says he's happy as long as I'm not at home surrounded by ghosts and silence." She hiccupped then, which did nothing to undermine the poetry of her words. "I thought that the party would stop for at least a day so that everyone could mourn, but the people must have their fun."

I cleared my throat and did what I'd been hoping to do all night. My chance to make the tragic character feel a little better had arrived. "I went to see Fabian for a while, but it felt wrong. This life you all lead is a thrill, it really is, but it's not what I pictured myself doing when I was a boy." I stumbled over the words then as I thought she probably still considered me just that. "Or rather… What I mean is that it feels like I'm on holiday here, and I can't imagine that real life is anything like this."

She raised her glass again but didn't drink. "It all felt real when I had Augustus. It felt as though we'd be able to keep dancing until we were old and grey. But it wasn't the parties or the drink or the wild schemes that made me happy; it was him."

I doubted there was anything I could do to cheer her up, but it struck me that sorrow is its own special form of medicine. Perhaps what she needed more than anything was the chance to cry.

"That's really rather wonderful, don't you think?" I asked and, as she could only sigh in reply, I soon continued. "The fact that you found something so fulfilling, even if it was just for a fleeting moment. That must be very special."

She closed her eyes ever so slowly and, when she opened them again, she was smiling. "Oh, Chrissy, you are an angel. ''Tis better to have loved and lost than never to have loved at all,' is that what you're saying?"

I felt my cheeks turn red and went to sit down beside her. "Oh, yes. I suppose I am. You probably think I'm terribly naïve, but I was in love with our maid Alice for years before she got married to a nice fellow on the estate. And then I met a girl in the north of England who seemed to like me. She even wrote me a lovely letter, but I'm evidently no epistolarian, and I suppose she got bored. But I still can't say I have any regrets." I must have sounded terribly sorry for myself.

Pandora put one arm around me and rested her head on my shoulder. "Those girls were fools, Christopher. Sheer fools. What woman in her right mind would reject the advances of such a fine gentleman as yourself?" I imagine the alcohol in her drink was having its intended effect, as her eyes would no longer come to rest on anything.

I took a deep breath and tried to push away my pity. "I could feel sad and give up on ever being loved, but what good would that do me? I know that I'll meet someone amazing one day and… well, maybe she won't be the slightest bit interested in me, but perhaps the one after that will. And you, Pandora… you're practically a princess. You could give up your mansion and your army of servants. You could forget all about your beautiful dresses and never comb your hair again, and people would still love you."

She was sobbing ever so quietly now. I could feel her tears on my cheek, and I was rather proud of myself for knowing what to say. "Gosh, Christopher. How on earth did you become so wise?" She sniffed and laughed (and also hiccupped) and every sound she made was musical. "If you talk like that to the next girl, she'll fall down at your feet. In fact, you should make a note of every word you just said and sell it to the newspapers or publish it in a book for men all over the country to spout. You're an absolute poet."

I didn't reply – it would only have made me sound conceited. Instead, I gave her time to think of the man she loved so deeply. With her arm still around me, I knew what it must be like to have a big sister. Despite the tragic circumstances, she'd made me feel quite confident for once.

When her tears subsided, and my body ached from sitting on that hard floor, she spoke again. "I feel like such a fool for not spending every moment that Augustus and I had together asking him endless questions. There's so much he never told me about himself." Her eyes finally seemed to focus on a point in mid-air. "I think sometimes that I loved him without really knowing who he was."

This was the moment at which I should have abandoned my attempt to be her friend and asked her why the police could find no record of a man named Augustus Harred. I should have twisted the conversation around to a topic that could have shed light on why her mysterious fiancé was murdered. But I didn't have it in me. I would have felt like a terrible rotter to needle her like that, so it was a good thing that my grandfather appeared to do the job.

"Truer words were never spoken," he said, wandering into the room with his eyes fixed on the paintings, just as I had. "You didn't know Augustus because Augustus didn't exist. There's no trace of him before two years ago, which, if I'm not mistaken, was around the time you first met."

He turned to see the shock on Pandora's face, but she would not answer him.

"That's what you were implying, wasn't it, dear? I'm sure you were swept up in the romance of it all and never thought there was any hurry to get to know one another. But, as today has gone by, you've begun to realise just how little Augustus told you about himself. You've started to wonder whether you knew him at all."

When her reply broke from her lips, it emerged as one distended cry. "I loved him and nothing else mattered." Her breathing became faster, and she pulled her arm away from me to support her head in her hands. "I suppose I loved that unknowable side to him as much as anything else. I never pushed him to talk, but it was clear that there were some things he couldn't bring himself to discuss."

"Such as?" Grandfather had become more insistent. His words exploded across the room like tiny hand grenades.

"Well, such as..." A silence that could have lasted for hours followed her words, but Grandfather had no time to wait.

"Such as the war?"

Nodding her head ever so slowly, her eyes remained glued to that single, invisible point halfway between us and the far wall.

"I imagine that you dismissed any suspicions you had." The room was so quiet that I could hear my grandfather's breath between sentences. Suddenly, the world of the Gargoyle Club seemed far away. "I'm sure you told yourself that he had suffered enough on the front line and didn't need you badgering him."

Pandora swallowed, her throat audibly dry in spite of the half-finished cocktail she'd been sipping. "He looked so lost whenever someone mentioned it that I couldn't bring myself to ask." Her cheeks were moist once more and her words were shot through with sorrow. "I never thought badly of him, but I did wonder what had happened over there. I used to run my finger along the scar on his face and dream up heroic stories about his time on the front line."

I felt as though I were trespassing on their conversation and didn't make a sound. Grandfather walked over to us, his manner somehow gentler, and he reached out to take our hands before he spoke. "I don't blame you, child. It seems unlikely that any of this is your fault. But we need to discover why your fiancé was murdered, and I believe you can help."

He paused for a moment and his eyes traced out her features as though he wished to one day paint her himself. (Having seen examples

176

of my grandfather's artistic efforts, I can tell you that his skills didn't quite match up to Augustus's.)

"You must know something," he said, when Pandora remained quiet. "Some secret that he couldn't keep. Some truth that he couldn't fully hide that will tell us who Augustus Harred really was."

There in our circle, it seemed as though we were praying for understanding. There's no way to say whether that petition was answered. But a sense of confidence descended upon Pandora, and I think that she now realised the part she had to play. She pulled her shoulders back, straightened her neck and, in a cold, formal voice, replied, "We never spent our Sundays together."

"That's interesting, my dear. Yes, that could be very helpful." Grandfather dropped my hand in order to move closer to her. "And do you know where he went? Did he ever tell you?"

"No, I..." Her voice faltered, but she fought her indecision and delivered a response. "He always said that he was visiting an elderly aunt in the countryside. He said she was too frail for visitors."

Grandfather pulled back a little. He had detected something in her words which would have remained a mystery to me. "And yet, you didn't believe him?"

A hint of shame or perhaps doubt appeared on her face, and she closed her eyes as to respond. "I did at first. I trusted him implicitly, but it went on for so long that I began to question whether he was lying." She peeked back out at us and shook her head. "You're going to think me quite silly, but I'd read a newspaper article about a bigamist. You know, one of these chaps with three wives in three different cities. Well, I panicked and worried that Augustus had another family somewhere."

"You followed him?" I asked, finally reading between her words.

"Yes." Pandora did her best to tamp down her emotion, but I could see how hard it was for her to say the words. "I was a fool. He was no bigamist. I followed him to the station one day, and he really was visiting an old lady out in the country. He got on at Charing Cross and took the Hampstead Tube to Edgware. I felt so dreadful for not trusting him, but then he bought some flowers at a florist's and the jealousy reared up within me. He went on foot to a large house in a park half an hour from the station. I thought that he would catch me, but he never looked back. A poor old dame in a wheelchair greeted him on the front steps of the house. The flowers were for her, and I walked back to the Tube cursing myself for ever doubting him."

Grandfather stood up and allowed her story to swirl around in that great big brain of his. "Thank you, dear child." He paused, as though what he had to say next was too much to ask of her. "I'll need you to tell me everything you can about the house you visited."

CHAPTER TWENTY-SIX

Thankfully, it was too late to go shooting off in search of a vaguely described manor in the wilds of Edgware, and so we accompanied Pandora to Stafford House before heading back to the Ritz. She looked quite terrified at the thought of spending the night alone in that enormous old hall with only her infinite number of servants for company. I was rather tempted to suggest that she take a suite at the hotel with us but didn't want to anger my grandfather.

For all I knew, she was the culprit and had killed her fiancé for not telling the old lady all about his lovely girlfriend. Yes, now that I came to think of it, that did seem like the sort of thing over which a lover might kill her partner. Why Pandora would have murdered Baron Pritt was a mystery to me, but perhaps it was practice for the real thing. After all, she had been the one to discover him after his supposed heart attack.

I put such dark thoughts from my head and said goodbye. She kissed us both on the cheek before parting, and Grandfather had some final words of comfort to offer. "You must contact us at any moment if you need the slightest thing, my dear. I really mean that. This may be goodnight, but it is far from farewell."

She had a little sniffle at this, and who could blame her? I kept my fingers crossed that she would not turn out to be a maniacal killer, though I'd long since learnt that I mustn't trust pretty ladies with gentle voices.

The night was not at its coldest, and I had plenty of coats with me, so we went on foot through St James's to our home for the night. I rather hoped that the revelations we'd unearthed would enable us to identify our second victim (and perhaps even the murderer himself) but, as usual, Grandfather kept me in the dark.

"I'm not going to tell you if you haven't worked it out on your own," he reiterated for the thousandth time.

"Can you at least confirm that Augustus Harred is Stefan Müller?" I thought myself dastardly clever to have come to this conclusion. "And, if he is, why was he holding his own cufflink?"

"Are they serious questions, or are you guessing?"

I had to consider his point. "A little of both, perhaps… but it fits together, don't you think? Stefan Müller discovered a valuable compound that made Baron Pritt a fortune. He went away to war and fought for Germany. When he returned to Britain, he had to change his identity to hide who he really was and couldn't receive the money he was owed. When he crossed paths with Terence Pritt on the treasure hunts, he lost his mind and decided to kill the man who'd taken advantage of him." I don't know where all these ideas had come from, but my brain was finally filling in the gaps in the case, and I was over the moon. "I'm onto something, don't you agree?"

"You have a wonderful imagination, Christopher." He shook his head but, taking pity upon me, offered a deal. "I'll answer all your questions if you can tell me the name of the second killer in your scenario."

I can't say I projected a great deal of confidence at that moment. "Oh... that's a very good question. I... Well, we... Or rather, yes! It's Cyril Fischer!"

"That's who you think killed Augustus?" His tone suggested that I'd have had more luck if I'd pointed the finger at Queen Mary.

"No... of course not. I think it was..."

"You're guessing, Christopher." He chanted his response in that *I'm-always-right-and-you-haven't-the-first-idea* voice of his. It made me even more desperate to know what he knew, which, I suppose, was his intention.

There were two small points which made me feel better about my failure to solve the case. Number one was the fact that I'd be spending the night in my very own room at the Ritz. Though I come from a wealthy family and wanted for nothing, my quarters back at Cranley were colder than the North Pole and the blankets were so scratchy that getting into bed felt like I'd taken shelter under a mantle of stinging nettles. My dormitory at school was, remarkably, even worse. I had a rock-hard bunk in a room of thirty boys, but there would be none of that tonight. I was going to enjoy every luxury known to modern civilisation.

And point number two? Well, Delilah would be there to sleep at the end of my ship-sized bed and keep my feet warm.

Perhaps I can be forgiven for having other things on my mind than murders, dead men with no pasts and missing German chemists. When Grandfather stopped in the lobby to make a phone call to his colleagues in the police, I ran up to our suite and turned the hot water on full. I filled the beautiful conch-shell bath with soap and bubbles right up to the rim.

Oh, it was heavenly, and the only thing that detracted from my pleasure was Delilah, who kept trying to get in alongside me. When I finally managed to explain that this was a *people bath,* not a *dog bath,* she sat on the floor looking sad. I went back to thinking over the facts of the two murders whilst she whimpered with her head on her paws.

After approximately five minutes, I was certain of one thing; this was by far the loosest, most intangible case we'd investigated. With my grandfather apparently homing in on the culprit, I still wasn't entirely sure who we should include on our list of suspects. In fact, this was the best I could conjure up…

Fabian Warwick – My grandfather had suggested he was in love with Pandora, though I really couldn't imagine it. The only evidence against him was the fact that he didn't like his uncle. It was true that we'd seen a darker side of him since Augustus's death, though, and I couldn't entirely dismiss the possibility that he was our man.

Lady Pandora Elles – No. No. No. I refused to accept that she could be involved after the tender scenes of that evening. She clearly loved her fiancé and had no reason to want him dead. And that's my final word on the matter! My final word!

Cyril Fischer – Now, this was more like it. Cyril was in love with the (first) dead man's wife and would presumably gain financially and romantically with Baron Pritt out of the way. What's more, he fought in the war – unlike his younger acquaintance Fabian – which might link him to Stefan Müller or at least a lone German cufflink. Oh, and another *what's more,* he wouldn't have needed to tamper with the clues in order to direct Augustus to the wrong place, because he was the one who wrote them. Not only did I still believe he was the likely suspect, but he also had a very silly smile to which I never quite warmed.

Baroness Pritt – We'd barely considered her as a suspect but… why not?

Leopold Twelvetrees – Though he was very rude (and unusually sweaty) the first time we met him, we'd failed to find a single piece of evidence to link him to the crimes. Knowing my grandfather's capacity to surprise me, he was probably our man.

Marjorie, the treasure hunt assistant, Gargoyle Club cloakroom attendant and restaurant worker – well, now I'm really scraping the bottom of the barrel. Though present at several key moments, she'd barely said a word to any of the significant players in the case except to hand them the clues for the games or take their coats. Moreover, I would like to take this opportunity to mention that I found it rather tragic that a young lady such as her should require three jobs to make ends meet. I wonder when she found the time to sleep!?

Of course, the suspect list in itself failed to account for the evidence we had discovered. I still didn't know who Augustus Harred was or why anyone would have wanted to murder the poor fellow. I really had to wonder if he was the missing chemist, Stefan Müller, back from the dead. Augustus was old enough to fit the description, and it would have linked the two murders. The only problem with this idea is that no one seemed to like Baron Pritt enough to seek revenge on his behalf. If anything, most people seemed happy he was dead.

As the old saying goes, *the enemy of my enemy is my friend*, which means… Oh, I don't know. It was all too confusing for me. On previous investigations, at least I'd had some idea in my head of why the victims were killed. I couldn't begin to fathom what had happened this time.

Perhaps it had something to do with the Gargoyle Club, or Augustus's art. Or what if Baroness Pritt was in the background pulling everyone's strings to get rid of her odious husband? If Augustus found out what she'd been up to, she might well have taken a gun and shot him dead beside Westminster Abbey. That made as much sense as anything else. I had no doubt that I was a million miles away from the truth, and that my grandfather had collected a whole tranche of evidence that I had somehow ignored, but this was the best I could do.

Blasted murderers! Why do they always have to make everything so complicated?

With my mental exertions complete, I cut my time in the bath short and allowed Delilah ten minutes to wash her long, silky coat before bed. I really should have prepared her towel in advance, though. She jumped straight out when her time was complete and shook and shook until every inch of the room was wet. I didn't feel quite so clean after that.

Into my pyjamas I jumped. Under the sheets I went. Out of the sheets I pulled our soggy dog, and fast asleep I fell. Tomorrow we would uncover the secrets of the man who called himself Augustus Harred but, for now, I was happy to be snug and warm, cocooned in soft cotton.

CHAPTER TWENTY-SEVEN

To my amazement, when I woke up the next morning, Grandfather was in no hurry to rush off anywhere.

"Are you feeling quite yourself?" I asked over breakfast.

Our suite of adjoining rooms at the Ritz was even grander than the comparatively meagre apartment we'd occupied at Claridge's. Every fitting was awash with gold leaf, which sparkled in the light that broke through long windows onto a wall of mirrors. I felt as though I'd been transported in my sleep from the bustle of London to the calm opulence of Versailles. It really was a rather nice room.

"Of course I am," he replied with some petulance but instantly smiled when our cook appeared to aid in the delivery of our meal. "This is just delicious, Henrietta. I can honestly say that you are the only person on this earth who prepares devilled kidneys precisely to my liking."

Cook was clearly moved by his warm words. "Oh, M'Lordship. I can't say how happy that makes me. Really, I can't." She blushed, curtsied and hurried back to the adjacent room where she was creating our feast.

Kidneys, devilled or otherwise, are not a favourite of mine, and I started with some toast smothered in butter and Seville marmalade.

"Your orange juice, M'Lord," Todd announced rather grandly as he brought our drinks. "And hot chocolate for young Master Christopher." He gave me a wink as he said this.

There were still six months before I would be old enough to join the army or move out of our family home(s), and I wondered whether he'd treat me with such familiarity once I was eighteen. To tell the truth, I didn't like the idea of growing up if it meant I would lose my friends at Cranley Hall. I secretly hoped they would still indulge me until I was at least twenty-one.

"The police have identified the bullet," Grandfather looked up from his paper to inform me. "I have already been on the phone to Chief Inspector Darrington at Scotland Yard this morning and it turns out that, like the cufflink, the bullet that killed Augustus was German. They believe it was fired from a Mauser C78. Which was quite a distinctive gun by all accounts."

"Was it wartime issue?" I asked, hoping this would simplify things.

"Sadly not. They'd been made for over thirty years before the war and were quite common, or so Darrington informs me."

This did little to help clarify the details of the case but made me more curious as to why he seemed so relaxed.

"Jolly good. So shouldn't we be thundering across London by now to right some wrongs?"

"To which wrongs are you referring?"

I wiped a spot of sweet milk from my chin as I considered his question. "Well... all of them. Murder, theft, deceit and whatnot." I forced myself to eat one last crumpet. It would have been rude not to, and I always hated disappointing Cook.

"There's plenty of time for that. We have two pieces of business to conduct today. First, as I am sure you can imagine, we must travel to Edgware. Darrington set a team of officers working overnight to find a house which matched the description that Lady Pandora provided."

"Large, with an impressive garden?" I sought to confirm. "That can't have been easy."

"And no more than a two-mile walk from Edgware station on the Hampstead tube." He sipped his drink before continuing. "As it turns out, there really aren't too many grand houses in the area. The officers found the place in a little under ten minutes, leaving them free to head home to their beds. The records are very old but, as far as the police can tell, Cannons is one of the Earl of Newport's properties. Darrington has given me unofficial permission to see who lives there before the police go themselves this afternoon. We'll set off after breakfast."

"Oh," I said, surprised by just how simple the process had been. "That sounds nice."

As it turned out, nice was just the right word for the day ahead. Grandfather was in such a leisurely mood that he suggested we go to matins at St Martin-in-the-Fields before Todd charted our course to the countryside. The distant winter sun shone down upon the car without warming us, but there was an elegance to the day that no other season can rival.

We wound through the knotted streets of the city where, even on a Sunday, carts, buses and automobiles blocked our path northwards. But then, upon reaching the outskirts of London, it was as though someone had fired a starting pistol and the Rolls Royce was unleashed. She positively growled with excitement as we shot up the A5 to our destination and the promise of answers to the list of questions which was expanding by the minute in my brain. As good a footman, bodyguard, dancer, fly fisher and friend Todd could be, he was never so happy as when behind the wheel of a car, and he smiled the whole way there. As did Delilah.

"We're going to the countryside, girl!" Grandfather told the wonderful beast, whilst ruffling her ears. "You must be sick of the sight of paving slabs and tarmacadam. We're on the way to a big park. You'll be able to run around all morning, and I've heard tell that there's even a lake for you to enjoy a swim."

I personally doubted that Delilah would go anywhere near a chilly lake in February, but it would give her a chance to chase some ducks. Either way, she barked with anticipation for the next five minutes until we arrived.

I don't suppose I had a fixed idea in my mind of how the house would look, but if I did, it was nothing like the reality we discovered.

"Cannons once belonged to The Duke of Chandos," Grandfather explained, as Todd slowed the car and we rolled smoothly onto the property, which did not appear to possess a gatehouse or guard.

"You mean your friend Bobbie?" I asked most foolishly.

"No, Christopher, not my friend Bobbie. The *first* Duke of Chandos who lived in the eighteenth century. He built this place as a monument to his wealth and influence, then proceeded to lose both when the South Sea Bubble burst. It was considered one of the finest houses in England and once counted George Frederick Handel as its resident composer."

We drove past the lake as he explained all this, and I caught my first glimpse of the property through two rows of broad oak trees.

"Grandfather?" I began, wondering if I was about to ask another very silly question. "How do you know all this?"

He looked a little sheepish and cleared his throat. "Well... I might have had a quick peek in the hotel's Encyclopædia Britannica this morning but, I can assure you, I knew most of the details myself."

Before I could laugh at him, we emerged from the avenue of trees to discover the house in all its... well, grandeur wasn't quite the word for it. Cannons was an English baroque manor house with a pedimented façade and several classical statues on the roof. It was also falling to pieces. One of the central columns of the entrance appeared to have been removed, several windows were broken, the brickwork was coming away all over, and it looked as though no one had tended to the once ornate gardens in some decades.

"It must have been quite the spectacle in its day," Grandfather continued with a sigh. "The duke's son sold all the great works of art and even the fixings two centuries ago. It's been a mere shadow of its famed splendour ever since. Records from the middle of the last century suggest it fell into the possession of the Earl of Newport. He possesses a large estate in Wales, and so I can't be sure who we'll find here today."

Delilah had jumped from the window before Todd stopped the car. It was her barking that must have alerted the occupants to our arrival. An elderly gentleman emerged from the front door and stood eyeing us wearily. I suppose the fact we were driving a sparkling new Silver Ghost would have reassured him we were not tradesmen coming to waste his time.

I thought he would shout at us to demand an explanation for our presence there, but he stood quite passively, as we got down from the vehicle, and Delilah ran in circles about the place. She was fit to explode with pent up energy after nearly an hour spent in the car.

"We're terribly sorry to intrude," my grandfather said, walking towards the house with his hand extended. "My name is–"

"Lord Edgington, if I'm not mistaken." This old man studied my old man before continuing. "I'm Lord Newport."

For a moment, I wasn't sure whether he was going to welcome us into his home, but propriety evidently got the better of him and he took my grandfather's hand in his.

"May I ask why you've come here? We have a telephone. You might just as well have rung."

Grandfather looked at me, of all people, as though I might know what to say to the poor man. To my surprise, I did. "We're sorry to disturb you, Lord Newport, but we thought it better that we came in person. I am Lord Edgington's grandson, Christopher Prentiss, and we're here to talk to you about your son." I'm not sure I'd ever spoken so formally in my entire life.

"Harald?"

I wanted to gasp then but managed to control myself. "Yes, indeed. Harald. May we talk to you inside?"

I pointed towards the house, and he hesitated a moment longer before motioning for us to follow him. Todd stayed behind to keep an eye on Delilah, who was quite manic at the promise of all that space she had to explore.

The interior of Cannons was as grand and dilapidated as the exterior had been. Paint was flaking off the wall, the elaborate mosaic floor was missing half its tiles and there were sun-stained rectangles all along the corridor where no doubt masterful paintings would once have hung. The former owners had sold off the most valuable parts of the house piece by piece, and I had to cross my fingers that the same fate would not befall Cranley.

We walked past vast salons, now free of a single stick of furniture, a ballroom with nothing but stone where a grand floor would once have been, and a billiards room with nothing left to play. It was a ghost house, a building struggling for its very last gasps of breath.

"My wife, Lotte, is in the winter garden," Lord Newport said when we'd been traversing the place for some time. "She's not so mobile as she once was, and it's the only wing of the house that is heated."

I had no reason to doubt the man. Walking through that old hall reminded me of the time I played hide and seek in the family tomb at Cranley Hall. I instantly regretted entering the icy spot, and I'd had nightmares about it ever since.

As we reached the far end of the long, rectangular dwelling, the rooms suddenly became more comfortable, and I had to assume that this was where the remaining inhabitants spent their time. There was a rather exquisite dining room, several plush lounges and a library in which I would have happily enjoyed a book beside the impressive marble fireplace. It made me wonder why, if they had the money to furnish this wing of the house in such luxury, and another estate elsewhere, they employed no servants.

"We used to spend more time in our main house in Wales," Lord Newport explained, as though wishing to answer my puzzled expression. "But Lotte worries about our only son and prefers to be close to London."

I must say, I was half out of breath when we got to the conservatory.

189

It was truly the jewel in the crown of the once grand house and looked untouched by the march of time. The window frames were perfectly white, great, healthy palm trees occupied the four corners of the room, and the thickly glazed glass, which made up the ceiling and three of the walls, trapped in the heat of the weak sun.

"Lotte, darling?" Lord Newport cast his voice ahead of us before we entered the room. "There are some visitors who would like to talk to us about Harald."

The old lady was sitting in a wicker wheelchair in the middle of the room. She'd had her eyes closed to enjoy the warm air but opened them now as she turned to welcome us. At first, her faint smile suggested she was pleased to see us but, as she registered the famous detective's presence, her expression changed.

"No," she cried out, her fear giving way to pain. "No, not Harald. Please, not my boy! I already lost him once."

CHAPTER TWENTY-EIGHT

Like figures in a doll's house, the four of us froze where we were. There was no stopping the tears that descended the frightened woman's cheeks. I could tell that my grandfather wished to ease her suffering, but her inference was correct: we came bearing bad news.

Finding no words to comfort her, Grandfather cast his eyes to the Grecian floor.

"I tried to protect him," Augustus or Harald or whatever-his-name-really-was's mother wept. "After the war, we left the family estate and tried to keep him away from people who wished him harm, but he grew tired of hiding here." She had an accent that was most definitely not British.

"Calm down now, my love." Her doting husband rushed forward to soothe her. "Getting upset will do no one any good." Unlike his wife, he could have easily blended in with the ranks of the English aristocracy. Standing at her side with his hand on her shoulder, he looked up at my grandfather to ask the most painful question imaginable. "Is it true? Is that why you've come?"

I rarely felt sorry for my beloved mentor. For a man of seventy-five, he lived his life with such passion and determination that it was difficult to pity him. And yet, on seeing the task he faced, I could have cried.

He gave a silent nod, and Lord Newport collapsed to his knees to embrace his wife. The two of them were united by their love for their son and by the grief that was tearing through them. Grandfather gave them time to make some sense of their emotions and then, taking a seat on a raffia chair, began his tragic explanation.

"I am deeply saddened to have to tell you what I'm about to say. Just one week ago, I was acquainted with your son. I came to think of him as a truly kind person and I know that Christopher would say the same. I don't know if you've seen the newspaper reports but, on Friday night, a man was shot dead in Westminster. I was there on the scene to confirm that the body which the police discovered was that of your son's."

Augustus's father looked up at us then but could not find his voice.

"I'm here to ask you about Harald." Grandfather retained his

191

solemn bearing. "It is my wish to not merely fill in the gaps in a terrible story but to bring the man who killed him to justice. Whatever past he might have had, no one deserves such savagery."

"I told him not to leave us… So many times, I told him." Lady Newport's voice was directed into her husband's shoulder and, at first, I could barely make out what she said. She pulled free from him to take some air and found the strength to continue. "After he came back from the war, we knew it wasn't safe and kept him here with us. We lived together for five whole years, but he wanted a life of his own. After a trip abroad to see my family, he made the decision that he wanted to live in London. He changed his name to hide who he really was, but I told him it wasn't enough. Some people never forgive and most never forget."

It wasn't just her staccato delivery that made it difficult for me to follow her story. I couldn't understand why Augustus would have locked himself away from the world for half a decade.

"He had German blood, is that right?" Grandfather's voice was gentler than I might have expected. There was none of the aggression and grit with which he normally spoke. "I assume you are German, madam?"

"I consider myself British!" she said most indignantly. "I moved country when I was twenty-one and have lived here twice as long as in my motherland."

Augustus's father squeezed her hand and explained more calmly. "My wife and I both have German ancestors. My grandfather was a Prussian Landgrave who married an English duchess. Our surname is Augheim, but I inherited my title through her."

So Augustus Harred's real name was Harald Augheim. It was not the most creative pseudonym.

"I wasn't trying to upset you." Lord Edgington bowed his head respectfully as he spoke. He clearly needed them to trust him if he was going to learn Harald's story. "I have known many fine Germans. I don't believe a whole nation of people became monsters overnight when our nations went to war. If I took exception to you, I'd have to stop talking to half my friends as well. So many British aristocrats can trace their families abroad."

He paused to let them consider this before asking his next question.

"I understand that Harald fought in the Great War. Is that correct?"

Lord Newport looked at his wife and stroked her cheek with great tenderness. They were close opposites. He was thin-faced and birdlike, while she had the figure and comportment of Queen Victoria in her old age.

"Whatever else you've heard about him wasn't true," she promised. "He fought for Great Britain – the country of his birth. He never told us the details of what happened in Germany, but it doesn't change the fact he was a hero."

Grandfather's quick eyes scanned her face for a moment as he extracted the fact that she wouldn't reveal. "Are you saying he was captured? That must have been torturous for you both, and Harald, of course. I know men who've spent time in prisoner of war camps, and it does not sound pleasant."

"He wasn't kept in a camp," the father whispered. "And perhaps that's what killed him."

Unnerved by her husband's quiet confession, Lady Newport seized the conversation. "He was no traitor. I don't care what people say. He enrolled in the British army because the Kaiser was a warmonger. Harald may have been caught, and he may have done some petty jobs for the Germans, but he gave away no secrets. He was nothing like Septimus Marchant."

Lord Septimus Marchant. I knew that name. P.C. Simpkin had told me about him in the Black Museum. He'd sent state secrets abroad during the war and was executed for his crimes. His treachery caused the deaths of hundreds of men.

Some of his wife's anger spread to Lord Newport. "Septimus was a monster, whereas our son merely used the fact he could speak two languages to avoid living in squalor in a camp. He had cousins in Germany; he didn't see the men who had captured him as inherently evil. So, yes, he translated some documents and helped send messages to the British to broker peace as the war was coming to an end. But every last thing he did served to avoid bloodshed, not cause it."

Hoping to make sense of their story, I watched my grandfather's reaction, but he was truly implacable. Either Augustus was a traitor… or he wasn't. That was as much as I could say for certain.

"Did his captors treat him well? Is that what you meant when you said that avoiding the camps might have brought about his death?"

Again they looked at one another, again they struggled for an answer and, again, it was Lady Newport who found the courage to reply. "You're twisting the facts just as the authorities did when he returned. Harald served his country. It wasn't his fault he was wounded in battle and captured. The fact he was kept with German officers and not subjected to harsh conditions meant that he avoided Typhus and influenza and who knows what else."

I felt their pain then. This was not what they should have been doing on the day they learnt of their son's death. Whoever Harald really was, they should have had the time to grieve instead of being forced to defend his memory.

I could take it no more and had to say my piece. "I knew your son as Augustus Harred, and he was awfully nice to me." I'd been floating about in the doorway but took a few steps forward to where a colourful picture of two dancing bodies was hanging on the wall. "I thought he was a wonderful painter. This is one of his, isn't it?"

His father nodded, and I took my time examining the cheery scene. The two figures were depicted in contrasting shades of red, which blended into one another so that it was hard to know where one finished and the other began. I had the unshakable feeling that I was looking at a portrait of his parents in happier times.

"It's lovely," I said, quite sincerely, and I was reminded of the feeling I'd had when I'd first entered his studio at the Gargoyle. "I truly think he was one of the most talented men I've ever had the fortune of meeting. You should see the portrait he painted of his fiancée."

Their heads flicked in my direction, like two pigeons at the sound of falling birdseed.

"Harald was engaged?" It was hard to know what Lady Newport was thinking at that moment. A mix of apprehension and surprise crossed her face, as though she couldn't bring herself to believe what I was saying.

Grandfather watched me, uncertain whether he should let me say another word but unable to interrupt.

"That's right, Lady Pandora Elles. Perhaps you've heard of her?" I looked at the painting one last time before turning to cast my gaze around that pretty conservatory. "She didn't know about any of this,

194

of course. Augustus told her he was coming to see an elderly aunt each week on his Sunday trips. She didn't know he was the Earl of Newport's heir, or that he'd been captured by the Germans. All she knew... all she still knows, is that she loved your son. She's just as heartbroken as you both must be, and do you know what I think?"

It was a rhetorical question, but I waited a little too long to answer it, and Lord Newport produced a careful, "No."

"I think that she'll still love him regardless of the stories she hears. I'm certain that nothing you've told us today could change that. If you say that Harald wasn't a traitor, she'll believe you. And so do I."

I thought this was just the perfect moment to end our interview and head back to the car. I thought it would shine a ray of hope on that dark day, but my grandfather had to ruin everything.

"Septimus," he said, quietly at first, and then once again a little louder. "Septimus! You called Lord Marchant by his first name because you knew him, didn't you?"

CHAPTER TWENTY-NINE

I should probably describe the tension in the room at that moment and the expressions of horror on their faces, but I'd really rather not if it's all the same to you. I felt dreadful for these people – absolutely dreadful. Their only son had been murdered, and I wasn't in the mood to browbeat them into telling us what we needed to know.

My grandfather evidently held a contrasting opinion on the matter. "Harald and Septimus would have been around the same age. So, what was it? Did they go to school together? Eton, was that it?" His diplomatic manner had gone off somewhere on holiday, and he was once more focused on the case. "That must be it. How could I not have realised before?"

"It changes nothing," Lady Newport said, and her husband rose to standing. I thought for a moment that he would throw a punch at the heartless detective, but he resisted, and my grandfather would not be cowed.

"For your own sakes, you must tell me what you know." He had no time for tact and rattled off his demands like a man reciting a shopping list. "Tell me what happened, and I'll make sure that the man who killed your son receives the punishment he deserves. You said that someone wished to harm your son. How did they find out he'd been captured?"

He waited for their response and, as they showed no sign of granting his wish, he started to pace. "I'm sorry. I'm sorry, I'm getting ahead of myself. But this is very important. When we found Harald's body, the killer had placed a cufflink with the initials S.M. in his hand. I explored various other theories, but the one that makes the most sense is that it belonged to Septimus Marchant."

He finished his speech and stood perfectly still with his palms open to convince them of his good intentions. There was a stalemate at play. Harald's parents didn't know whether to trust us, and we had tried everything we could to persuade them. When the silence there was finally broken, it was not by the fragile voice of Lord Newport, as I might have expected, but another fiery proclamation from his wife.

"They were at the same school, but they barely knew one another." I thought this was all she would tell us but, after a few moments of silence, she spoke again. "It was at Oxford that they became friends. Septimus visited us at home in Wales one summer, and we adored him. He was full of grand ideas and grander plans. He claimed he would become prime minister one day, and I must admit that I believed him."

She shook her head and peered through the windows at the pale sky. "We never saw him after the fighting began, but Harald told us that his friend had changed in that first year. Septimus thought that the Kaiser was certain to win and did all he could to position himself for a change of ruler. He used his family's contacts in politics, the press, the army and industry to get a position close to the heart of the government. He believed he could end the war and save millions by sacrificing thousands."

It was Lord Newport who finished the story. He pulled himself up to his full height and stepped towards my grandfather, his words finally coated with the anger that was running through him. "As I've already told you, Septimus Marchant was a monster. He deserved the sentence he received before a firing squad on Tower Hill. But my son was nothing like him. When the authorities interviewed Harald after the war, they were looking for Septimus's accomplices. It was clear that he'd convinced several other figures of his way of thinking. But I swear on my life, Harald was not one of them."

Silence filled the room. It was an oppressive, clawing force that seemed to push in at me from all sides and tighten my throat, so that my words left my mouth in a pitiful croak. "Perhaps whoever killed him thought otherwise."

I could see from his restless gaze that my grandfather's mind was now ablaze with possibilities. I really couldn't see how any of it fitted together with Baron Pritt's murder, or even how it would reveal the killer, but he clearly believed he had found the solution.

"And all this because your son chose an alias that was foolishly close to his real name." He shook his head in a gesture of sorrow and bemusement.

"I told him not to do it, but he thought it was all such fun." The earl's voice wavered in plainly spelt despair. "He said that if he couldn't be himself, he'd change as little as possible." His words came out in an extended screech. "I told him to change his name to Charles or John or Robert, but he wouldn't listen. He was the most stubborn, impetuous boy I've ever met and... and I don't know how we'll cope without him."

Lady Newport wheeled her chair closer and reached up to clasp her husband's hand in her own. "He was like that from the moment he was born, and we could never change him." Her husband looked down at her and, true to what I'd seen of their relationship, she had the last word. "I'm not sure we ever really wanted to in the first place."

It was this that finally brought her husband to his knees. Unable to manoeuvre her chair any closer, Lady Newport placed her hand on his shoulder and looked up at her uninvited guests.

"Thank you for coming here today." With a sad smile, she looked at the painting over my shoulder. "I mean that genuinely. I'm glad it was you and not a stranger in a uniform. But my husband and I now must be alone. I'm sure you'll find your way out."

My heart ached for her. I hated to leave without another word and, had I known them even a fraction better than I did, I might have put my hand on hers to express my condolences. In unison and without a sound, Grandfather and I turned to leave. We walked out of the conservatory and along the interminable corridor to the neglected garden outside, where the sun still shone.

Delilah had just as much spring and energy as when we'd arrived, and my grandfather whistled for her to come. He nodded to Todd, who knew his master well and hurried back to the car to get us on our way. Five seconds later, Delilah jumped through my door, looking as though she couldn't wait to tell us about the adventure she'd enjoyed. Grandfather retained his stony silence until we drove off the estate, and I found the courage to say something idiotic.

"It's fascinating, of course, and very much changes our understanding of why Augustus was murdered, but I don't see that it helps us say for certain who killed him."

In response, Grandfather looked a little surprised. "Don't be naïve, boy. We didn't come here to identify the killer; I worked that out yesterday. We came here to discover why anyone had to die in the first place."

"You mean you've known all this time, and you didn't tell me?" I was a little hurt. "What if he kills again?"

A rather smug grin formed on his lips which his impassive

moustaches could do nothing to hide. "I can promise that will not be the case."

"So will you at least tell me his name, and why he's been going around murdering people?"

Grandfather surprised me then. Instead of scoffing at the suggestion, and telling me I should do the work myself, he leaned across the back seat of the automobile to place a hand on my shoulder.

He looked me squarely in the eyes and said, "Yes, I will."

I was overjoyed to hear this. For once I wouldn't have to look an idiot in front of all our suspects as my grandfather asked me questions which I couldn't possibly answer. I got comfortable in my seat, hoping to settle down for a thrilling story of spies, international espionage and wartime valour, but that's not quite what happened.

"Todd, find an open newsagent," he turned to our driver to command. "If we're lucky, there'll be one near the station. I need some paper and writing equipment."

I was somewhat baffled by his behaviour, though this was nothing new. "What do you need paper and pencils for? You're not going to set me a test, are you?"

"No, of course I'm not." He finally scoffed at one of my ideas – it had been a while. "As a matter of fact, I'm not sure that I hold with examinations in the first place. Why should we consider a child's ability to memorise lists of facts and quotes to be a good indicator of his abilities? Unless you're planning on a life of academic–"

I had to interrupt him then. I have no doubt he could have elaborated on such a topic for some hours. "The murders, Grandfather! Can we please stay focused on the investigation?"

"Oh, very well." He tutted and his eyes disappeared up into their sockets for a moment. "I need the stationery to write an account of the events of the last nine days."

This was not the answer I desired. "But why don't you just tell me what's been happening?" My normally patient manner had deserted me.

"Because you would forget half of the details, and then where would we be?"

As Todd stopped the car in front of the newly built Edgware underground station, I considered where we *would* be if I forgot the details of the case. I wasn't sure that I knew the answer.

"Wait a moment," I said before he could escape from the car. "Why do you need me to remember anything?"

He closed the door behind him and looked in through the window. "That's the best part of it, Christopher. You'll see."

CHAPTER THIRTY

I should have known that Lord Edgington was incapable of doing anything so mundane as revealing the name of a killer in the back of a car travelling south on a quiet A-road. He had never been able to resist the lure of the theatrical.

So, instead of having my every assumption of the case realigned by his exhilarating explanation, I read my book. As he composed his opus in a smart leather notebook with sparkling gilt edges, I enjoyed a dose of Dickens. He wrote at great speed, filling each page almost as quickly as I could read a chapter in my mystery. Whenever the point snapped on his pencil, he would take a new one and continue with his writing, barely breaking his concentration or taking a moment to breathe. It looked quite exhausting.

By the time we arrived back at the Ritz, he'd finished his work and presented the book to me with a courtly wave of the hand.

"I think you'll find everything you need to know is contained within. Take Delilah inside, order whatever you wish from the restaurant, and I will meet you at ten o'clock tonight in front of Guildhall."

He ushered me out of the car, and Delilah was already on the pavement waiting. As a general rule, I found that, when my grandfather told me not to worry, I should be mortally afraid and, if possible, lock myself away somewhere safe.

"Wait. Where are you going?"

He smiled at me then and I felt a wave of grandfatherly affection, which he sometimes did a good job of hiding. "I have four important calls to make. First, I will go to the Gargoyle Club and the offices of The Chronicle. Then, if I have time, I will call in at Stafford House and, finally, but most importantly, I must speak to Chief Inspector Darrington at Scotland Yard. I'm not expecting it to be an easy conversation, but we'll need him on our side if my plan is to work. Have a lovely afternoon!"

Before I could ask anything more, that conniving conspirator Todd had driven off. I have no doubt that, if my grandfather provided any sort of instruction to new members of staff at Cranley Hall, it would contain just as much advice on how to make their master look mysterious as tips on running a large country house.

The Silver Ghost disappeared along Piccadilly, and I stood gazing after it quite hopelessly. I was unsure what to think of anything that had occurred that week, year, or at any point in my short existence, for that matter. Delilah barked to knock me from my reverie, and we returned to our suite. As I had rather a lot of reading to do, and my grandfather's handwriting was more difficult to interpret than most Egyptian hieroglyphs, I decided to order lunch up to the room. I say *lunch* but we'd already missed elevenses, I hadn't had a scrap of brunch and it was getting on for afternoon tea. I probably complain too often about not eating enough, but I honestly believe that without strict and regular mealtimes, the British Empire would crumble.

I sat on my gigantic bed – which was fit for two kings, at the very least – and devoured a roast dinner while I worked my way through grandfather's story. I'd ordered Delilah a pork chop, so that she didn't whine and try to steal scraps from my plate. This also meant that I was free to concentrate on Grandfather's fascinating tale – in which I was, at the very least, a supporting character.

Reading a good book is always a pleasure and the polymathic Lord Edgington certainly had a way with a pencil. It was not the dryly structured case file that I'd been expecting but a novella, complete with subplots, unexpected developments and a serpentine narrative that kept me guessing as to what would happen with each turn of the page.

I don't mind telling you that my jaw fell wide open a number of times. Though, I must say, I felt a little cheated by the ending. Grandfather often made it sound like my ideas were pure poppycock, when, more often than not, there was a modicum of sense in my thinking. Admittedly, I had not picked the right killer, or determined why the two men had died, but I had at least considered our culprit as a possible suspect, which is surely an impressive feat in itself.

I was coming to the end of the slim volume, feeling quite as emotional as if I had discovered some previously unknown work by Charles Dickens, when there was a knock at the door to my room. Delilah jumped up from the puffy ottoman she'd been sleeping on to see who was there, and I was only a few steps behind her.

"Master Christopher Prentiss?" a young courier from the hotel enquired.

"That's right."

He needed no further invitation and, glancing over his shoulders, called, "This is the room, boys."

I stood out of his way as he bustled inside with a large black box in his hand that might well have come from Lock & Co, the hatters on St James's Street. He was followed by two tradesmen in smart brown overalls, who were carrying what appeared to be garment bags in either hand. One final lad, my age or thereabouts, held two more boxes. Going by their cylindrical shape, they almost definitely contained hats... or cakes. I've never looked particularly handsome in a hat and was crossing my fingers for some variety of rich French gateau.

"Just leave them on the sofa, gentlemen," I said, as though I was perfectly used to issuing orders to staff. Delilah, meanwhile, gave the men a good sniff.

As soon as they had filed out again, with each of them offering a workmanlike nod as they passed, I rushed over to inspect the delivery. I opened the square box first, as it was the hardest to imagine what it might hold. Upon popping the lid free, I was faced with a long-nosed, golden mask which was encrusted with tiny gems. Delilah looked just as puzzled as I was.

I seized one of the bags next to discover an exquisite black velvet cape. I donned the two props and stood before the mirror in my bedroom, positively terrified of my own reflection. The elongated nose I now bore had a grotesque, beak-like quality that made me look quite monstrous. The cape, however, was much more to my taste and I would have happily worn it to an opera, or perhaps around the house on a cold day.

My inquisitiveness could be contained no longer, and I opened the other packages to find two smart suits, one black and the other grey, which could have been modelled on my grandfather's favourite apparel. Somewhat inevitably, the round boxes contained not cakes but two matching top hats. This explained why my grandfather had ordered his tailor to measure me the day before, though I was unable to guess why he wanted me to dress up in such a fashion. Hoping for more answers, I ran back to the notebook to finish reading.

The final paragraph was set apart from the main bulk of his explanation.

I'm sure you'll work it all out as soon as you see what I've bought you. (Oh ye of too much faith, dear Grandfather!) *As we heard Cyril*

205

mention yesterday, there is a masked ball this evening to celebrate 'Carnival', much as they do on the continent. Dress for the occasion, and I will see you at the aforementioned location at ten tonight. With your remaining time, I would recommend studying the notes I have provided herein. I plan to invite a number of guests, and they will all be eager to discover our killer's identity. I've placed my trust in you, dear boy, and I know you will not founder.

Slumping back onto the bed, I thought about sleeping off the shock. I wasn't the type of cove to stand in front of a crowd reciting the evidence we'd accumulated or the intricate mental exertions that led us to finding the culprit. I was much more of a spectator than a performer. More the sort who might cheer from a balcony with a bag of boiled sweets than climb upon a stage to exhibit my talents. No matter how many times my mentor might give me opportunities to prove otherwise, I was simply not born to be the brave detective at the centre of an investigation.

I was terrified of making a jabbering fool of myself in front of who knows how many onlookers. Sadly, Grandfather wasn't there for me to argue my case and a realisation set in.

"There's only one thing for it, Delilah," I told the soppy puppy, who was hiding from me beneath a Queen-Anne-style chair. I took my mask off so that she would no longer be scared. "I have some studying to do."

Homework on a Sunday isn't encouraged, even at my fun-hating school, but Grandfather was right. I had no desire to disappoint and didn't want to turn up unprepared for the great Lord Edgington's big event. I gobbled down the last of my lunch and read his composition through twice more before it was time to leave. When I put on my all-black costume and stood in front of the mirror, a rush of confidence washed over me. All of a sudden, I felt great certainty that I might possibly, just about, be up to the challenge.

Delilah whimpered rather tragically when I went to leave without her, and so I told her the truth. "Honestly, if you don't like the look of me in this mask, you certainly won't want to come with me tonight."

I'd never realised before that dogs can shrug. I didn't think they had the shoulders for it, but that's exactly what happened. She stood for a moment, ducked her head with a nonchalant shudder and walked back to her spot at the end of my bed. It left me quite speechless.

I took a taxi to Guildhall, but not before I'd surprised an old lady in the lift and had to apologise for scaring her half to death. I arrived at the designated meeting place: the City of London's ancient town hall, with its glorious, spired façade looking like it had been cut off from some gothic cathedral. The large square in front of the main building was deserted except for a few children kicking about a tin can, but they disappeared when I swept in with my cloak flowing behind me like Dracula.

I stood in the middle of the yard, with plenty of time to consider why my grandfather had chosen that particular spot. It was another mystery that would soon be solved. The paved square was illuminated by dim yellow streetlights attached to the great oblong church of St Lawrence Jewry on one side and the gallery on the other. My nerves grew more strained the longer I waited and, when I saw the first masked spectator arrive, I thought I might explode.

Slowly, more figures appeared from the various lanes that flowed into the square, like rivers into the sea. A crowd soon formed around me in a circle. I tried to recognise them from their silhouettes and the style of their clothes. I was fairly certain that a chap in a gold cape and metallic green mask – looking more like a phantom than a man – had to be Fabian Warwick, and the golden curls of the woman beside him could only belong to my dear Lady Pandora. There must have been thirty people in total, and every last one of them was silenced by the pageantry that my grandfather had set in motion.

I wondered whether all of our suspects were present and I should begin but assumed that the ever-resourceful Lord Edgington would have devised some sign to show me when he was ready. A couple standing in front of the Guildhall made me think of Baroness Pritt and her lover, but it was impossible to identify anyone with absolute certainty.

And then it happened. I doubt that many in the crowd would have seen it, but I did. In the five exits from the square, men in black uniforms appeared but came no closer. It wasn't just for the history of that famous spot or the dramatic shadows that danced across the yard that my grandfather had sent me there. It was the ideal place for the police to trap our killer. There would be no escape, and this gave me the confidence I needed to begin my speech.

CHAPTER THIRTY-ONE

"We are gathered here today…" No, that wasn't right. I cleared my throat and tried again. "Some of you may not know why you were brought here. You may know nothing of the events that have unfolded over the last two weekends or the wickedness that has taken place, but you soon will."

For a moment, I wasn't sure that I knew much better than them, and I had a sudden urge to pull grandfather's notebook from my suit pocket and simply read it out loud. Instead, I held my nerve, took a deep breath, and continued.

"Two men are dead. Innocent or otherwise, they died too young. The first on a treasure hunt organised by one of the leading lights of the *Bright Young People*, as our sensationalist newspapers have christened you all." At this, Fabian took a theatrical bow to confirm his identity, but I wouldn't be distracted. "Baron Terence Pritt was not a popular man, but he was a rich man. A man who had no qualms about taking advantage of the opportunities that came his way."

I had to shout to be heard, so it was quite a relief when the circle contracted, and I could relax my voice. "He apparently died of natural causes. The pathologist diagnosed a heart attack, though there was a wound on his head and his face had turned a shade of blue that might normally be associated with strangulation. This was the first piece of evidence which led us to believe that his death was suspicious. You see, Pritt was a lean, lithe man in his prime. He had no great problems with his health, but he did have plenty of enemies who might have wanted him dead. His immense wealth was built on the back of an idea stolen from a man who could not claim the fortune he deserved, a man named Stefan Müller who went away to war and was never seen again."

I turned slowly on the spot as I told my tale, trying ever so hard to maintain the deep, mysterious notes in my voice. "When we discovered the name of the man who Pritt had betrayed, it made me wonder whether he had survived the war or perhaps a loved one had taken revenge on his behalf. But matters were complicated when a second weekend of games and excitement arrived, and a second victim died. Augustus Harred was a fine painter, a loving fiancé and in no way the man he claimed to be. Born into a rich Anglo-German family, he went away to fight for Britain and came back a pariah. Augustus was an outcast who spent five years hiding from figures who wished him harm after he was captured in Germany early in the war. But Augustus, or Harald Augheim as he was christened, wanted to live. He met a beautiful woman on a French train and decided to change his name to be able to engage with the world once more."

I could feel the atmosphere change as I moved from one piece of evidence to the next. Though I could make out little of my audience's faces behind their ornate Carnival masks, and jester hoods, I could see their eyes. I knew that they were trying to solve this complex mystery, just as my grandfather had before them.

"Someone discovered the truth about my friend Augustus. Someone worked out who he really was and chose to murder him in a shadowy spot, just a few hundred yards from Parliament, knowing that he could melt into the background in moments. In the dead man's hand was a single cufflink with a German hallmark and the letters S.M. etched on the back. S.M. for Stefan Müller? Or S.M. for Septimus Marchant?"

There was an intake of breath from the crowd at the mention of that infamous name. "Lord Marchant shared military secrets with our enemy during the Great War and was executed for treason, a mile from this very spot. He was at university with Harald Augheim, and it seems quite likely that the pair hatched a scheme together to infiltrate the two sides of the conflict and pass information between one another."

Pandora let out a cry at this moment, which admittedly made me feel like a rotter, but at least it reminded me to hurry up with the story. "So two men died, neither was truly innocent, but who among us can make such a claim? Should we ignore murder just because we may not have approved of the lives the victims led?"

I was the only performer in a one-man show, and so I answered my own question. "No, of course we shouldn't. But what could tie Baron Pritt and Harald Augheim together? Why did these two men meet their fate in such a sad and public fashion? Over the course of this weekend, I've thought of little else. I wondered what savagery could excuse such ruthless acts but, so often, the truth is much smaller and more mundane than our imaginations allow."

I paused to look at Pandora. I wanted to tell her that everything would be all right. I wanted to reassure her and soothe her pain, but it was hard with just a look and so I kept talking.

"My grandfather, the unsurpassable Lord Edgington, former superintendent of the Metropolitan Police, divined countless motives. He considered whether the men could have been murdered for as simple a reason as passion or jealousy. Pritt's wife was in love with a younger man, and yet the estranged couple seemed resolved to the decline of their marriage, and they had little to do with one another. Harald Augheim was engaged to one of the most eligible young women in Britain, but Lady Pandora Elles is too intelligent to surround herself with jealous suitors, and we found no evidence of any such person.

"The more we learnt of these two men, the harder it became to tie them together. They had friends in common, but this is London, and they were well-known figures from the upper echelons of society; such links are far from rare. They both had an S.M. in their lives, but Stefan Müller and Septimus Marchant are dead and neither left vengeful families behind to do their bidding. There were so many winding alleys to explore in their pasts, but what if that was what the killer wanted? What if there was no dark history or hidden connection that we needed to uncover? What if this whole case was a tangled trail that had been designed to lead us away from the truth?"

I raised my voice once again as I prepared to deliver the first great surprise of the evening. "There was nothing to link the two murders because Baron Terence Pritt truly did die of natural causes. The wound on his head occurred when he hit the dashboard of the car he was driving. His face had turned blue because a cardiac infarction had stopped the blood from reaching the key organs around his body. There was no killer there that night, only happy treasure hunters, the event's organisers, and the odd member of the press." I paused, very much for effect. "And yet, his death would spark the idea of what was to come."

I wasn't used to commanding such unwavering attention. It must have been the dramatic costume I wore. Perhaps I should dress like that for my Latin oral exam at school. Either way, it felt rather wonderful, and I moved on to the final stage of my tale, probably enjoying the dramatic intonation of my voice a little too much. I was no Claude Rains, after all.

"If we exclude Pritt's death for the moment, what remains? We've already ruled out the possibility that Harald was murdered by a love rival. We found no evidence of debts or debtors and, as one who met him, I can attest that the man I knew as Augustus was a gentle, thoughtful soul of whom I quickly became fond.

"The cufflink then? That will surely explain this discrepancy. Whoever murdered him must have known who he really was. But how? His parents remained in hiding and Harald retained no ties to the life he had led. He came to London as little more than a bohemian, wishing to make a living from his talent as an artist. Whoever discovered his secret would have needed to know how to research a man's past. A lawyer or police officer, for example, would be well equipped in that department. A politician may, from time to time, have to engage in such activity but, more than anyone else, it is journalists who are most skilled at digging the truth out of old files and documents. If anyone could uncover the fact that Augustus Harred was Harald Augheim, a journalist could."

A murmur travelled about the ring of onlookers, picking up pace and volume as it went. "When reported in the London papers, Pritt's unexpected death caused a renewed rush of public interest in the lives of the Bright Young People. Copies flew off the newsstands all week as journalists desperately tried to find some new story to report. Lord Edgington himself has been followed by an opportunistic reporter. When that flash of interest died away, something new had to be conceived, but how could a newspaper story be extended beyond its natural life?"

A short stroll around the group had not only given me the chance to stretch my legs, I had taken the time to examine every woman there and now darted forward to pull a white plaster mask from its owner's face. The mask's elaborate red and yellow feathers did nothing to hide Miss Craddock's brown ringlets, and she stood before me in apparent shock.

"Peggy Craddock was there at every treasure hunt. She was the first journalist to arrive when Baron Pritt crashed his car, and it was the popularity of her articles that kindled The Chronicle's sales. The people of this city were desperate to know if some conspiracy had brought about the wealthy industrialist's death and, when no answer could be provided, Miss Craddock decided to create a conspiracy of her own. She knew the names of the characters who commonly took part in the treasure hunts, and a little research led her to the discovery that there was no record of an Augustus Harred. She had found a ghost, a ghost who no one would miss should he suddenly disappear."

A gasp went up from Pandora and she stepped towards her new enemy, but Fabian was too quick and held onto her as tightly as his skinny limbs would allow.

I had reached the final lines of the final act of an inordinately complicated play and would not be distracted from my task. "But that wasn't all. If Harred didn't exist, there must have been a reason for his subterfuge. With a word to her contacts in government and a dig through the archives, I wonder how difficult it would have been to discover the rumours of a British soldier who returned from Germany under a cloud of suspicion. A soldier who had been linked to the crimes of the traitor Septimus Marchant."

I was mere inches away from our culprit and released my next questions in a rather loud whisper. "Is that why you did it? Did you feel justified in murdering a man who you believe betrayed our country?" I watched her for five whole seconds. At first, she showed no sorrow or guilt, no feeling whatsoever, in fact. But just as I was about to turn back to the crowd, I saw the slightest quiver of her lips. "Peggy Craddock's star was on the rise. We heard from her boss last night that, despite her lies to the contrary, she would be rewarded for her good work. But she wanted more."

In a slow, sad movement, a man nearby removed his mask to examine the killer more closely. Leopold Twelvetrees looked as gaunt and unhealthy as when we'd first met, but his expression was one of true sorrow. There was no time to think about him, though. There was more evidence to reveal and secrets to tell, and I turned back to fire my accusations at the deceitful Peggy Craddock.

"You obtained and planted a cufflink, not for any moral reason, but simply to add more intrigue to the story you would print. You went to the Gargoyle Club on the day of the treasure hunt and ensured that you could direct your victim to a place where no other competitors would see you. Disguised as the White Rabbit, you lured your victim to his death before shedding your garb and reappearing as Peggy Craddock of The Chronicle. No one suspected you because you'd always been there, lurking in the background, searching for a story." I paused one last time and held her with my gaze. "You killed a man because–"

I had the perfect line planned and everything was going just as I had hoped when two men in the circle jumped forward. The taller of the two shouted, "Now!" to interrupt me mid-flow. I heard the thudding feet of countless officers come surging into the square and I was really rather disappointed that I didn't get to conclude my speech when the men shot past Peggy Craddock to seize Leopold Twelvetrees.

CHAPTER THIRTY-TWO

"That was exceptional work, Christopher," my conniving grandfather announced, as his companion fixed the press magnate in handcuffs. "And you, too, Miss Craddock. You both played your parts to a T."

"Thank you, M'Lord." Peggy was all smiles. "But don't forget the exclusive interview you promised me." She had a wicked glint in her eye, and I was knocked back by the speed that it had all happened.

"Grandfather, you could have waited another five seconds," I chastised him. "I was about to deliver my big line."

He did not look too sorry about it. "Go on then. Why don't you say it now? I'm sure it will still have the same impact."

I considered his suggestion, but it was too late. "Hardly! Everyone knows she isn't the killer."

I turned to Twelvetrees, who was even more flabbergasted than I was. He looked rather like a tuna that had been hauled out of the water and was attempting to adapt to life on land. I didn't fancy his chances.

The chap who had clapped him in irons removed his mask to reveal good old P.C. Simpkin there at his boss's side. I spotted a few other key figures as well. Baroness Pritt was cuddling the life out of poor Cyril. Marjorie, the assistant, was watching keenly, and the rest of the crowd was made up of Gargoyle Club regulars. With the other officers securing the scene, Darrington marched over to us. He'd clearly been informed of the details of the case before despatching his men to assist with the elaborate operation.

"You were right about this young man, Lord Edgington," he said, as he shot his hand out for me to shake. "That was a top-notch performance. We couldn't be certain whether our suspect here would have a gun about his person, and you created the perfect diversion for us to capture him."

I must have blushed at all the attention, before realising that I could have been shot and no longer feeling quite so brave.

"Wait a moment," Fabian strode forward to exclaim. "I can't say I fully understood the intricacies of the narrative. Was it really Twelvetrees who killed Augustus?"

Grandfather winked at me as he replied. "Yes, but perhaps Christopher here should explain. He's so much better at these things than I am."

Not only was I quite out of breath from the excitement and all my chattering, I was also not quite certain I had memorised the rest of the details of Lord Edgington's account.

"Oh, no," I humbly replied. "I think you should have the opportunity to prove yourself, too."

His moustaches scrunched together, and he straightened his posture as though preparing to address a superior officer. A few of the onlookers had strolled off, headed to that evening's ball at The Cavendish, but most stayed to hear the end of the twisted saga. As the real detective began his tale, our killer stared off into space and would barely respond to the testimony of his guilt.

"It is true; Leopold Twelvetrees is a murderer. His distance from the victim was such that he must have believed he had committed the perfect crime, but there were a number of factors which gave him away.

"When I first read of Pritt's death, I did not consider it particularly remarkable. In fact, if the truth be told, I only set out to investigate the case in order to have a break from my long winter, shut away at home. On inspecting the body at the mortuary, we discovered certain irregularities which left open the possibility that the largely unmissed baron had been murdered."

He stopped to check that everyone was following the story. "We first crossed paths with Leopold Twelvetrees on the day after Baron Pritt had died. He claimed to be participating in the treasure hunt as a ploy to gain new readers, but this did not sound like the sort of endeavour that the wealthy proprietor of a newspaper might undertake. Furthermore, he had not even coordinated this attempt with his own reporter at the scene. He was also sweating profusely, at night, at the beginning of February. To me at least, this suggested either illness or, as I later discovered, that this man was a heavy drinker and was suffering from the effects of alcohol withdrawal."

"That's one thing I don't understand, Grandfather." For once, I felt entitled to ask a question in his summing up of a case. "Why did he go to the trouble of taking part in the treasure hunt? What did it gain him?"

"A very good question, Grandson." He was in a particularly effusive mood. "When we met Twelvetrees, he made it seem as though he was a regular at such events but, like us, he was there that night because he'd read an article in his own newspaper. It was not the death of Baron Pritt which caught his attention, but an otherwise inconspicuous name. The words Augustus Harred jumped out of the page at him, and he was determined to discover whether his suspicions were true.

"The hunt gave him the chance to observe the man he assumed to be Harald Augheim at close quarters. The next day, he would sign up to the club where Augustus had his studio and even commissioned a painting from him in order to spend time with the man and ensure he had picked the right target. Pritt's death was the perfect cover. Despite his claims that the baron had appeared nervous just before he died, by examining a list of participants, we discovered that Twelvetrees hadn't in fact been present that night and only joined the club the following day."

I was rather bowled over when he said this. Simpkin had shown me the very same list, and I'd failed to spot the significant omission. I didn't feel I needed to contribute this information, though, and my grandfather kept talking.

"He had nothing to do with the event and, from what the police have unearthed, barely knew the industrialist in the first place. And yet, the fact that I was investigating what had happened to Pritt told Twelvetrees that any further loss of life would inevitably be tied to the first death."

I watched the harsh light of the electric bulb behind me ripple across my grandfather's expressive face as he led us from one piece of evidence to the next. "Confident that he had located the traitor Harald Augheim, Twelvetrees knew that the police would not be able to link him to the baron, and so he had a free hand to exact his revenge. It was easy enough to pop to the Gargoyle Club and rearrange the clues from the game of Hares and Hounds. As a member, he could come and go as he pleased. With that one act, he had ensured that Harald would be alone in Westminster at the beginning of the challenge, when any potential witnesses would be busy elsewhere."

He came to a sudden halt and turned from the bulk of the crowd to address the prisoner. "You walked straight up to him as though you'd won the game, isn't that right? He thought you were coming to gloat when, in actual fact, you pushed the gun to his chest to muffle the sound and fired at point-blank range. With the deed done, you started off in pursuit of your own target in the game."

Silence gripped that sad scene, and I could never have predicted what would happen next. Twelvetrees laughed. His great, trembling roar cut through the still city night to echo about that elegant plaza, before the voice of the devil reverberated in my ears. "Oh, I shot him. I killed that double-dealing traitor, and it may be my greatest achievement. I'll make sure they inscribe it on my tombstone."

"Well, I have some good news for you, then." Grandfather spat out the dry rejoinder. "You won't have long to wait."

There was a pause as the odious creature in handcuffs glared at his accuser, and Grandfather gloried in his role. With an insouciant smile, Lord Edgington moved on to the last part of the mystery.

"This villain placed an expensive German cufflink into his victim's hand. When I saw the hallmark, I couldn't be sure where it was from, but I should have known the initials S.M. immediately. Septimus Marchant was a popular young chap before the war, and I'd come across him a number of times. But it was what he did to this country that has gone down in infamy. When I realised it could be his cufflink, it was another avenue which, with the help of my former colleagues in the Metropolitan Police, I was obliged to explore."

Chief Inspector Darrington looked proud to be included in his old colleague's appraisal and listened intently to every word my grandfather said. I, meanwhile, took this moment to watch Pandora. She was surely the person who would suffer most in the aftermath of Twelvetrees's crime but was not crying out in agony as I might have expected. She was calm, and I realised that, just like the police, she had been forewarned.

My favourite schemer continued his tale. "Of course, we might have failed to identify the culprit if it hadn't been for the mistakes he made. They say all killers slip up over time, and Twelvetrees went a step further. When one is hellbent on revenge, you can be sure that passion will override common sense. He realised that leaving the cufflink at the scene of the crime had been a foolish idea, but it was his fear of discovery that ultimately gave him away.

"On the same night that I noticed an unfinished painting of Leopold

Twelvetrees in Augustus's studio, he came to me to reveal more information on Baron Pritt. He said that he had found evidence of a man named Stefan Müller. A young chemist from whom, the rumour mill would have us believe, Pritt stole his most valuable product."

"If I may, Superintendent," Darrington raised one hand to add an important detail. "My colleagues and I had explored this possibility and found the details of a chemist who had worked for Pritt, fought gallantly in the war, and died in Flanders. His name was not Muller at all, but Jeremy White. He wasn't German but a Geordie, born and bred in Newcastle."

Grandfather nodded his thanks to his unofficial subordinate and expanded on the point. "I knew nothing of this last night, of course but, with the evidence I had independently secured, had enough on Twelvetrees to be sure of his involvement in the crime."

This was clearly a lot for everyone to comprehend, and Cyril was the next to ask a question. "We know how Twelvetrees killed Augustus, but you still haven't told us why he would do such a thing. He's incredibly wealthy and has everything a man could want in life. Why did he risk losing all that?"

Grandfather seemed to shiver then, and I doubted it was down to the winter air cutting through him. "Because Lord Leopold Twelvetrees doesn't see the world as you or I do. He believes that justice should be delivered no matter the cost. He'd waited since the end of the war to enact his plan and would not let the opportunity go to waste."

"So Augustus really was this man Harald?" Fabian asked with some distaste in his cultivated voice. "And he really was a traitor in the war?"

His eyes on the dead man's fiancée, Lord Edgington measured his response. "That's correct. Harald was a traitor and Twelvetrees was set on punishing him. But it was only when I travelled to see Harald's parents that I understood the whole story. I knew that Twelvetrees was a fanatic. I saw it the first night we met, as he gave up his alcoholic crutch in order to have the focus he needed to pursue his goal. What I didn't realise, though, was exactly what he was so zealous about."

It was my grandfather's turn to stroll about the place, looking into the eyes of each person there. Our killer was the only man who wouldn't return the detective's gaze. Since his short-lived outburst, Twelvetrees's vision had been fixed upon the paving stones beneath our feet.

"When I realised that the initials on the cufflink could refer to the traitor Septimus Marchant, I assumed that whoever killed Harald had considered him just as culpable of crimes against this country as his notorious accomplice. But this hypothesis did not make absolute sense. For one thing, I saw Augustus's papers and there was no doubt that they were genuine. Though we could find no trace of his name in any records, his passport was official, which made me believe that someone within the government had obtained it for him through official channels. That would not have been possible if any suspicion remained that Harald was a spy.

"Furthermore, though it was widely believed that undiscovered accomplices had helped Septimus Marchant to communicate with Germany, no one was ever arrested and, as Harald was imprisoned in a German castle from 1915 onwards, he couldn't have been to blame. When I spoke to his mother yesterday, she reminded me that her son's university pal, Marchant, had any number of important connections, from politicians to press barons."

Our culprit took this moment to spit on the ground at his feet, but he couldn't distract his inquisitor, whose voice swelled in final judgement. "Leopold Twelvetrees didn't kill Harald Augheim because he'd betrayed Britain. He killed that brave young man because he was a double agent. He'd tricked his German captors into trusting him, and it's my belief that he used his position there to uncover Septimus Marchant's plan."

"I killed a murderer," Twelvetrees shouted, the words bursting out of him like a siren. "Septimus was unique. If he'd achieved his goals, he would have cut the war short by years. Just before he was arrested, he managed to leave me a message in the usual way and included one cufflink so that I'd know it was really from him. The note explained that he feared he'd been uncovered and didn't have long to escape. He couldn't be sure how the government had identified him but believed that a friend from university was behind it. He did not provide the name, and it was too dangerous during the war for me to investigate.

"Once the fighting was over, and suspicion had died down, I looked into the fate of his Oxford classmates. Some had been lucky enough to live, while many had died in battle. But there was one soldier who had been captured in Germany, returned to Britain and faded from existence thereafter. I knew then that Septimus's blood was on Harald Augheim's hands, and that I would kill to put it right. I avenged the death of the brightest young man born in the last fifty years. Septimus was a visionary, and his death may well be the greatest injustice of the last decade."

My grandfather would not be baited by such claims and, at the end of his pathetic speech, Twelvetrees had little voice remaining. He was a sick man with a twisted mind. He'd murdered a British hero and forsaken his countrymen. As Simpkin escorted him away to a waiting van, I felt nothing but disgust.

Lord Edgington's eyes fired across the square, and he bellowed out one last thought. "The only question I have left is whether it will be murder you're ultimately hanged for..." He took a deep breath then to propel the final words even further. "...or treason!"

CHAPTER THIRTY-THREE

A week to the day later, we gathered in Westminster to pay our respects. The snow had finally returned and our drive into the city took twice as long as normal. I'd never thought I would miss my grandfather's speedy driving but, as we entered the third hour of the journey and I hadn't been able to feel my fingers already for ninety minutes, my usual priorities were temporarily realigned.

The roads in the centre of London were quiet for once and, under that pretty white sheet, it felt as though the city was closed for redecorating. We parked the car on Parliament Street to walk along the icy pavement to the Cenotaph, mere yards from where Harald had breathed his last. My grandfather had contacted the dead man's parents, who appeared to have adopted Pandora as their own. Fabian was there too, dressed conservatively in a plain black suit with only a speckled green handkerchief in his breast pocket as a nod to his usual tastes. For once, Delilah had expressed no interest in joining our excursion and was presumably still asleep in front of the fire in the library at Cranley Hall.

"Grandfather," I mumbled when we got out of the car. "I've been thinking about it a lot, and I've come to the conclusion that you cheated."

He looked at me in a manner which told me he did not agree. "May I ask in what way?"

"You used the police to do much of the detective work for you. I thought you normally took pride in doing everything yourself."

"I'm afraid I must disagree, dear boy." He brushed off the criticism with a smile. "Another lesson you must learn is that, when faced with an insurmountable array of evidence, one should always share the load. This case was too big for one man and his dog... and even his grandson. But I shared what the police revealed just as soon as I knew anything, and you had all the information to which I was privy."

I suppose he was right. After all, he'd used the police to rule out possibilities that he considered unlikely so that he could concentrate on the core facts of the case. There were a few things that still needed clearing up, though.

"I understand that Leopold Twelvetrees supported Lord Marchant's treachery, but I'm not entirely sure why. What was it that made him kill Harald all these years later?"

Grandfather furrowed his brow and turned the question over in his mind. "If you'd met Septimus Marchant, you wouldn't need to ask." He looked dead ahead to where the others had gathered, and I was uncertain whether he would offer anything more in the way of an explanation. "He was younger than my children by some years but, as you know, in the English aristocracy, everyone is connected to everyone. I can honestly say that he had the most magnetic personality that I've come across. People fell to their knees to adore him. So, no, it does not surprise me that he was able to bend important figures in British society to his will, or that another man would kill in his memory." He stopped walking, his eyes still on our friends. "I have a suspicion that you know what such an attachment feels like."

He was referring, of course, to my friendship with Fabian Warwick. A man who few could resist and who, much like Septimus Marchant, could use his power for evil, good, or (more likely in Fabian's case) the pursuit of endless, idle pleasure.

"You're right. I do," I confessed. "But that doesn't mean I'd betray my country like Twelvetrees."

"Leopold Twelvetrees didn't betray his country."

I'm sure there was an answer to this that any normal person would have been able to produce. Instead, I stopped walking and possibly looked a little bilious.

"Well, he did, but only one of them." He gave me another moment to consider this. "His name, Christopher. How many Leopolds do you know?"

"Just the one, but... Ah, I see." Why hadn't I made that connection before? Twelvetrees must have had German parentage. "Fine, but there are thousands of people in Britain with foreign blood. That doesn't mean they would–"

"Are there thousands of people in Britain with *German* blood who drive the exact same *German* car as the *German* emperor who started a war between Britain and *Germany*?" He looked a little introspective and lowered his voice. "I didn't trust Leopold Twelvetrees from the moment I met him. And his imposing black Mercedes 37/95 was only one of the reasons." He shook his head then, as if appalled once more by the man's crimes. In time, his moustaches evened out, and his tone brightened a fraction. "I must say, though, Chrissy, you're improving. You don't have nearly so many questions compared to our previous cases."

"Well, there is one more thing," I whispered, as we caught up with the other mourners. With even our footsteps muffled by the snow, I had no wish to draw attention to myself. "I don't understand why Harald didn't tell his parents or fiancée the whole story. If they'd known the truth, perhaps they could have saved him."

"Harald was a spy, Christopher. He had signed the Official Secrets Act and was not permitted to discuss the mission he had completed, even with his family. If he had not been such a good soldier and an honest man, things would have run a different course, but I have no interest in such hypothetical scenarios."

His words died away as we joined the small group standing in the cold. Pandora wore a long white dress beneath her black coat but, as she stood before the war memorial, I saw her once more as Alice. There was something so pure yet curious about her, and I was certain I would always remember her just like that. The silent tears she cried, with Lord and Lady Newport on either side of her, following suit, made my heart ache. I know that moments of sorrow serve to heal tender wounds, but it seemed terribly unfair that she would have to suffer so.

As she laid a simple bouquet of five white roses on the steps, I noticed two figures watching the informal ceremony from a distance. One of them I recognised as Chief Inspector Darrington, who was dressed in his full ceremonial uniform with several medals on his chest and silver braid on the lapels. The man who stood next to him, however, was far harder to describe. There was simply nothing remarkable about him. He was a short chap in a beige trench coat. His shoes and hair were black, and his face was exactly what you would see if you asked a small child to draw a very normal-looking man. I forgot about him almost immediately, and my turn soon came to approach the large stone monolith.

The cenotaph was built as a tribute to all the souls lost in that unequalled and appalling conflict. It was a testament to the hundreds of thousands of soldiers whose bodies would never return to Britain. As I stood solemnly in the cold, with my grandfather there beside me, it was not just my friend Augustus who I pictured, but the legions of his peers who were buried in foreign fields. I closed my eyes and prayed that we might learn our lessons and that such senseless destruction would be consigned to history.

When all the mourners had taken their turns, the formal atmosphere seemed to dissipate. Discussion became lighter, shoulders de-hunched, and Harald's mother even managed to dry her eyes.

Darrington finally approached us but made no reference to his companion. "My condolences to you all. It is a tragic state of affairs when a young man is murdered in the heart of the capital simply for serving his country."

There was some quiet agreement before he put a proposition to us. "If I may be so bold as to suggest we get inside somewhere warm to raise a glass to Harald? There's a hotel a few streets from here which can accommodate us."

He motioned in the direction of St James's and Grandfather nodded his consent. We got back inside the Aston Martin as, even if we'd wanted to walk, the path was too slippery for a man of Lord Edgington's supposedly advanced years.

I'd never heard of St Ermin's Hotel before, but it was rather impressive. A horseshoe-shaped courtyard gave on to a particularly grand lobby where a team of staff was on hand to assist us. The nondescript fellow in the trench coat led our group, and I got the impression that he had prepared everything in advance. He sailed through the hotel to a back room which contained a small bar and various cosy nooks, with comfortable chairs and a few tables.

"Grandfather, who is this fellow?" I asked under my breath before entering.

His eyes seemed to flare in reply. "Patience is a virtue, Christopher. All will soon be revealed."

Oh, what a surprise. He knew more than me for once!

A barman in butlering attire saw to the refreshments, and then discreetly removed himself from the room. Fabian did not look comfortable there and eyed the stranger in our midst, who was busy removing papers from a battered leather Rosebery bag. Without discussion, we pulled some chairs over to congregate around him.

"You don't know me," he began, barely looking up from his task, "and I'm not going to tell you who I am. Chief Inspector Darrington put in a request with his superiors for me to come here today and explain a few significant points. I will leave these files for you to peruse for one hour, after which time it is very unlikely that you will see them, or me, ever again."

He spoke in a dull, flat tone, as though reading out the index to an encyclopaedia. "If any of you were to disseminate the information you discover here this morning, the British government will deny all knowledge of it." He looked up at us without a hint of a smile. "Certain members of the organisation in which I work suggested that we force you to sign a secrecy agreement, but I don't think that will be necessary."

I should probably have worked out that this almost comically dreary fellow was some sort of spy.

"We appreciate you coming to talk to us," Lady Newport declared with a stately bow of the head.

"It's very good of you," my grandfather agreed, and our host began his presentation.

"I am at liberty to share two files with you this morning. You must understand that, under normal circumstances, members of the public would be kept in the dark on such matters. But the case of Lieutenant Harald Augheim is far from normal." A spark of interest coloured his voice then, and I had to wonder if he wasn't quite as boring as he would have us believe. "You can read the full details for yourselves, but I will summarise the mission he carried out before I reveal the contents of the second file."

He pointed at the documents as he spoke and took a moment to observe his audience. "When the Great War broke out in 1914, very few people with connections to Germany were allowed anywhere near the front line. German communities in England were heavily monitored, and men of fighting age were interned. One of my superiors realised how useful a patriotic Brit with German blood could be, though, and we sought out a good Kraut of our own. We found Augheim at Oxford and did what we could to vet his suitability. I was lucky enough to meet him back then, and I can say with some certainty that he was no fan of Kaiser Wilhelm. From the very first day, it was clear that he would embrace the mission we had devised."

227

I watched Harald's mother clutch her husband's hand more tightly, while Lord Newport closed his eyes to stem the tears. They were clearly still unable to accept their loss, and I wondered if they were praying that this new version of events would provide one final twist and bring their son back to them. I have a similar feeling whenever I re-read a book. I cross my fingers every time I return to 'Oliver Twist' that, this time, Nancy will enjoy a happier ending.

"The intention was for Lieutenant Augheim to be captured by the Germans in north-east France during the First Battle of the Marne. It was no easy feat to place him close enough to German territory without getting him injured, but the plan came off. Once he was taken, we had no contact with our man for over a year. To be perfectly honest, we feared the worst. But as I'm sure you're all aware, Harald Augheim was a man of some talent, and he did what was required of him.

"The German army thought that he would be a real feather in their caps. A *good Tommie,* if you like. They kept him away from the front line and entertained him as one of their own. It is true that he was required to produce translations of English texts and even write propaganda on their behalf, but he was largely translating falsified documents that we had released."

I was pleased to see Pandora smile a little more with every new revelation of her hero's bravery. It seemed that even our mysterious speaker had begun to relax a little, too. His delivery had become pacier as he detailed the dead soldier's achievements.

"One of the reasons we had deemed it necessary to plant a man in Germany was due to the suspicions we had that there was already a spy in Whitehall. Over time, it was clear that someone was feeding the enemy information, but we couldn't identify the source. Lieutenant Augheim was under strict instructions not to compromise his position unless he had significant intelligence to share with us. While we never expected him to learn details of military operations, the information he obtained turned out to be even more useful. He found our traitor."

His voice became a touch more animated, a little less monotonous. "I discovered after the war that he'd befriended a German general who could be chatty when he'd had a bottle of Riesling. This chap thought they were ever so fortunate to have a man hidden in the British government and boasted about it on several occasions. When Augheim heard the name Septimus Marchant, he knew that his moment had come."

Fabian released a sharp breath at the news of the danger Harald had faced. We were all trapped within the account by now and, though the man's speech could have been more dramatic, the story itself certainly compensated.

He addressed the grieving parents. "The details of how your son managed to communicate such information to his compatriots are not included in the file and will remain a secret. But I can tell you that he was never safe from that day forward. The fact that he avoided detection until 1918, when he was liberated from capture, is a real miracle. The government could never openly acknowledge the contribution he made to the British war effort for fear that it would reveal the tactics that we used, but I can tell you that everyone in the know will forever be grateful."

He allowed us a moment to savour the details of this selfless act. Out of loyalty to king and country, Harald had kept his own counsel and paid a heavy price. Through his actions, he may have saved the lives of thousands, but he was granted no protection on his return from the war. Sadly for all of us, Septimus Marchant hadn't been working alone.

The plain-faced spy shuffled in his seat, before placing one finger on the other manilla folder. "For the most part, this second file contains very few names. Until one week ago, it was labelled simply Persons N. We did not know what to call the party who aided Marchant in his treachery and might never have known if it weren't for Lord Edgington."

My grandfather was standing behind my chair and put his hand on my shoulder at this moment. In his own way, he was a modest man. Though happy to discuss his abilities, he rarely crowed over his achievements. Yet, looking back at him, I could tell how proud he was to have earned such a compliment.

"In our interviews with Twelvetrees this week, we have learnt a great deal. His mother was born abroad, and my colleagues have discovered a room in his manor house which is filled with paraphernalia from the Prussian army and the time of German unification. It seems unlikely that he would have needed much persuading to betray the country of his birth. He claims there were other men who worked with Marchant – a whole club of them, in fact. We hope to locate the others in time but, in his arrogance as he boasted about his treachery, he has revealed something even more important. We have finally come to understand how he communicated Marchant's findings to the Germans.

"I must confess, we feel rather foolish not to have uncovered it before, as Twelvetrees placed hidden messages in his editorials in The Chronicle. The code was not so complicated that one of our experts back in..." I think that he was about to tell us who he worked for but caught himself just in time. "We would have broken their code, but we simply weren't looking in the right place. Perhaps that, more than anything else, is what cost Lieutenant Augheim his life."

This was the only moment when the curious fellow expressed something which might be described as a recognisable emotion. Swallowing hard, he tucked one lip under the other and had to pause for some moments before continuing. "Harald was a brave man. On behalf of the British government, I am truly sorry for the failings which led to his death."

Pandora stood up to put her arms around the old couple's shoulders. I watched as the three of them held onto one another like a huddle of poor souls lost at sea. With this scene playing out, the nameless official prepared to depart.

"Ladies and Gentlemen, I will send a subordinate to collect the documents in exactly one hour. I thank you for your time and bid you good day."

That was how he left us. Without fanfare or farewell, he took his empty briefcase and slipped from the room, leaving seven civilians in charge of a small pile of secrets.

Fabian looked as though he had fainted into his armchair and stared up at the plain white ceiling in a daze. Chief Inspector Darrington was alert but aloof, standing beside the door as though expecting an intruder, and the three people who loved Harald most still hadn't come up for air.

I stood to give Grandfather my seat and, in a whisper, encouraged him to read.

He held my gaze for ten long seconds, then nodded and opened the first file. I think we were all a little surprised to see my friend Augustus looking back at us from ten years earlier. He was clean-shaven, with no scar on his cheek and his hair looked a lot darker than when I'd known him, but it was unmistakeably him.

Clearing his throat and rolling his shoulders, like an actor preparing for his big entrance, Grandfather took his glasses from his pocket and started to read,

"Lieutenant Harald Daniel Augheim, born October 17th, 1891. Died February 13th, 1926. Recipient of the Victoria Cross from His Majesty King George V in a closed ceremony at Buckingham Palace in the spring of 1919. Lieutenant Augheim put himself in considerable danger by crossing the front line to obtain essential information from the enemy. He was instrumental in uncovering the plot to undermine the British war effort by the traitor Septimus Marchant..."

As my grandfather took us through the key moments of one man's incredible life, nobody made a sound. Sobs were held back, our breathing became more muted, and I didn't dare swallow for fear of disturbing the hush that now seized the room. The investigation was complete. The guilty had been punished, the innocent victim avenged, but the case would never leave me.

The End (For Now...)

READ MORE LORD EDGINGTON MYSTERIES TODAY...

- **Murder at the Spring Ball**
- **Death From High Places** (free e-novella available exclusively at benedictbrown.net. Paperback and audiobook available 2022)
- **A Body at a Boarding School**
- **Death on a Summer's Day**
- **The Mystery of Mistletoe Hall**
- **The Tangled Treasure Trail**
- **The Curious Case of the Templeton-Swifts** (Coming Summer 2022)

Check out the complete Lord Edgington Collection at Amazon.

The first three Lord Edgington audiobooks, narrated by the actor George Blagden, are available now. The subsequent titles will follow through the year.

Get another
LORD EDGINGTON ADVENTURE
absolutely **free**…

Download your free novella at
www.benedictbrown.net

"LORD EDGINGTON INVESTIGATES..."

The sixth full-length mystery will be
available in **Summer 2022** at amazon.

Sign up to the readers' club on my website to know when it goes on sale.

ABOUT THIS BOOK

Since I started this series almost exactly a year ago, I knew I wanted to write a book focused on the Bright Young Things. I like Evelyn Waugh's early books and, from about 1928, he was at the heart of this brief, exclusive social movement. By 1926, however, the term was already all over the newspapers and the forerunners of the scene were enjoying their treasure hunts and games of Hares and Hounds all over London.

Perhaps the most unlikely part of this story – when the soldiers in Buckingham Palace advanced on a mass of drunken revellers – actually happened, and the captain of the guards had to call for backup when the smart set descended. They really did get up to some incredible things including all sorts of themed parties. There was an infamous one at a swimming baths, which was full of the social celebrities of the day and the water was covered in bobbing champagne corks and flower petals. There was a "white party", and a party where you had to "come as you were twenty years ago," – where parents wore their chicest attire from two decades earlier, and the younger generation dressed as babies.

There were a lot of parties and elaborate balls, but they also went on scavenger hunts and would have to retrieve strange objects in the dead of night or pass themselves off as foreign dignitaries. Some of the tasks they engaged in sound more like interactive theatre than what we would normally consider a game, and the Gargoyle Club on Dean Street was often their stage. All the details I included about that glistening venue were based on reality and I'd rather like to have gone there in its prime.

Important names such as Cecil Beaton, the Mitford sisters and, "the brightest of the Bright Young People" Stephen Tennant, still hadn't clubbed together in 1926 and so I created my own band of sensational characters for Chrissy and Lord Edgington to interact with. I like the Bright Young People so much because they remind us that every generation has had a brat pack who scandalised polite society. Looking back through history, we see it really is nothing new. The press is still obsessed with hedonism and celebrity and enjoys nothing more than to report on the loves, adventures and misdeeds of whichever group are popular that year. While the Bright Young People of the 1920s did

236

it with more style than the reality TV stars and footballers that you can read about today, very little else has changed.

This is my second murder mystery set mainly in the English capital. (Greater) London is the city of my birth and I still love it just as much as when I was a kid going up to town for visits with my high-flying auntie Marilyn. When researching the book, I absolutely adored discovering the seemingly endless stories that relate to each important building and neighbourhood. In the absence of a country house for the action to take place in, I hope that I have sewn together a tapestry of some of the most incredible parts of London.

Along with the famous clubs and hotels Chrissy visits, one place that was particularly important for me to include was Guildhall in the centre of the City. The history of London's town hall is amazing (the building was constructed on top of the Roman amphitheatre, and once had its own pair of giants!) but my reason for loving it is a lot more personal. My father Kevin worked in the building helping to organise grand functions for visiting diplomats when he was in his twenties. He had all sorts of stories to tell about the banquets he got to attend, though the most memorable ones include the time the master of ceremonies mispronounced the name of Princess Alexandra's husband – who, as it happens was second cousin to those Bright Young Things, the Mitford sisters. Apparently, the Honourable Angus Ogilvy did not like being introduced to a hall of bigwigs as Agnes.

Then there was the time when my father had to stand in line for the entrance of Emperor Hirohito of Japan. Kevin Brown was a very principled man, and he would later claim he had to resist the urge to "kick him in the shin" for allying Japan with Nazi Germany in the Second World War. As these books are dedicated to Dad, it was nice to fit in another reference to him. My father came from an immensely poor background and left school at sixteen with only three O-levels, but he achieved a great deal in his life. I hope he's looking down as I write this, having a good laugh at the name Agnes!

If you loved the story and have the time, please write a review on Amazon. Most books get one review per thousand readers so I would be infinitely appreciative if you could help me out.

THE MOST INTERESTING THINGS I DISCOVERED WHEN RESEARCHING THIS BOOK...

I can honestly say that this book was the most fun to research and the hardest so far to write. Setting a book in twenty different locations across an ancient city that has changed a lot in the last century means I had to stop every other sentence to check my facts. This also means I discovered all sorts of wonderful things I never knew before.

For example, I found out that the first royal telegram to people turning one hundred years old was sent in 1917 by King George V. There were 24 telegrams sent that first year whereas, in 2014, nearly eight thousand were sent by our current queen. I also had to learn about old coins as I was born post decimalisation. Before 1971, there were twenty shillings in a pound. The shilling was made up of twelve pennies (referred to as 'd' after the Roman coin *denarius*) and there were also halfpennies and quarter pennies, known as farthings. In addition, there were three-penny coins (thruppence), and six-penny coins (a tanner). A shilling was known as a bob, but a two-bob coin was a florin, and five shillings made up a crown. Perhaps strangest of all, there were two hundred and forty pennies in a pound. Simple!

This system had been in place for hundreds of years, and the roots of the pounds, shillings and pence system can be traced back to the eighth century. Though complicated for shoppers today, each coin's weight related to its value so that one pound coin was equivalent to a pound of sterling silver, and a penny was a pennyweight of silver. Things got even fiddlier as prices were often expressed in shillings, so that what might seem logical to count as 75d would have been six shillings and thruppence. I never had to deal with such complexities, but my mother has fond memories of helping out in her family shop in South Wales in the forties, when shillings and pence were in use.

To my amazement, I found out that the word *yuck* did not exist until 1966, which makes me wonder what onomatopoeic sound people used to express disgust before that date. I had to create my own sound to help Chrissy make his feelings known about entering a mortuary. *Beurggg* will do nicely and is similar to the sound French people make.

I knew early on that I wanted to have a jobbing female reporter at the centre of the story and that my hardworking wife would be tasked with creating a newspaper to open the book. What I was less sure of was the role of women in the press in the twenties, but I soon found that, as in so many fields at the time, they were beginning to cut a path into this male-dominated arena. C. A. Lejeune became The Observer's film critic from 1928 until 1960, she was a good friend of Alfred Hitchcock's and had started writing for various papers by 1921.

It seems the First World War went some way to opening up the world of work to women, and there were several notable female reporters during the war, including Mary Boyle O'Reilly who dressed as a peasant and Dorothy Lawrence who passed herself off as a soldier to get close to the action. The newspaper in this book, The London Chronicle, was a real title, though it had already disappeared a century earlier. It had the distinction of being the first paper to publish the Declaration of Independence in Europe.

My journalist Peggy Craddock takes her name from one of my readers who deserves a mention for her own incredible life. Aged eighty-nine, and possibly sharper than I am, she's an avid reader, despite having double vision brought on by a bite from a paralysis tick. She volunteered at the Centre for Peace and Conflict Studies in Sydney for twenty-five years and established their resource centre which was named after her. She was also a teacher for much of her life and has written an autobiography which I look forward to reading, just as soon as I don't have a book to write or edit.

Perhaps my greatest thrill in my research came when looking over a map of London and discovering all sorts of new things about it. London is a city that, for every square centimetre on the page or screen, can lay claim to a million stories. I loved plotting the treasure hunts, and collecting small, fascinating anecdotes about the different places that Chrissy and his grandfather visit. One sad example was the fact that the boating lake in Regent's Park had to be made shallower in 1867 after a disaster in which forty people died when the frozen cover they were skating on cracked. It's hard to imagine a puddle in London freezing these days, let alone a lake.

Over in St James's Park, it wasn't because of Chrissy's poor ornithological knowledge that he mentioned pelicans, there really are a small colony of them and they have been there for hundreds of years. The first birds were given as a present to Charles II in 1664 by a Russian ambassador and they have been replaced over the centuries whenever one dies. As Lord Edgington points out, they don't fly away because their wings are clipped, though there is one bird there at the moment who was found in an English garden and is free to fly away. He goes to London Zoo each day to enjoy a second meal but otherwise returns to see his friends in the park. No doubt he's a fan of fish and chips.

I particularly love the names of the churches in London. All Hallows-by-the-Tower, St Giles-without-Cripplegate, St Lawrence Jewry and St. Botolph-without-Bishopsgate may sound like I've made them up, but they are all real churches. I wrote this whole book with an antique map by my side to check that the locations actually existed in 1926, as the city has changed immeasurably. This was especially the case with Tube stations, half of which have evolved or disappeared over the decades. Mark Lane station was closed to make way for Tower Hill and names that we rely on like the Northern Line and Victoria Line were not in use in the twenties.

In fact, the Northern Line, or Hampstead Tube, as it was colloquially known back then, had only just been extended north to Edgware a couple of years earlier. This was a happy stroke of luck as it led me to my most incredible chain of coincidences. I chose Edgware merely because it is still the end of one branch of the Northern Line. From there I looked for an old house that no longer exists and found Cannons. In real life, it turned out that Cannons was owned by the first Duke of Chandos. By chance, in my third Lord Edgington novel, 'Death on a Summer's Day', the victim is the fifth Duke of Chandos. But even more surprisingly, the real first duke of Chandos's wife was his cousin Cassandra Willoughby, who spent much of her life supervising the rebuilding of her family's mansion at Wollaton Hall. And Wollaton Hall… wait for it… just happens to be the house on the front cover of "Murder at the Spring Ball", the first novel in this series. Whatever I researched, I found these wonderful coincidences and – while this can be put down to the fact that a massive amount of wealth and power was controlled by a small, inter-marrying group of aristocrats – I still find those connections magical.

Cannons itself was considered one of the most exquisite houses of the day when it was built in the early eighteenth century. Replete with the embellishments of the finest artists and every old master going, it hosted all sorts of dignitaries, including, as Edgington explains, the live-in composer George Frederick Handel. However, its glory was short lived as, when the second duke of Chandos inherited the estate, he did not have enough cash to keep it going and had an auction to sell off every last thing in the house from the Titians to the staircase and tap fixings. The house's columns now hold up the portico of London's National Gallery and, just twenty-three years after this absolute palace was completed, it had vanished altogether. Incredible!

Another important house in the book is Stafford House, which I am happy to say is still standing, though now known by another name. Back in the nineteenth century, the area of Mayfair and St James's was full of palaces and mansions, and this one, originally built for George III's son, the Duke of York and Albany, was rated as the most valuable private house in London. Such notable figures as Chopin, Giuseppe Garibaldi and Harriet Beecher Stowe visited over the years and, popping by from neighbouring Buckingham Palace, Queen Victoria apparently said to the owners, "I have come from my House to your Palace." At the beginning of the twentieth century, it was bought by a soap magnate and renamed Lancaster House before being donated to the government, who still use it today for exclusive events and also to house their wine cellar.

Moving away from the grandeur of Mayfair to the grime of London's underworld, I must mention a man who has a hand in this novel's events without appearing in person. Sir Bernard Spilsbury was a pioneering pathologist who became synonymous in Britain with advances in the nascent field of forensics. It was Spilsbury who recommended police carry the "murder bag" containing gloves, swabs and tweezers, that Edgington makes use of. He was involved in countless high profile

241

murder cases, including the trial of Dr Crippen, the 'Brides in the Bath' case and the Brighton trunk murders. His reputation was so great that juries would side with him regardless of any other evidence, and he was known for his formidable manner in the courtroom.

The cases of Charles Peace, the violin-playing burglar, and Frederick Bailey Deeming, the Jack the Ripper suspect, were exactly as P.C. Simpkin describes, and artefacts relating to such men remain in the Scotland Yard Crime Museum to this day. The infamous "Black Museum" is only open to serving police officers but is full of gruesome wonders. I was overjoyed to discover, just as I was setting out on a career as a crime writer, that my good friend Natalie's stepdad had retired from the flying squad to become the museum's curator. He's told me all sorts of incredible stories and answered invaluable questions for pretty much every book. So if police procedure in my stories is the slightest bit realistic, you can thank Paul.

The museum itself was founded in 1874 in order to store prisoners' property that could be useful to the investigation of future crimes. To begin with, it did not have a curator but was established and run by a serving Inspector and his police constable assistant. Over the years, countless morbid artefacts have been amassed, including shrapnel from terrorist bombs, cleverly concealed weapons, poisoner's vials, and the despicable Dennis Nilsen's bathtub (which I would not recommend looking up if you're of a squeamish nature). Pretty much everything I mentioned in the story really exists, and there are several great books on the contents of the museum that are fascinating for fans of true crime.

Chrissy has yet to cross paths with a female officer, but they were already in existence. The first British woman to join the police was Edith Smith in August 1915. Four years later, the number of female recruits in the Metropolitan Police had risen to one hundred and ten, though they were not allowed to arrest anyone and went about in special "Women Police Patrols". Even their numbers soon tailed off and, though there were brief success stories, it was not until the 1970s that male and female officers were de-segregated. Around 30% of serving police officers in Britain today are female, so some things have clearly changed since Edith Smith's day. My daughter Amelie would like to be a police officer when she grows up, though her main motivation is that she thinks it will help her avoid jail, so who knows what else she's got planned.

Speaking of ground-breaking women, one part of the story was inspired by my father's secretaries when he worked for our local court service in the 1980s. Joy and Doris were two tiny old ladies of whom you could never imagine having such incredible lives. One day, my father's rather pompous boss asked whether he could trust them with a simple task. Joy informed him that she had signed the Official Secrets Act during the second world war and never revealed the sensitive information she had overheard in the cabinet war rooms under Westminster, where she served as a secretary to Churchill and the British generals and politicians who held meetings there. Doris, meanwhile, had worked in Bletchley Park on the Enigma machine breaking German codes, and neither of them had spoken of their work for decades after the war. I stayed in touch with Joy until she died in her nineties, and she was truly inspirational.

I needed to find an extinct name to use for Augustus and, according to the internet at least, Harred fitted the bill. It sounds odd to imagine surnames disappearing entirely, but apparently it can happen. The first world war itself may have hastened the extinction of some names, when whole male lines of families were killed. Changes in spelling and hyphenation have a similar effect. Apparently, the actors Bill Nighy, Helen Mirren and Hugh Bonneville (Lord Grantham from 'Downton Abbey') all have names with fewer than fifty people remaining. As the number one most common surname in London and the third in the UK, I think the Browns would take a major disaster to wipe out. And yet, having provided my parents with their only grandchild, I still feel protective over it.

The story of Augustus is purely fictional, but there were traitors executed at the Tower of London, including several who used invisible ink. In fact there was something of a battle during the course of the war to come up with a substance that would be unreadable without knowing the exact reagent to reveal the text. For every development the Germans made, the British and French chemists would come up with a solution and, even after the war, the Germans believed there was a mole in their ranks spilling their secrets. In reality, it was just good science that sank them. Hurray for scientists!

Speaking of Germans, life in Britain for ex-pats during the first world war was not much fun. There was widespread paranoia about German spies infiltrating from within, and the government soon enacted legislation to appease the public. Germans were not allowed to travel more than five miles from their homes in Britain, all German clubs and publications were banned, and German-owned businesses were closed down. Even worse was the internment of all German-born males aged seventeen to fifty-five. At the beginning of the war, there were over 50,000 Germans in Britain, but over half that number were locked away. By 1919, approximately two thirds of the original number had left.

Two places in the book that, structurally at least, still exist today are The Criterion restaurant and Café de Paris in the West End. The Criterion is one of the most beautiful restaurants in Britain (no question) and my wife and I were lucky enough to have afternoon tea there before it was turned into an Italian restaurant with many of the stunning period features hidden by modern nonsense. Café de Paris, meanwhile, continued as a plush cabaret venue until very recently. We had a fun night there a few years back but, though it survived heavy bombing during the Blitz, it did not make it through the economic downturn caused by the pandemic and has been closed ever since. Let's hope that both venues are revived, with all their period grandeur, very soon.

I think that this is the first book where Lord Edgington gets to sing some solos and I was tempted to write an original song for his club appearance, but I love "Burlington Bertie from Bow" and couldn't resist it. A girl sang it in a school assembly when I was about eight and I've never forgotten it, though it was originally written in 1915 by William Hargreaves for his wife Ella Shields who would dress as a man to perform it. Another Music Hall staple is "The Boy in the Gallery" in 1885 by George Ware which I chose simply for the fact that it sounds ridiculous to hear Chrissy's grandfather singing it.

Last but not least, I'd like to mention the Marquess of Edgington's speed-demon tendencies. In 1926, the national speed limit was twenty miles per hour. However, it was so rarely observed that, by 1930, Britain did away with speed limits altogether. So the idea of Chrissy's mad grandfather shooting through the countryside in his powerful sports car at sixty miles an hour is actually quite realistic.

244

ACKNOWLEDGEMENTS

Writing this comparatively complex book was a challenge, and it would probably have been a disaster without the help of three people who read and re-read it in a very short time (Joe, Kathleen and Bridget, you're the best!). I also couldn't do it without my incredible wife, Marion (who has about seventeen jobs as my graphic designer, business manager, web designer, cook, chauffeur, gardener and many more roles to boot) taking up the slack when I'm shut away in my writing room for twelve hours a day. I'm also not sure I'd have the drive to be so productive if it wasn't for my daughter, Amelie, who happens to be the greatest human on the planet.

Thank you, too, to my crack team of experts – the Hoggs and the Martins, (**fiction**), Paul Bickley (**policing**), Karen Baugh Menuhin (**marketing**) and Mar Pérez (**forensic pathology**) for knowing lots of stuff when I don't. Thanks to my fellow writers who are always there for me, especially Pete, Rose, Suzanne and Lucy.

Thank you, many times over, to all the readers in my ARC team who have combed the book for errors. I wouldn't be able to produce this series so quickly or successfully without you, so please stick with me, Izzy and Lord Edgington to see what happens next…

Rebecca Brooks, Ferne Miller, Melinda Kimlinger, Deborah McNeill, Emma James, Mindy Denkin, Namoi Lamont, Katharine Reibig, Sarah Dalziel, Linsey Neale, Karen Davis, Taylor Rain, Terri Roller, Margaret Liddle, Esther Lamin, Lori Willis, Anja Peerdeman, Kate Newnham, Marion Davis, Sarah Turner, Sandra Hoff, Karen M, Mary Nickell, Vanessa Rivington, Helena George, Anne Kavcic, Nancy Roberts, Pat Hathaway, Peggy Craddock, Cathleen Brickhouse, Susan Reddington, Sonya Elizabeth Richards, Još Presler, Mary Harmon, Beth Weldon and Anny Pritchard.

"THE TANGLED TREASURE TRAIL" COCKTAIL

We've largely stuck to European cocktails until now, but if anyone was to be aware of bold new innovations (in many fields) it would be the Bright Young People. One of the main reasons that this page exists in these books is the fact that, by 1926, cocktail culture had invaded Britain from the States. If you read a non-fiction account of the smart set of London back then, everyone was drinking them.

I like the idea of Fabian and his friends sipping on lurid green grasshoppers, a drink which had only been in existence since 1918. A lot of cocktails have murky or contested origins, but it seems pretty clear that the grasshopper was created in the second oldest restaurant in the French Quarter of New Orleans. A bartender called Philibert Guichet made it for a cocktail competition and won second prize. His restaurant, Tujague's, is still open and you can still drink Grasshoppers there a century later.

I also like it because it contains crème de menthe. Whenever anyone asked my dad what he wanted to drink, he would not so hilariously reply, "A pint of crème de menthe!" in reference to a Monty Python sketch which he thought was very funny.

Ingredients...

> **30ml green crème de menthe,**
> **30ml white crème de cacao,**
> **30ml cream**

To prepare, just combine the ingredients in a shaker and shake with crushed ice before straining it into a cocktail glass. In summer, you can also supplement the cream for mint choc chip ice cream for an even sweeter treat. Though I'm not sure that cocktail purists would agree with such a practice.

The idea for the cocktail pages was inspired by my friend and the "Lord Edgington Investigates…" official cocktail expert, Francois Monti. You can get his brilliant book "101 Cocktails to Try Before you Die" at Amazon…

246

CHARACTER LIST

Baron Terence Pritt – wealthy metal magnate, recently deceased.

Baroness Ermentrude Pritt – Pritt's wife

Cyril Fischer – her lover

Fabian Warwick – "Enfant terrible" / social celebrity of his day

Augustus Harred - acclaimed artist.

Lady Pandora Elles - his charming fiancée, heir to the Elles family fortune

Peggy Craddock – journalist

Leopold Twelvetrees – press baron / Peggy's boss

"Young" P.C. Simpkin – likeable officer, old colleague of Lord Edgington

Chief Inspector James Darrington – former colleague of Lord Edgington

Regular Characters

Lord Edgington, The Marquess of Cranley – our seventy-five-year-old detective. A wealthy landowner who previously worked for Scotland Yard.

Christopher "Chrissy" Prentiss – Lord Edgington's seventeen-year-old grandson, and a cake connoisseur.

Cook (Henrietta) – Cranley Hall's increasingly itinerant cook

Todd – Lord Edgington's chauffeur and one of Chrissy's heroes.

Delilah – the smartest and most adorable golden retriever in the history of literature.

WORDS AND REFERENCES YOU MIGHT NOT KNOW

The flea's eyebrows! – there were lots of phrases like this used in the twenties to say that something was great. The cat's pyjamas and the bee's knees are more famous examples.

Decolletage – a low neckline.

Insalubrious – seedy, unhealthy.

Gulled – tricked.

Ragpicker – an old-fashioned word for a person who collects scrap materials. Today we're more likely to say rag and bone man.

Pied à terre – an expression to describe a property within a city that is used occasionally. Normally in contrast to one's more extensive property elsewhere.

Intellection – mental activity / act of understanding.

Sternutations – sneezes!!

Growler – a slang term for a horse-drawn carriage, so called for the sound of its wheels over the cobbled streets of London. Often a taxi.

Megrims – Similar to how we now say down in the dumps or to have the blues - to be moody, miserable and depressed.

Atlantes – the plural form of the Greek god Atlas. In an architectural sense, it's a male form which holds up a roof.

Cozening – to defraud through deception. Rather brilliantly, this comes from the French cousiner which means to cheat by pretending to be a cousin. I wonder if that is a common problem in France.

Skipjack – fop or dandy.

Cogitation – concerted thinking.

Dyspeptic – suffering from indigestion or, in this case, having an irritable, depressed, misanthropic nature.

Compeer – a companion or peer.

Diddled – slang for being tricked.

Trap set – the word used in the early part of the twentieth century for a drum kit.

Epistolarian – a letter writer.

Landgrave – A German title. Previously it meant a count, but by the nineteenth century it referred to a sovereign prince.

Polymathic – having many talents or a great range of knowledge.

Hurray for words! Aren't they wonderful?

THE IZZY PALMER MYSTERIES

If you're looking for a modern murder mystery series with just as many off-the-wall characters but a little more edge, try **"The Izzy Palmer Mysteries"** for your next whodunit fix.

"A CORPSE CALLED BOB"
(BOOK ONE)

Izzy just found her horrible boss murdered in his office and all her dreams are about to come true! Miss Marple meets Bridget Jones in a fast and funny new detective series with a hilarious cast of characters and a wicked resolution you'll never see coming. Read now to discover why one Amazon reviewer called it, *"Sheer murder mystery bliss."*

AB♀UT ME

Writing has always been my passion. It was my favourite half-an-hour a week at primary school, and I started on my first, truly abysmal book as a teenager. So it wasn't a difficult decision to study literature at university which led to a masters in Creative Writing.

I'm a Welsh-Irish-Englishman originally from **South London** but now living with my French/Spanish wife and presumably quite confused infant daughter in **Burgos**, a beautiful mediaeval city in the north of Spain. I write overlooking the Castilian countryside, trying not to be distracted by the vultures, hawks and red kites that fly past my window each day.

When Covid 19 hit in 2020, the language school where I worked as an English teacher closed down and I became a full-time writer. I have two murder mystery series. There are already six books written in **"The Izzy Palmer Mysteries"** which is a more modern, zany take on the genre. I will continue to alternate releases between Izzy and Lord Edgington. I hope to release at least ten books in each series.

I previously spent years focussing on kids' books and wrote everything from fairy tales to environmental dystopian fantasies, right through to issue-based teen fiction. My book **"The Princess and The Peach"** was long-listed for the Chicken House prize in The Times and an American producer even talked about adapting it into a film. I'll be slowly publishing those books over the next year whenever we find the time.

"The Tangled Treasure Trail" is the fifth novel in the "Lord Edgington Investigates..." series. The next book will be out in the summer and there's a novella available free if you sign up to my readers' club. If you feel like telling me what you think about Chrissy and his grandfather, my writing or the world at large, I'd love to hear from you, so feel free to get in touch via...

www.benedictbrown.net

Printed in Great Britain
by Amazon